E PRAISE
USE BROKEN

"*House Broken* beautifully strips down the layers of family until all that is left is what's most important—love, forgiveness, understanding, and healing."
> —Jennifer Scott, national bestselling author of
> *The Accidental Book Club*

"Don't be fooled by the cute dog on the cover; there is nothing cute about this book. It's fearless, even dangerous, interested in telling the truth about complexities of behavior (human and animal) and not interested in being reassuring. Yoerg, like a dog in the book, bites down and doesn't let go. I very much admired her book."
> —Richard Kramer, author of *These Things Happen* and
> award-winning TV producer and writer

"A powerful tale of the ways in which families hurt and heal . . . gorgeously written with characters that shine."
> —Eileen Goudge, *New York Times* bestselling author of
> *Swimsuit Body*

"With an unflinching eye, Sonya Yoerg has created a riveting tale exploring the power of family secrets. *House Broken* is a novel that will burn itself into your memory."
> —Ellen Marie Wiseman, author of *What She Left Behind*

continued . . .

Written by today's freshest new talents and selected by New American Library, NAL Accent novels touch on subjects close to a woman's heart, from friendship to family to finding our place in the world. The Conversation Guides included in each book are intended to enrich the individual reading experience, as well as encourage us to explore these topics together—because books, and life, are meant for sharing.

Visit us online at penguin.com.

"Sonja Yoerg's smartly written debut, *House Broken*, tells the spot-on tale of the challenges of navigating the three different families so many of us are part of—the one we grow up in, the one we marry into and the one we create with our partners. With impeccable prose and marvelous wit, Yoerg shows us that for almost every dark pocket of pain a family's history hides, there is, ultimately, a ray of light and love."   —Julie Lawson Timmer, author of *Five Days Left*

"*House Broken* is a sparkling and insightful debut. Sonja Yoerg paints her characters and her plot with the finest brushstrokes that will have you turning each page faster than the last."
                        —Emily Liebert, author of *When We Fall*

"Sonja Yoerg creates a compelling tale of a family gone awry and the ultimate cost of maintaining shameful secrets. *House Broken* is everything I love in women's fiction . . . beautiful writing, strong characters, a dash of mystery, and the hope for redemption."
                —Lori Nelson Spielman, international bestselling author of
                                                        The Life List

HOUSE BROKEN

SONJA YOERG

NAL
ACCENT

NAL Accent
Published by the Penguin Group
Penguin Group (USA) LLC, 375 Hudson Street,
New York, New York 10014

USA | Canada | UK | Ireland | Australia | New Zealand | India | South Africa | China
penguin.com
A Penguin Random House Company

First published by NAL Accent, an imprint of New American Library,
a division of Penguin Group (USA) LLC

First Printing, January 2015

 REGISTERED TRADEMARK—MARCA REGISTRADA

LIBRARY OF CONGRESS CATALOGING-IN-PUBLICATION DATA:

Yoerg, Sonja Ingrid, 1959–
House broken/Sonja Yoerg.
p. cm.
ISBN 978-0-451-47213-7 (paperback)
1. Women veterinarians—Fiction. 2. Mothers and daughters—Fiction.
3. Alcoholics—Family relationships—Fiction. 4. Family secrets—Fiction.
5. California—Fiction. 6. Domestic fiction. 7. Psychological fiction. I. Title.
PS3625.O37H68 2014
813'.6—dc23   2014019908

Printed in the United States of America
1   3   5   7   9   10   8   6   4   2

Set in Sabon   •   Designed by Elke Sigal

For Rebecca and Rachel, my sun and my moon

ACKNOWLEDGMENTS

I'm grateful to my agent, Maria Carvainis, for taking a chance on me and giving this book, and my career, the full benefit of her expertise, enthusiasm and guidance. I'm also indebted to Maria for placing me in the skillful hands of Claire Zion, who didn't mind that I "came from nowhere." I'm lucky to have these incredible women on my team.

Thanks to Jeanne Lyet Gassman for insightful comments, and to Helga Immerfall for reading, and for caring. My teenage daughters, Rebecca and Rachel Frank, were thoughtful, patient readers and accepted my new life as a writer with nary an eye roll. Rachel, special thanks for keeping Ella true.

I owe so much to my writing buddy, Julie Lawson Timmer. We shared a foxhole during the Query Wars, when doubting ourselves was habitual. Thanks, Julie, for reading and helping and cheering and making me glad to be a writer just so I could know you.

And thank you, now and always, to Richard: for granting me the luxury of time to write; for critique and encouragement, in perfect balance; for waiting until I finished my second novel to tell me you didn't think I had the patience to write the first; and for giving me the freedom to dream.

HOUSE BROKEN

CHAPTER ONE

GENEVA

Dr. Geneva Novak stared at the X-ray clipped to the light box on the wall. She tilted her head sideways and squinted at the contents of the dog's stomach. The iPod was obvious—it faced her—but the object protruding from the large blurry mass stumped her. Rectangular, with two bright white bars. Only metal lit up like that.

She clenched her jaw. This would be the third time she would have to operate on Zeke to remove things he'd swallowed, things his owner shouldn't have left lying around. After the second incident, she had talked to the owner at length about how to protect his dog. She recommended he walk Zeke daily, so the dog wouldn't turn to mischief out of boredom, and suggested he either keep his apartment orderly or confine the dog when he left the house. Nearly all dogs come to love their crates, she reassured him. Geneva had written down the instructions and told him he could call her anytime for help. But when Zeke's owner brought him in this morning, he confessed he hadn't followed through on anything. And the outcome was illuminated in black and white on the wall.

Eyes still on the X-ray, she pulled a hair band from the pocket of her lab coat and secured her dark hair into a tidy bun that would fit under her scrubs cap. Her cell phone, abandoned on the desk behind her, warbled. She touched the icon. A message from Dublin. *It's Mom*, it read. *Call me.*

Geneva sighed. "It's always Mom."

Holding it by the edges as if it were rigged to explode, she placed the phone on the corner of her desk, and took a step back. Her mother, represented by three letters on a tiny screen, had intruded on the sanctity of her workplace and unbalanced her. Exhaling completely, she pulled her broad shoulders down and back, a habit from her yoga days that helped her focus.

She didn't have to call Dublin, not right away. For all he knew she could be in surgery or have back-to-back appointments all afternoon. She might have left her phone on the kitchen counter this morning, or the battery might have died. Whatever had happened—whatever her mother, Helen, had done this time—could wait, ideally forever. Geneva had Zeke to take care of and another surgery after that. Helen was better off in Dublin's hands in any case. Hadn't he been dealing with her for years? And what could Geneva do from five hundred miles away?

Down the hall in the treatment room, a dog barked, setting off several others. Rosa, an intern from Marin High School, appeared in the office doorway, clutching a stack of files to her chest. She rocked on the toes of her red sneakers and grinned at Geneva.

"Zeke's almost done with his fluids, Dr. Novak. He'll be ready for surgery in about fifteen minutes."

"That's great. Thanks." She turned toward the image of the mysterious object imprisoned in Zeke's rib cage. "Hold on a minute, Rosa. If Zeke's owner is still here, can you ask him if he's also missing a charger?"

"Are you serious?"

"Bull terriers are notorious for their dietary indiscretion." She noted Rosa's blank expression. "They'll eat anything. Still, Zeke's taste for electronics has less to do with genetics than boredom. Zeke was made a geek, not born one."

Rosa laughed, tossed her braid off her shoulder, and disappeared.

The call to her brother would have to wait. She took a last look at the X-ray, flicked off the light box and went to change into scrubs.

· · ·

At three o'clock Geneva finally unpacked her lunch. Her cell phone vibrated under the paper bag. Dublin again. She couldn't avoid this any longer.

"Hi. I was going to call you."

"Yeah? You got my message? Good. Listen, I know you're slammed at work. When aren't you, right? But I just need a minute, okay?" Dublin's tone sounded more frenetic than usual. She sat up straighter. "Here's the story, Ginny. Act One. Lights come up. The set's deserted but there's an empty vodka bottle on a side table. You can't miss it."

"Dublin, just tell me what's going on. You can write the scene later."

"I am telling you. Welcome to Act Two. Mom crashed her car. One leg is pretty mashed up for starters. God knows what else. She wasn't too drunk to remember her seat belt, so we can expect an Act Three."

The blood rushed from her head. She lowered the phone from her ear and stared at it with a mix of disbelief and anger. The seconds ticked by on the call timer. She listened to Dublin's voice, now small in the palm of her hand. How easy it would be to quiet him, to hear nothing more about her mother. She could simply slide her finger an inch to the right. What was technology for if not such a convenience?

She raised the phone to her ear. "Sorry."

"You okay, Ginny? Didn't you hear me shouting? I was about to call reception and have them check on you. Don't scare me like that."

"I'm really sorry." A car accident. How often had she asked her mother to get in the habit of taking taxis when sober, so she would automatically call one when she had been drinking? Helen's opportunities to train herself were diminishing. Was it even noon when she had the accident? Geneva pictured the buckled hood of her mother's blue Mustang, shattered glass on concrete, the rear doors of an ambulance. "Was anyone else hurt? Please tell me she didn't kill anyone."

"She didn't kill anyone, but the cop at the hospital said she took out a few parked cars along Wilshire. The last one was an armored truck in front of a bank. The drivers thought she rammed them on purpose, so one of them drew his gun on her. That brought the cops pretty quickly. Everyone kept their heads, though. The only thing that went off was the air bag."

"My God." She dropped her forehead onto the heel of her hand.

"I know. Even I can't write stuff this good."

"Are you still at the hospital? Which one?"

"The Good Samaritan. And no, I was there but didn't get to see her. I had to pick up Jack."

When Dublin's son, Jack, was diagnosed with autism four years ago, Dublin's life had gone from rosy to harried. He and his wife, Talia, had a complex tag-team schedule, which was already subject to the mercy of L.A. traffic. A trip to the emergency room wouldn't have been easy. Geneva felt a stab of guilt for Dublin's burdens, then immediate gratitude for her two healthy children. Then a bit more guilt for that.

"What can I do, Dub?"

"Stay tuned." He gave her the phone number of the hospital, and said he'd leave a message when he heard from the doctor.

.   .   .

Geneva called Zeke's owner after the surgery and told the young man it had gone well. She gave him general directions for postoperative care and promised to leave a detailed instruction sheet at reception.

She was about to say good-bye when he asked, "Any chance the iPod still works? The way these vet bills keep piling up, I can't afford another one."

She suppressed the urge to hang up. "I didn't test it," she said evenly. "And I didn't match up the socks I found in there either.

There were three this time. And two pairs of women's under-wear."

"For real? That dog is nuts."

"Nuts? Hardly. Are you waiting for Zeke to reform himself? He needs you to take charge. Do the things I suggested before. Exercise him every day. A tired dog is a good dog. Don't give him the run of the house when you can't monitor what he's doing. And, at the risk of sounding like your mother, pick up your socks."

. . .

Geneva sent off the last urgent email of the day and noticed Constantine Corso leaning against the doorframe. Burly and square-jawed, "Stan" looked less like a veterinarian than a retired hit man.

"Zeke vacuuming his house again?"

"Yes. And he'll be back. I'm not sure it was ethical to have sewn him up. Perhaps a Ziploc closure next time."

"A lot of dogs eat things they shouldn't, Geneva. Their owners can't always stop them."

"But they should try, Stan. That poor dog."

Her cell phone buzzed from inside her lab coat. She pulled it out. Her brother again.

"You want me to show you how to answer that?" Stan teased.

"I'm not a Luddite," she replied, more sharply than she meant to. "I just think connectivity is oversold. Case in point. Here we were, having a nice little chat about the moral quandaries surrounding sock-eating dogs, when this electronic buttinski interrupts with a message I know I don't want." She held the phone aloft. "I'm tempted to feed this to Zeke." She slapped the phone onto the desk.

Stan lifted his eyebrows. She bit her lower lip and turned to the window. Outside, a woman in a blue coat holding a cat carrier walked down the path. A small girl skipped ahead of her. Geneva let out a long breath. Stan stepped into the room and sat in the chair across from her.

"Care to share with the class?" he said quietly.

In the three hours since she had talked to her brother, she hadn't paused to think about her mother. In fact, she'd made a point of not thinking about her, and not only because of the demands of her job. The *It's Mom* message gave her a familiar wrench-in-the-works feeling because each incident involving her mother upended her life. Last time Helen had left a pan unattended, and while she was out cold on the couch, the kitchen curtains caught fire. Taking a nap, she had said. The repairs and insurance claim took weeks to sort out. A year before that, her mother was stranded in Vegas and, having reached the cash limits on her accounts, hawked her jewelry and burned through the proceeds. As in the past, there would be consequences. Legalities. Arguments. Reparations. And, eventually, promises to do better. Those were the worst.

She considered what to tell Stan. A few years ago, he had met her mother during a rare visit. Helen had embarrassed everyone by flirting ostentatiously with Stan in front of his wife. But Stan knew no more about Helen than Geneva revealed—not a great deal.

"Geneva?"

She leaned back in her chair. "I'm sorry I snapped at you. My mother's had a car accident."

"Oh, no. How bad is it?"

"Serious but not life threatening, as far as I know. My brother was updating me." She tapped the phone on her desk.

"Can I do anything?"

It's my life and I can't even control it, she thought. What could anyone else do? "I've kept someone waiting in Room Two for twenty minutes. It's my last appointment. You free?"

"You bet," he said, getting up. "And let me know if you'll need time off."

Dublin's message was a list: fractured knee and leg, broken nose (from the air bag, she presumed), dislocated shoulder, possible concussion, monitoring for internal injuries, stable. He had placed the word *stable* in quotes. She smiled thinly at the quip, then winced as she imagined her mother in a hospital bed, in a hip cast, her nose taped across the bridge, and bruises blooming under her closed eyes.

. . .

Geneva lifted the leash off the hook behind the door and hung up her lab coat. She left her office and stopped by reception to remind the assistant to check on Zeke later that evening.

Outside the treatment room, she peeked through the window in the door. Rosa was bent over a computer next to Diesel, Geneva's Great Dane–chocolate Lab mix. The dog had recognized her footfall in the corridor and sat up expectantly, his head cocked to one side. She pushed open the door and called to him. He trotted across the room and sat in front of her, his nose at her waist, and lifted a paw. She held it and inspected the strip of adhesive tape on his forelimb. Tom, her husband, had brought Diesel to the clinic that morning to donate blood for a dog that had been hit by a car.

She stroked Diesel's ears flat. "How's my brave boy? Ready for the steak I promised you?"

. . .

The marsh wasn't on her way home. By the time she stood on the path that ran along Pickleweed Inlet, the shadow of Mount Tamalpais had turned the water midnight blue. A pair of kayaks, pointed toward Sausalito, slipped along the eelgrass at the marsh's edge. She walked Diesel only a short distance, not wanting to tire him after the transfusion. Raising her binoculars, she scanned for unusual shorebirds. A dowitcher probed the sand and a handful of sandpipers huddled close before scattering like children at recess. The head of a harbor seal surfaced twenty feet from shore. It regarded her briefly, then vanished, leaving the merest ripple.

The binoculars had been a tenth-birthday present from her father, Eustace, who died less than two years later. The weight of them on the strap around her neck calmed her as she looked across the water at the reeds on the distant bank, Diesel's shoulder against her thigh. Her father had no particular love for birds, but Geneva tagged along when he hunted turkey or small game in the lush Carolina wood. He said searching for songbirds would keep her occupied during the long, quiet mornings in the woods. Walking behind him on the narrow paths in the predawn glow, his back as broad as the trunks of the ancient cottonwoods around them, she felt safe, and because of that, happy. They only spoke occasionally, when he would drop to one knee and show her some animal sign—a new opening in the bramble or a print in the dewy moss—his voice so low it sank into the damp mulch at their feet. He never minded when there was nothing to shoot, and she never minded when there was. The harsh crack of the rifle and the limp rabbits and doves represented the practical cost of the joy of those mornings.

That marked the beginning of her interest in animals, and the beginning of who she was to become. When her father died, she felt forsaken. A few years passed before she also felt cheated. Her eldest sister, Paris, was nearly an adult when he died, and his love for her was blinding, uncommon. Geneva, by comparison, was a child in the shadows. He had missed out on her entirely.

She turned toward the car. Tom would be wondering where she was. She would have to explain why she hadn't called him about Helen. He would nod with understanding. And when he asked if she wanted him to go with her to L.A., she would watch for the measured disappointment on his face as she admitted she hadn't decided whether to go.

CHAPTER TWO

GENEVA

The porch light shone in the dusk when Geneva pulled into the dirt driveway shadowed by redwoods. She parked in front of the barn next to her brother-in-law's Explorer. The sign above the barn's carriage doors read, in art deco lettering, TREEHAUS. Nine years earlier, Tom had designed and built an elaborate two-story tree house for a wealthy friend. When it appeared as part of a spread in an architectural magazine, he quit his job as a graphic designer and set up a woodworking shop in the four-stall barn. Although he now specialized in building custom staircases and hadn't made a tree house in years, the name stuck.

Geneva wasn't surprised to find the kitchen crowded with Novaks. Tom, his four siblings and their families lived in one another's pockets. Today, Ivan, Tom's brother, perched on the butcher block island, beer in hand. His twin sons and Geneva and Tom's son, Charlie, all in baseball jerseys, gathered around a large bag of chips. Tom stirred the contents of a saucepan, his back to the door. She had to smile when five heads bearing the same Dennis Quaid grin turned toward her. Diesel pushed past her, bounded over to Tom, then to Charlie, butting his forehead against their stomachs in greeting. At fourteen, Charlie was almost as tall as his older cousins and as long-limbed as his father—and Diesel. Geneva still saw the toddler in him. A warm pulse spread under her skin.

Tom took the dishcloth from his shoulder and wiped his hands. "Long day?"

"Very."

"Spaghetti's on the way."

"Smells wonderful."

Ivan jumped off the counter. "You want a beer?"

"Maybe later, thanks."

Charlie looked up from scratching Diesel's chest. "Hey, Momster, is the dog okay?"

"The dog?"

Charlie shot her a quizzical look.

Of course, she thought. The transfusion. That was today. It might as well have been last week. "I was confused. There was another very sick dog today. But the one that got hit by the car is doing just fine, thanks to Diesel."

Cars hitting dogs. Dogs eating socks. Intoxicated mothers ramming armored cars. Geneva's head filled with cotton, and the kitchen suddenly became too confining. She turned away. "I'm going to change."

She left her shoulder bag on the bench near the door and headed down the hallway. Ella's door was closed—which meant

Do Not Disturb—so Geneva didn't pause. She entered the bedroom at the end of the hall, not bothering to turn on the light. A red light blinked on the bedside phone. She crossed the room in the dark and pushed the button. The attendance officer from the high school reported Charlie had missed first period.

"I dropped him off in town on time." Geneva spun around to see Tom silhouetted in the light spilling from the hallway.

"But apparently he was tardy again."

"Those late starts on Wednesdays seem to be a problem for him."

"Then he shouldn't be allowed to go to town before school. Those are the rules."

"I realize that, Geneva. He's very persuasive. As you know."

"That's why we agreed to be firm with him. No bending the rules for a wink and a smile."

"It's easy to talk about rules when you're not around to enforce them. I have to be the heavy."

"Or not." She spun away, fed up with his laxity. Wasn't it just last week she had warned him that with both kids in high school they had to maintain discipline?

He approached and put his arm around her shoulders. She flinched. He let go and said, "I didn't come in here to argue about Charlie. I came to see if you were okay."

She might have said that if he was so worried about her wellbeing, he could try not undermining the parenting decisions they had made. Together. But she didn't have the energy to act out her part of the script.

In the darkness, she felt smaller than usual, as if she were contracting. The voices in the kitchen receded.

Tom swiveled her to face him and lifted her chin. "Are you okay?"

She nodded. Holding it together was her strong suit. But all at once a band tightened around her chest. Her nose stung as she fought back tears.

"No."

. . .

Ivan and his sons left after dinner. Ella, sixteen years old, cleared the table. Her blue eyes hid behind fine blond bangs. She was dressed entirely in gray, as she had been for the last six months. When Geneva had noticed the pattern, she asked Ella if it was a statement. "A nonstatement, Mom."

Ella stacked the dishes. Geneva leaned against the counter and finished her wine.

"Did you work at the library after school today?"

"Yeah."

"Was it busy?"

"Not really."

"Still reading *Pride and Prejudice* in English?"

"Yeah."

"Liking it any better?"

"Not really."

"Why's that?"

"Too many words." Ella wiped down the table, tossed the sponge in the sink, and headed to her room. "Nice chatting with you, Mom." She gave the word *Mom* a sarcastic twist, as if it might not apply.

Geneva caught Tom's eye and raised her eyebrows.

He shrugged and pointed at the laptop screen. "There's space on a flight Saturday at noon. Knee surgery's scheduled for Friday, right? You'd have a couple days to get organized. You could even make Charlie's game on Saturday morning."

Geneva loaded plates into the dishwasher. "I know I should want to see her, Tom. Honestly, though, I'm not feeling much like the attentive, loving daughter."

"But you do love her."

She closed the dishwasher and faced him. "That word. I don't see how it's relevant. The question is whether it makes any difference to her—or to me—if I appear at her side."

He frowned. "You're angry."

"Furious." She folded the dishcloth and pinched several spent blossoms from the miniature rosebush on the counter. "I'll go see her. But for Dublin. No reason he should deal with her alone. And because I'll feel guilty if I don't."

"Do you want me to come?"

"Thanks, but I'm reluctant enough without having to worry about who's going to look after the kids." That was an excuse. What she didn't want was Tom monitoring her bedside manner. Maybe Tom should go and she should stay.

"Ivan and Leigh would take them. Or one of the others."

She didn't doubt it. Tom's family functioned as an organism. Eighteen years in, Geneva still marveled at the Novak family's cohesion and adaptability. If someone was ill or distressed, siblings arrived like macrophages at an infection, efficiently absorbing the duties of the other family into theirs. They drove children to school and sports practices, stocked refrigerators, walked dogs, and texted updates while working and shopping until all of the organism's parts were up and running again. Even Tom's parents, who were in their late seventies, would not be left out. During months when birthdays, anniversaries, and holidays were thin, the elderly Novaks invented occasions. Recently they'd hosted a barbecue to celebrate the first anniversary of their new barbecue.

As much as Tom's family embraced her, Geneva was an outsider. Her family was too different. Helen had named her four children after European cities to give them the sophistication lacking in their one-horse South Carolina town. But to Geneva their names had come to represent their distance from their mother and one another. She hadn't seen Paris in ten years, and Florence, two years younger than Paris, rarely left Manhattan. Only Geneva and Dublin phoned and visited each other regularly. If it weren't for her brother, she might as well have no family of her own.

"You stay with the kids, Tom. I'll be fine. Really."

"She'll be glad you came. You'll see."

She smiled at his insistence on remaking her mother into a version of his. Or maybe he believed her mother could change. Geneva knew better. The woman had been on a steady downhill slide since her husband's death. The trajectory had been hard for Geneva to discern early on. At first she was too young and wholly dependent on her mother to stabilize her fatherless world. A child sees what she wants to see. Once she entered middle school, she began to understand emotions could be complicated—even paradoxical— and attributed her mother's self-destructive behavior to grief. Geneva, patient and watchful, waited for Helen to come around. But the strength that should have returned to her mother never appeared, or never for very long, and Geneva finally realized she was waiting for a mother she never had. Six years after her father's death, she left Aliceville (and her mother) for college and for good.

Helen's life increasingly took on a haphazard quality, with a recent emphasis on *hazard*. Tom avowed that every incident provided an occasion for positive change, but Geneva disagreed. She believed the best predictor of future behavior was past behavior. In her mother's case, this did not bode well for the future. Her mother was too old and too stubborn a dog to learn new tricks.

Charlie came into the kitchen. "All done with my homework. Can I watch TV now?"

Geneva turned to Tom. "I didn't have a chance to check his grades online today. Has he earned back weeknight TV?"

"How'd you do on your history test?" Tom asked.

"Mr. Shaw hasn't finished grading them."

"And you're up to speed on everything else?"

"Yup."

"Okay. One show."

"Thanks, Pop." Charlie left before Geneva could object.

"I'm willing to wager a week's worth of dishes there's a history test in his backpack," she said.

He closed the laptop and got up. "You worry too much. I wasn't much of a student either, and I turned out all right." He moved to the living room couch and picked up a magazine. Conversation over.

It wasn't Charlie's grades that concerned her, but his character. Habits were hard to break; a child cutting corners and bending the rules was the same as a dog with a habit of digging. Look the other way, and a hole becomes a tunnel, and the dog is somewhere on the far side of the fence.

Did she worry too much? Maybe. But if she erred on the side of excess concern for either of her children, she had her reasons.

If you worry too little, you might find out too late.

CHAPTER THREE

GENEVA

Geneva held a mechanical pencil above the Saturday *Los Angeles Times* crossword folded in her lap. During the hour she'd sat next to her mother's hospital bed waiting for her to wake, she had entered only half a dozen words. Her stomach growled. She had rushed from Charlie's baseball game to the airport in San Francisco and missed lunch.

The setting sun pierced the haze and reflected off the matrix of glass and steel outside, throwing lurid shafts of orange light into the room. Flying in, she'd seen the smog that enveloped the city, held low by an inversion. Her eyes burned during the taxi ride and even now the back of her throat was raw. She had difficulty understanding why anyone, let alone thirteen million people, chose to live here. She'd trade palm trees and smog for redwoods and fog any day of the week. She took a sip from the Starbucks cup on the bedside table, recrossed her legs, and resumed tracking her shadow as it moved glacially across the brace on her mother's leg.

Five years earlier, shortly before Helen turned sixty, she'd announced her intention to leave her native South Carolina, declaring the last of a string of interchangeable Southern gentlemen to be much less fun after a hundred dates than after three. Besides, she said, she'd had her fill of snakes, sweet tea, and red-faced women who rested their chins on their bosoms. Her first choice was to live with Florence and her husband, Renaldo, in Manhattan. She packed and waited for Florence to offer her a closet-sized room in their walk-up. When the invitation failed to appear, she brushed it off, telling Geneva that New York was too expensive and "chock-full of Yankees." Dublin was her next choice. This time she didn't wait to be asked. She sent her belongings ahead of her and flew to Los Angeles for the easy glamour of room-temperature life amid palms. She purchased a condo a few miles from Dublin's house in Sherman Oaks.

In the hospital bed, Helen lay slack as a marionette doll abandoned by a puppeteer. Someone had brushed her platinum-blond hair away from her face, which accentuated her cheekbones and magnified the bruises under her eyes. Her lips were chapped and colorless. She would hate that, Geneva thought, recalling how her mother reapplied lipstick at the table after every meal. Without makeup, Helen appeared more vulnerable. Maybe "war paint," as she called it, was exactly that—it emboldened her, or at least made her appear stronger. In the beige confines of the hospital ward, she lay stripped of her accessories. No war paint, no spectator pumps, no oversized sunglasses. And no Dutch courage.

A nurse in a kelly-green uniform entered with several paper cups on a small tray. She introduced herself to Geneva and gently tapped Helen's uninjured left shoulder. The doctors had immobilized her right shoulder after repairing torn cartilage and resetting the joint. When Geneva received news of the surgery she knew her mother's recovery time had doubled. She wouldn't be able to lean on a walker for weeks.

"Time for your medication, Mrs. Riley."

Helen opened her eyes a little. "Am I still here, for Pete's sake?"

"Yes, you are. And your daughter has been waiting for you." The nurse nodded at Geneva on the far side of the bed.

Helen's face lit up as she slowly swiveled her head. "Florence?"

"No, Mom. It's me."

"Oh. Geneva. I didn't realize."

The note of disappointment was slight, but it pierced Geneva like a dart. She turned away and pretended to admire the view. Her mother lifted her head an inch, then sunk into the pillow. "Is my water over there somewhere?"

Geneva picked up the cup, adjusted the angle of the straw, and handed it to her. "I got here a while ago."

"Have you spoken with your sister? She was so upset about my accident!"

Geneva had two sisters, but her mother spoke of only one. After thirty years, her mother's erasure of Paris still registered.

"I called Florence yesterday after I spoke with your doctor. She's fine. I mean, we're all upset, Mom." She noted a defensive tone had crept into her speech: I'm a good daughter! I'm here, aren't I? She told herself not to be pathetic. "How are you feeling? You were sleeping so heavily."

"I don't do anything but sleep." The nurse picked up Helen's wrist, silently counted pulses, then moved to the end of the bed and picked up the chart. Helen looked Geneva in the eye. "Every time I wake up I pray I'm not here anymore."

The ambiguity of the statement hung in the air between them.

The nurse handed Helen her pills, ensured she had swallowed, then wrote the time in the log. "A few more days, Mrs. Riley. Then you can go home."

Geneva reminded herself to talk with Dublin about home care assistance after Helen's release. It might be a while before she could get around.

"Who brought those dahlias?"

"I did, Mom."

"They're my favorite."

"I know."

The nurse asked Helen about headaches and the level of pain in her shoulder and leg.

"It's tolerable, but I don't much care for that medication you've been giving me. Makes me feel I'm floating along like a bunch of balloons in a breeze. Why can't I choose my own medication? It's a free country, isn't it?"

"Mrs. Riley, we've gone over this . . ."

"I know, I know. Hospital policy. Too much policy and too little sense, if you ask me. It's only a drink, for Pete's sake." She turned to her daughter with a look that said this would be an appropriate moment for Geneva to speak up and demonstrate her solidarity. Geneva's face was noncommittal, so Helen changed direction. "Have you seen Dublin? Do you know when he's coming?"

Geneva was used to this question, and the anxious tone accompanying it. Her mother was always searching for one of her children. It started when Paris was fifteen. Geneva, at nine, would walk into the house, and her mother would be standing at the window, hands nervously flattening the front of her skirt. Her first question was always "Have you seen Paris?" Geneva didn't understand her concern because Paris wasn't ever hard to find. If she wasn't at the school library or the one in town, she was at the mayor's office with their father. For as long as Geneva could remember, Paris wanted to follow in their father's footsteps and become a lawyer. She applied herself at school with remarkable dedication, determined to be the top of her class as Eustace had been. After she graduated, she secured an internship at the State House in Columbia, and moved there. Several months later their father died, and after the initial shock wore off, Helen began asking Dublin and Geneva if they'd seen Florence, the next eldest. Didn't her basketball game end an hour ago? Why isn't she back from her friend's house? Then Florence graduated and left to play college basketball at Chapel Hill. She was too busy to return home often, so Helen shifted her focus to Dublin. When Geneva started high school, she began to wonder if she would finally become visible to her mother only after she left her behind. It never happened.

"He should be here soon, Mom. It's rush hour, so it's hard to say exactly when."

Ten minutes of stilted small talk later, her brother blew into the room like a dust devil, wearing the same leather jacket he'd had since college, his brown hair rumpled as if he had been roused from a nap. His smile was tense at the corners. He flung his arms wide, and Geneva sank into his bear hug. They were the exact same height. Bookends, Helen had called them.

"It's good to see you," she said.

"You, too, Ginny." He placed his hands on her shoulders and appraised her. "You look like hell. Good hell. Hell that's keeping up appearances. But still hell."

"Thanks."

"That's enough cursing, Dublin." Helen tried to sit up. "Aren't you going to say hello to me?"

He gave her a hard look. "I'm weighing my options."

"What ever are you talking about?"

"I got to hand it to you, Mom. I did not see this coming. Blindsided, sucker-punched, bushwhacked . . ."

"See what coming? Geneva, what is he talking about?"

"I have no idea."

Dublin sat down. "She has no idea. You know why, Mom? Because I just found out myself. Yeah. Only a few minutes ago from the friendly folks downstairs in the billing department. Correction. They *were* friendly. Now, not so much. But that was my fault."

"Oh, the billing department! This is about money, is it? Don't worry yourself. I've got plenty."

Dublin looked pointedly at Geneva, then back to his mother. "Had."

"Had?"

"You *had* plenty of money. But then you had a little accident and, oh, yeah, before that, you canceled your health insurance. . . ."

Geneva put a hand on his arm. "What?"

"They admitted her because the card in her purse looked valid. For three days, no one followed up. But the formerly friendly folks in billing informed me that Mom will be transferred to a county facility in the morning unless she forks over cash for the bills she's racked up so far." He addressed Helen. "Unless, Mom, you've got insurance coverage somewhere else?"

"Well . . ."

"Of course not! Too easy!"

"It must be a mistake," Geneva said. "Mom, you didn't cancel it, did you?"

Helen threw her hands in the air. "They wanted to raise my premium! It was already so high. I figured I'd be eligible for Medicare before long. I never go to the doctor. Why spend all that money when I'm in perfect health?" She fixed Geneva with her bright blue eyes, daring her to contradict.

Geneva gripped the railing at the end of the bed. "That's the nature of insurance. As I'm sure you know." She pushed down on her frustration and anger. "Dublin, what's the damage?"

He cocked his head and studied the ceiling. "A five-series BMW with all the extras. But if she stays here a few more days and you include the outpatient care she'll need, you're looking at a Porsche, and a pretty nice one."

"Who's buying a car?" Helen asked.

"Not you," he said. "Ever again."

"Anyway, they took away my license."

"That's not the point."

"I still have car insurance."

"That was lucky, wasn't it, Ginny? Can you imagine the fucking mess if she'd canceled that, too?"

"Dublin! I asked you to quit your cursing. Honestly!"

Geneva shook her head in dismay. "Mom, I don't understand you. Don't you care?"

"About the money? I've been poor. I'm not afraid of it."

Dublin said, "I'm guessing it's worse when you're old."

"I've got news for you, son. Everything's worse when you're old." She rubbed her temple. "The two of you have given me a headache. Why don't you let me rest? Go find something else to get your panties in a twist about."

· · ·

Geneva sat in a lawn chair in Dublin and Talia's backyard in Sherman Oaks. She pulled her sweater closed and crossed her arms against the evening chill. Through the window, she listened to Talia read to Jack and admired her slight Russian accent. Talia had lived in the United States since the age of sixteen, but her vowels still emerged deep and rounded. She was reading the same chapter for a third time. Three was Jack's number. Three slices of apple on his plate. Three flicks of the light switch when he entered or left a room. Three knots for his shoelaces. At dinner earlier that evening, Geneva had joined them at the dinner table and Jack had refused to eat. "I have dinner with three people, not four!" His ten-year-old brother, Whit, had said, "Guests don't count. Just pretend she's not here." Before Dublin and Talia could intervene, Geneva picked up her plate and moved to the nearby breakfast bar. "Is this okay, Jack?" He'd bent his head and began eating.

Light from the kitchen fell in parallelograms on the patchy lawn. A stack of empty planters leaned against the fence next to a bag of potting soil, perforated by rot. Weeds grew under the rusted swing set, next to a sandbox where hundreds of tiny soldiers—a green army and a brown one—had been painstakingly arrayed for battle. Jack's work, Geneva thought.

The back door creaked and Dublin stepped out. "Like what we've done with the place? I call it Postmodern Disintegration."

"It's lovely. You've really made it look as though it were simply neglected."

"Only a trained eye such as yours could spot the difference."
He took the chair next to her.

She nodded toward the swing set. "Remember when Charlie
and Whit knocked Ella off the slide? I thought her head would
never stop bleeding."

"And Jack—what was he? Four? He ran around in circles for
hours afterward with his hands over his ears, screaming, 'No!
No! No!' The neighbors were threatening to call the cops. Those
were the days."

"Jack seemed okay tonight." She knew enough not to use the
word *better*. A good day was a good day, not a trend.

"He likes you."

"And I like him. He doesn't seem so strange to me."

"I'll resist the obvious reply." He grinned at his sister. "I'm
guessing it's your animal behavior thing."

"My 'animal behavior thing'?"

"You don't take him personally. You just go with what he
gives you, work with what he will do instead of what he won't.
His specialist says it's the best route forward."

"Maybe it is from years of working with animals—and their
owners. No one's behavior surprises me anymore."

"Except Mom's."

She laughed. "Except Mom's." She drummed her fingers on
the armrest. "What are we going to do? It's going to be weeks
before she can get around on her artificial knee."

"I thought they wanted her using it pretty quickly."

"They do, but in therapy. She can't use a walker because of
the shoulder injury. With the insurance debacle, do you think she
can afford weeks of nursing care?"

"I'll look at it more carefully but I doubt it. Not decent care.

We don't want just anybody in her condo, driving her to therapy and all that."

"No. Although it'd be tempting to teach her a lesson by getting her someone really cranky."

"Or maybe a beefy loudmouth who sings opera all day."

"That's good!" She shoved him playfully. "Seriously, though. Who's going to be willing to put up with her drinking?"

"We could clear the booze out of her condo."

"Okay. Who'd be willing to deal with her then?"

They stared into the starless night.

She said, "Do you remember how she was when we were little, before she started drinking?"

"I do. She was fun—one of us."

"Yes, as long as 'us' didn't include Paris."

Talia appeared in the doorway. "You guys want anything before I collapse?"

Dublin said, "No, we're good. I've about had enough of this particular day."

"Ditto," said Geneva.

The writing was on the wall. Someone would have to take care of Helen. Dublin and Talia had too much to cope with already, and Florence's tiny Manhattan walk-up wouldn't work—and wouldn't be offered. This would be a perfect time for Paris to materialize, call a truce with their mother, and start making up for all the vodka-fueled disasters she'd missed.

Geneva listened to a siren wail in the distance and wished herself away.

CHAPTER FOUR

HELEN

Eustace Riley claimed it was Helen's butterscotch pie that did it. But even a Blue Ribbon dessert (two years running) was no match for that figure of hers at sixteen, and they both knew it. Any fool could see the way he looked her up and down. Then he pretended to wave hello to someone behind her, so she'd spin around and he could investigate her calves. As if she hadn't seen that trick coming.

That Fourth of July was hotter than a billy goat in a pepper patch. Eustace invited her to the show barn, where he claimed it was cooler. They leaned over the rails and laughed at the piglets pulling at one another's tails. He bought her a lemonade and wiped the sweat off the glass before he handed it to her. It struck her then what the difference was between a man like Eustace and the boys who'd been chasing her like bees from a shook hive. Eustace had manners and a confident air, as if he already had what he wanted before he thought to ask for it.

"You seventeen yet, Miss Helen?"

"Near enough."

And her daddy thought the same, though it surprised her some. Of course back then she wasn't thinking about the same things her daddy was—Eustace's family money and law degree, and getting loose of his daughter before she ended up damaged goods. Helen believed she had found True Love. Certainly her feelings matched up with what she read in those romances her mama hid behind the pickle jars in the pantry. The bare-chested pirate on the cover of one bore a likeness to Eustace, with his strong jaw and hair black as coal, though she'd never seen him with his shirt off and blushed to think of it. When her mama let drop that Eustace was thirty-two, she nearly fainted. Twice her age! But then she came around to look at it from another side. A man of such experience (and breeding) wasn't likely to make a foolish mistake, meaning he loved her and aimed to keep her. That thought made her bold and desirous, not only of Eustace but of leaving her childhood behind. As love goes at sixteen, Helen did love Eustace. And considering what was to transpire, her love was plenty true.

He courted her through the summer swelter. They held hands during the picture show and along the river walk in the evenings. If everyone in town gossiped about them, they gave no notice of caring. Helen held her head high, sure as sure could be that the opinion of the populace of Aliceville, and the entire state of South Carolina, mattered not a penny to her, not next to the attentions of a man of Eustace's stripe. He told her the townspeople had their jaws pinned to the floor because she was pretty. So pretty, in fact, he might just have to marry her. He let the comment fall real casual, but her heart jumped and her palms went clammy. He owned he wasn't in a particular hurry, but neither did he see any purpose in delaying the full measure of their happiness.

One evening in the middle of August they sat on his porch swing, sipping sweet tea and watching swallows cartwheeling across the sky. Eustace stood up and bent down on one knee. He held her hand light as a baby bird inside both of his. His eyes, dark and knowing, caught the gleam off the porch light. When she said yes, he kissed her like he was dying.

The next day they drove the thirty miles to Wilbur to see his folks. Helen's stomach exchanged positions with her heart the whole way there. Eustace's father came from a long line of tobacco farmers, but not the kind whose boots ever saw dirt. When Eustace and Helen arrived, the Rileys' girl saw them to the parlor, and kept her head bowed the whole time. Mrs. Riley's manners held up well, considering her only son was presenting her with a child as a daughter-in-law—and one from the wrong side of town. The elder Mr. Riley leaned his forearm on his belly as he sucked on a cigar. He eyed Helen over his bifocals. His eyebrows twitched like caterpillars on a hot plate.

"Young and frisky! Didn't know that was your taste, boy!"

She stared at her shoes.

Eustace's mother clucked. Then she barked at the girl to hurry up with the drinks.

．　．　．

Since she was six years old, Helen'd reckoned she wear her mama's wedding dress when the time came. It hung mysterious in a dark bag in her parents' closet behind Mama's funeral suit and the Bo Peep outfit she had sewn for a masquerade party twenty years before and worn to every Halloween party since, not that there'd been many. When Eustace asked for her hand, she expected her mama to offer up the dress, but it didn't happen. Helen suspected forces were at work, meaning Eustace. Sure enough, two weeks before the wedding day, Mama waltzed into Helen's room with a dress draped over her arms. "Eustace's folks brought this by. Modern, they called it." It was finer than any she'd seen. Lace appliqué over satin, with hundreds of tiny pearls stitched in a delicate flower and paisley design. She turned it over and counted thirty-four corset buttons down the back. Later, while her mama hung out the washing, she dug to the rear of the closet and pulled out the old dress. She fingered the dime-store buttons and yellowed fabric—not the Cinderella gown she remembered—and put it away.

Come the wedding day, Helen had dropped so much weight from nervous excitement that her mama had to stuff the bosom of her gown with cotton wool to make it fit proper. She would remember as much of that day as she might of a dream. One picture did stick in her mind: Eustace beside the preacher, taller by a head and easier, it appeared, in the house of the Lord. Satisfaction writ large across his face.

. . .

They celebrated her seventeenth birthday on the honeymoon. She'd never stayed in a hotel before. Never had reason to. Once in a blue moon Daddy'd drive them somewhere—to a lake for a swim, to a fishing hole he'd heard about and, on one occasion, clear into Columbia—but they'd always come home at the end of the day. He'd drive tired. Coming home from Columbia he'd swerved like a drunk, with only Mama's yelling to keep them out of the ditch. They'd already paid for home, he said, so that's where they'd sleep.

Not Eustace. They stayed a week in the Tower Suite at the Hotel Tybee near Savannah. Every day they walked the boardwalk, hand in hand, and swam in the ocean. Eustace laughed when Helen said if she stood on his shoulders she bet she could see Europe. But in the evening, while they were slow dancing on the lawn under the palms, he whispered that in Europe they would crown her, because that's how beautiful she was. His voice was honey pouring into her head. She was susceptible to such nonsense then.

She hadn't known what to expect when they went to bed, him bringing twenty years' experience under the covers with him. She should've guessed he wanted what he wanted and he got what he saw fit to take. He wasn't particularly gentle and he wasn't particularly mean—at least as far as she could judge. What did she know of such things? Mostly she was glad to fall asleep afterward and gladder still to see the light peeking around the drapes. She looked forward to each new day—piles of sweet, fat shrimp to eat, and the warm sand pushing up between her toes.

• • •

"Honeymoon's over," Eustace declared as he supervised the bellman stowing their cases in the trunk.

She missed the sea even before it disappeared from sight. He turned on the radio, hung his elbow out the window, and hummed along. She stared out at the houses in the towns they passed, wondering if any of them might contain the sort of life she was about to have. The fancy neighborhood in Raleigh intrigued her especially, and she wished they could slow down and have a closer look. But naturally she couldn't ask Eustace that.

They drove past the cemetery coming into Aliceville. Helen and all the other town kids always held their breath the whole way past, so as not to invite bad luck, but either she forgot or she decided she was no longer a child and took in air the way she usually did. Aliceville looked the same and it didn't. The drugstore, town hall, liquor store, and the other buildings along Main Street appeared to have shifted over a few feet. Maybe that's what marriage does, she thought. One day you're holding your breath lest a ghost fly up your nose and the next you're coming home as married as your own mother.

Eustace navigated the rutted drive leading to Helen's house and parked next to a shiny red Chevy truck with a dealer sticker in the window. Her daddy's rattletrap was nowhere in evidence.

"Looks like your daddy got himself a present," he said.

"That's not Daddy's. He wouldn't know where to look for that sort of money." Eustace raised his eyebrows, and she realized she'd contradicted him.

"Let's get your things, Princess."

They got out of the car. Helen noticed another layer of paint had peeled off the house. The weeds crowded the path and laid claim to the first step. Shame rose in Helen. She ran her hands down the crisp pleats of her skirt and reminded herself that although this ramshackle cottage might have been her home, it most assuredly wasn't any longer. Eustace had taken care of that.

Her daddy appeared in the doorway. He must've expected them because he'd put on a shirt. He swiped his mouth with the back of his hand, hitched up his trousers, and grinned.

"Welcome back! Look at you, Mrs. Helen Riley. You're brown as a nut." He gestured toward the truck. "How do you like it?"

"You picked a beauty, you did," Eustace said.

She said, "But, Daddy, how . . ."

Out of the corner of her eye she saw Eustace wink at him. Then her mama came and shooed everyone inside, reeling off a million questions about their trip. Helen would have to be content to riffle through her feelings another day, or forget about the meaning of that truck entirely.

. . .

Eustace's house was close to town. He let her do with it as she pleased, not that she had a firm idea of what ladies with money did with their houses, their gardens, or their husbands. She had help in every other day, which unnerved her some, as she wasn't used to having Negroes around. Louisa was about as old as her mama, and no doubt had children Helen's age. At first Helen busied herself in some part of the house Louisa wasn't, but soon decided it was foolishness. She learned Louisa didn't mind chatting as she shelled peas or scrubbed the floors. Helen asked a lot of questions about running the house, and would have asked more but for fear of appearing ignorant. One day she got up the nerve to ask Louisa what other ladies did all day. She laughed. Helen joined in and pretty soon the two of them were doubled over. They spent the rest of the afternoon making Helen's famous butterscotch pie.

The house was large, with a wide front porch and a shaded backyard. When Helen was alone, she stayed in the kitchen. If Louisa had done all the cooking—or if it was too hot to eat—she brought her sewing in there, or a book. The yellow gingham curtains and the ticking of the stove clock calmed her. Her mama came to call if she was already in town on other business. She never stayed long. She lit from chair to chair like a butterfly visiting flowers, then proclaimed she was needed at home and blew out the door.

Eustace left early for his law office in town or, if there was a trial, the court in the county seat. More evenings than not, he attended meetings of one sort or another, leaving Helen to her books and the radio. Weekends he took off hunting or fishing, but always returned in time to take her to a party, or the country club. She took great care with her appearance for these outings, knowing Eustace expected her to outshine the other ladies to such a degree that her age would be set aside. A quick study, she discovered which hairdos and styles of dress earned her admiring and envious looks from ladies and gentlemen alike.

She had been married only a month when she woke light-headed and queasy. She put two and two together and was equal parts scared and thrilled. Straight off she knew it was a girl. Eustace didn't realize, but they'd picked out the child's name at Tybee, the last night they sat on the beach. The moon shone like a silver dollar tossed on a velvet spread. Eustace had his arm around her. Same as when she lay against him in their hotel bed, he was the only thing between her and the on-and-on darkness. The salt lifted off the sea, and she breathed it in.

"What cities, do you suppose, would want me for a princess?"

"Paris, for a start."

What a beautiful word. It drifted lightly, like a promise to a child. "You been there?"

"A long time ago. With my family."

"Did you eat snails?"

He let out a bark of a laugh. "No. My mother tried to force them on me, but I got my way. Even then." He lay on the sand and pulled her on top of him. She felt herself blush, though not a soul could see her, not even him. There wasn't even that much moonlight. He put his hand on her breast and squeezed until she gasped. "And now I've got you."

CHAPTER FIVE

ELLA

Ella had been waiting forever for school to end. School was always boring, but today every single period seemed stuck in some bizarre time warp. In history class, Mrs. Bragarian droned on in super slo-mo. Normally Ella'd zone out or doodle her way across a few pages pretending to take notes, and the forty-seven minutes would dribble away. Not today. During biology, she snuck a couple of nonobvious looks—okay, more like stares—at Marcus Frye. But not even His Most Gorgeousness could distract her today. Which was another way of saying she was preoccupied.

When she finally got home, she stuck her head in the barn because her dad always wanted her to check in. Like some creeper in a panel van was going to haul her off between the bus stop and here. She waved hi and he waved back, but he didn't turn off the sander, so that was that. Prince Charles was playing baseball or hanging out with the Master Stoners or up to something else—what did she care? He'd been working all the angles since he was born. As long as it didn't involve her, more power to him. He wasn't home; that was the point. If he was, he'd be trying to get her to do his homework, or hitting her up for money or, worse, telling her a story about his friends. Daring Deeds of Dickheads. Awe-Inspiring Adventures of Assholes. And her mom was still in L.A. visiting her lunatic mother, the drunken stunt driver. She wouldn't be home until . . . When was it? Tonight? Tomorrow? Whatever.

The point was no one was around to bug her. She had all the peace and quiet she needed for the project she'd been thinking about since she woke up.

Last night she had this dream. She was standing in the middle of an enormous lawn that stretched all the way to the horizon. The puffy clouds overhead started linking up until the whole sky was a mass of cotton balls. Snow fell, but it wasn't cold. The snowflakes were ginormous, the kind you can see the shape of when they land on your skin for the split second before they melt. The snow got thicker, and swirled around her until she was in the middle of a snow tornado. It wasn't scary. She tingled all over with excitement.

Then the best part happened. The snowflakes turned into words. As they spun past, she read them, only it was more like knowing than reading. *Potent*. That was one. *Gamble. Heretical.* (She wasn't sure what that meant.) *Greening.* The dream went on for a long time, and when she woke up she could remember every single word. At school she thought about writing them down but knew that wasn't what she should do.

First things first. She pulled her stash of weed from the tummy of her Build-A-Bear and rolled a joint. Most kids were into alcohol, probably because it was a cinch to get and parents generally looked the other way. But booze was mundane and bourgeois. Weed was for artists and dreamers. Leaning out the window, she took a couple of hits, then spit in her palm and snuffed it out. It was good shit, and she didn't want to overdo it. She had work to do. After she put away the weed, she kissed the bear on the nose and gave the room a couple of squirts with orange oil spray. Her mom thought she was addicted to the stuff. Well, you could put it that way.

She found straws in the kitchen and fishing line in Prince Charles's room and went to work. Writing the words on little rectangles cut from index cards took her an hour. There turned out to be exactly one hundred, which creeped her out a little. Whatever. It's my brain, she thought. I have to learn to deal with what it dishes out. Making the mobiles took another hour and a half. It wasn't easy to get the length of the straws and strings right so the words balanced. She wondered if she should choose which words hung together, but scotched the idea. That was the sort of thing her mom would do. No, first her mom would organize them alphabetically or by parts of speech, then decide she needed a spreadsheet.

Ella climbed a stool and attached the mobiles to the ceiling. She was pretty sure she wasn't supposed to tack things to the ceiling, but this was necessary. Critical. Vital.

See? It was working already.

She'd been writing poetry since she could talk. Her very first one went like this: Kitten shark / kitten dark / Kitten bark, bark, bark. Made her laugh every time she thought of it. And, sadly, it was better than a lot of stuff she'd written recently. Which was exactly why she needed a revelation. She got that everyone's work changes as they get older. She got that it was normal to cringe at poems she had written three years ago. That was her rhyming phase, for Christ's sake! Sonnets were her next thing. She read every book about the Tudors she could find and her poetry got all Olde Tyme Englishy. Still rhyming, but more complicated with iambs and all that. She was so into it she forgot how to spell the regular way, and her grades in English tanked. After that she broke into free verse. So freaking pleased with herself you'd think she invented it. The breakthrough gave her a better window into growing up than getting her annoying period did. Her mom presented her with books like *How to Survive Being a Mutant Teenager* and *PMS: Nature's Battle Cry*, but all she wanted to read was Wallace Stevens. She tried to copy his style but realized she was out of his league—at least for now. Instead, she wrote some drifty pieces that might have been song lyrics for people too stoned to follow a verse. They didn't suck, considering her tender age.

But since then her poems were garbage. She couldn't even stand what she wrote last month. Total unmitigated drivel. Derivative drivel. She'd been hoping for some sort of epiphany. The wordstorm had to be it.

Ella lay down in the midst of the paper scraps. Above her, the mobiles stirred a little, twisting and rocking. She could make out the words from here—that was important. Her mind stepped from one floating word to another—*gallant, clapboard, feverish, necessity*—and she smiled.

It wasn't a swirling storm, like in her dream, but an ocean. Each white card was the crest of a wave, catching the sunlight like a diamond chip. She watched from above, suspended in the endless sky, while her words danced upon the water.

· · ·

She lay there for who knows how long. In a wordstorm-and-weed-induced trance or something. Then she gradually came out of it, checked her phone for the time, and remembered she had a shitload of homework. She learned a long time ago it was easier to do the work than argue with her mom about why she wasn't doing it. Her mom was fixated on the idea that Ella was smart, and so there could be no excuse for not getting As. In reality, there were lots of excuses. Not feeling like doing it, for example. Or not wanting to come off as a nerd with no life by handing in every assignment complete and on time. Because even if you weren't one of the cool kids (and she was 100 percent not), you had to at least fake having something going on other than school. None of the kids knew about her poems—talk about social suicide!—but they knew she was pretty good on guitar. A guy in her grade who was on the edge of cool almost asked her to be in a band. At least that's what someone said. That was enough to save her from Loserville. But nothing could save her from homework. Or her mom.

Most of the time it wasn't difficult. She'd hang out on her special chair in her dad's workshop and read or do math problems. He didn't insist on digging into her life, which was a relief. Sometimes she'd think out loud, and they'd end up talking. She adored the smell of wood and varnish, and the sound of the hand planer rasping like a baby dragon. The big saw was too loud to think around. Diesel hated it, too, so that's when she'd take him for a walk.

Prince Charles didn't do homework. He outsourced it. And he cheated. He'd had some close calls, not that their parents had a clue. His shenanigans had started early. In first grade he set up convoluted trading sessions at lunch so he'd end up with exactly what he wanted to eat. Didn't matter who had it, or how many trades it took. It was pretty funny, watching him work the other little kids, making them believe they really wanted a bag of wheat crackers more than a brownie. They'd start to cry or get mad, and he'd give them half of their brownie and tell them they wouldn't get that kind of deal the next day.

But Charlie wasn't little anymore. He'd get caught eventually, and it wouldn't be so cute. Not that it was any of Ella's business. She made a point of knowing some of what he was up to, in case it came in handy, and sometimes he got weed for her at a decent price, but other than that, who cared?

CHAPTER SIX

GENEVA

Monday evening traffic was light on the Golden Gate Bridge as Geneva headed north out of the city toward home. She lowered her window and a crisp breeze blew through. Twenty miles offshore a wall of fog sat on the water like a layer of meringue. Tonight, or tomorrow night at the latest, the fog would climb over the headlands and enter the bay. A few days later, when the land had cooled, it would shrink and gather itself again, waiting for the warm valleys to call it in. She loved the fog cycle. It was predictable, yet never the same. And the way it crouched offshore, then slunk inland, reminded her of an animal on the hunt. Fog made her think of redwoods, especially the ones along her driveway. From April to November they drank only fog, catching mist along their drooping branches. When Ella was five, Geneva led her under the largest of their redwoods. The fog lay thick as cream, and when they stood under the canopy beneath an umbrella, water fell in sheets around them. Ella looked up at her mother, wide-eyed and openmouthed, as if Geneva, and not the tree, had made it rain.

She drove past the redwoods and the house came into view. She and Tom had toured the property with a real estate agent a few months after they married. The wisteria over the porch and the apple trees in the yard lent a romantic note, but when Tom's foot went straight through the floorboards in the kitchen she had seen enough. He frowned as he inspected the rafters, the foundation and the roof, so she assumed he had come to the same conclusion. Later she learned his frowning was mostly for show. He told her the place was perfect.

"Are you sure?"

"Trust me."

He drove the price down, closed the deal, and set to work. For a year, they devoted evenings and weekends to the restoration. To save money, they mined the barn for lumber, hardware, and fixtures. They suspended interior doors on overhead rails, turned bridles and halters into drawer pulls, and installed a stable door leading to the garden to encourage a breeze on warm days. They saved for last a small bedroom with a view of the backyard. On painting day, Geneva stood by the open window because the fumes made her queasy. Tom dipped his brush in a can of daffodil-yellow paint and drew a smiley face on the T-shirt stretched over her rounded belly.

·   ·   ·

She left her roller bag and handbag next to the car and headed for the barn. Diesel lifted his head when she opened the door but didn't get up because Ella was using him as a footstool. Years ago, Tom had moved an old overstuffed armchair into the barn. If Ella couldn't be found in her room, she was in the chair reading or doing homework while her father worked.

Geneva breathed in the familiar scent of sawdust and realized how glad she was to be home. She called hello and walked around the workbench where Tom was sanding an artichoke finial.

He set down his work and opened his arms. "Welcome home." They embraced.

Ella waved. "Hey, Mom."

"Hi, Ella."

Geneva kissed the top of her daughter's head, happy she wasn't hiding in her room. At the same time, she couldn't deny feeling jealous that Ella usually chose to be with Tom. When she acknowledged her insecurity to Tom, he had pointed out he worked at home, and had more time. He also said Ella, a perennially quiet child, was no more talkative in the barn than elsewhere. But their conversations were not the point. Tom had a simpler relationship with Ella than she did, and with Charlie, too. When the children were small, Geneva was the undisputed center of their universe. She couldn't remember when it had begun to change, but it had. Maybe her personality was better suited to infants and toddlers, and Tom's to adolescents. If true, then her most intimate days with her children had passed. Her rational mind told her she ought to accept these changes, but that didn't make it hurt any less. And being the de facto disciplinarian didn't help.

She squatted in front of Diesel and scratched his ears. "How's everyone's favorite ottoman?" Diesel licked her hand and whined softly.

Ella said, "How's Nana?"

"Better. She should be out of the hospital in a couple days."

"That's good."

Geneva shrugged. "I saw your cousins. Whit was asking about you. He wanted to know if you had a boyfriend yet, or if you were still cool."

"He said that?"

"Yes. He's a riot. Like his dad."

"We haven't seen them in a while. Wasn't it Thanksgiving?"

Geneva smiled, gratified her family mattered to Ella. With the Novaks a constant presence, she didn't take her daughter's memory of Riley family events for granted. "Yes, Thanksgiving in L.A."

"Oh, yeah. Nana fell asleep at the table. Uncle Dub got all the Christmas stuff from the garage, and we strung up lights and decorated the table while she was out of it." She stopped to control a fit of laughter. "Then she woke up, looked around, and said, 'Must've been the eggnog. Merry Christmas!' "

Geneva winced. Perhaps some Riley family events were better forgotten.

"Ellie," Tom said as he put his tools away, "I'm about finished here. Give Diesel his dinner, would you?"

"Sure." She turned her book upside down on the chair and left, the dog at her heels.

Geneva picked up the book. She tore a corner from the newspaper on the floor, marked the page, and placed the book on a side table. "Ella was verging on garrulous. What's that about?"

Tom shrugged. "She's a teenager."

"It's just been so long since she said that much. At least to me. Anyway, did she do the practice SAT test?"

"I don't know. She was in her room a long time today working on something. You can ask her."

"Thanks. I love being the SAT police."

"You've got a knack for it."

"Someone has to be the parent."

He glared at her. "What the hell do you think I do?"

Whatever's easiest, she thought as she sank into the chair.

Tom swept wood shavings into a dustpan with short, sharp strokes. "Did you and Dublin get anywhere with finding help for your mother?"

"Tom, can we talk about this later?"

"I guess. But isn't there some urgency?"

Geneva sighed. "We called a few places that were recommended, but no one was available on such short notice. I'll call more tomorrow."

Tom stood in front of her. "I mentioned this on the phone, but I'm going to say it again. She could come here."

"And I'll say what I said on the phone: I can't see it working."

"Why not?"

"How can you ask that?"

"She's a sixty-four-year-old woman who had a bad car accident. And she's your mother."

"She could pay for the care she needs. She'd just have to curtail her spending."

"How much?"

"She'd probably have to move somewhere cheaper. Out of California."

"Away from her grandchildren."

"That she's so very close to. She called Charlie 'Barney' the other day."

"She's old."

"Any other tired excuses you want to trot out, Tom?"

"I don't see why you're so hostile."

"Because you're doing a stellar job of making me feel guilty."

"Honestly, Geneva, your guilt should be telling you something."

"Right now it's telling me that you're pressuring me. Try backing off."

"I only want you to do the right thing."

"Right for whom?"

"For everyone."

"Good luck with that." She instantly regretted her sarcastic tone. "Look. I know a daughter is supposed to help out her mother, especially if there aren't other good options. I get it. But why does that automatically override the fact that I don't want her in our house?"

"Maybe she's learned her lesson. Maybe if she's here, and she needs to rely on you, she'll see how to be a better person."

She wanted to laugh. A better person. So ridiculous, so trite. But Tom meant it. His face betrayed concern and hope. She had always been drawn to his earnestness and optimism, fascinated by his sunny worldview. She didn't consider herself a cynic, but next to her husband she was. She felt disappointed in herself even while knowing, in logical terms, that her attitude toward her mother was justified. At work, Geneva was precisely the person she needed to be. At home, however, she felt compelled by Tom, and sometimes by her children, to consider other possible versions of herself. More flexible. More forgiving. At forty she hadn't decided whether strength or fear kept her true to her real self—the tough, rational one.

"I wish it didn't have to be me."

"It's not you. It's us."

"I know, Tom. Thanks." That's what he deserved to hear, but she didn't believe it for a minute. When it came to her mother, she was on her own.

. . .

She'd first met Tom outside the clinic during her second year at the veterinary school at the University of California at Davis. One afternoon she left the building, intending to study at home in her studio apartment, then take a long walk before dinner. She pictured the container of vegetable curry she'd moved from the freezer to the refrigerator the night before and wondered whether she had finished the jar of chutney from the farmers' market.

A man sat hunched over on a bench, a dog's collar in his hands, and a leash at his feet. His shoulders shook with each loud sob, the sound half choke, half cry. Geneva stopped, unsure of what to do. Was it worse to ignore him or to intrude? She took a few steps toward her car, away from the crying man, and stopped again. It felt wrong to leave. She wondered for a moment if she recognized him, if that might account for the pull she felt, but couldn't place him.

She never cried in public. Even in the privacy of her apartment, she never gave in so thoroughly to distress. Perhaps she had as a child, but she couldn't recall a specific incident. When her father died, she must have broken down then, but she couldn't be certain. She could summon few clear memories from that time.

She walked to the bench and sat down. People went in and out of the clinic doors. Dogs stopped to sniff and pee on a worn patch of grass. An afternoon breeze lifted across the playing fields on the far side of the parking lot. She zipped up her jacket. The man's crying eased. He sat up, wiped his face with his sleeve, and stared ahead at the field where a group of men was getting ready to play soccer. He reached for Geneva's hand.

She struggled to comprehend why she was holding hands with a complete stranger—and an emotionally distraught one at that. But a deeper feeling, instinctual, told her she was exactly where she needed to be. For once, she listened.

The man turned to face her. His eyes were hazel. "He was a really good dog."

She squeezed his hand. "What was his name?"

"Larry."

She couldn't help a small smile.

"I know." He shook his head a little and shrugged. "It suited him." His expression shifted, suddenly aware of himself, but not embarrassed. "I'm Tom." He smiled at her.

Clarity. Not the certainty of a well-reasoned argument, or the satisfaction of a properly completed procedure. But clarity, like light itself.

"It suits you," she said.

Eighteen years later, she remembered the feeling, but dimly. On dark days she felt no more than the hope of its return. Her love for Tom was at sea in a fog.

. . .

At six the next morning, she arranged her swim fins, paddles, buoy, and kickboard on the edge of the community pool. A young woman in an ankle-length parka and ski hat sat atop the lifeguard stand, her knees hugged to her chest, and gazed vaguely toward the only other swimmer—a man whom Geneva recognized as a regular. On other mornings, they had nodded to each other across the lane lines but never spoke. She put on her goggles and pressed the lenses to ensure they were watertight. Goose bumps rose on her arms and legs. She entered the water feetfirst. Fog swirled above the surface of the pool, obscuring, then revealing the large lap timer three lanes away. She stuck a piece of paper detailing her workout onto the pool wall just above the waterline. The workouts came from a Web site. She printed out a month's worth at a time and stored them in her swim bag. She never read the workout until she entered the pool. If it called for lots of sprinting, or length after length of butterfly, she would be tempted to crumple it up and improvise. But once in the water, she was committed.

To her relief, the printout called for long sets to build endurance. She pushed off the wall and began the warm-up series. Each time her arms came out of the water, she felt the cold. Her legs felt heavy, and her flip turns were off by a foot. She concentrated on lengthening her stroke, on catching the water and pushing it past her. She imagined her body as a swimming machine, smooth and efficient. After twenty laps, she found her cadence. She unhooked her mind from the work of her body and let it drift.

To her surprise, the first person who snagged her thoughts was not her mother, but her father. He would have turned eighty a month ago, but she couldn't picture him as an elderly man. He was frozen in his late forties, upright and strong, with a touch of gray at his temples. When Geneva was three, Eustace Riley became mayor of Aliceville. His family's reputation and wealth had helped him garner attention, but it was his self-assurance that held it. It seemed natural to Geneva he should run their town—the only world she knew. He handled every situation within the jurisdiction of his family and his town with unguarded authority. And if he were alive today, he would know how to handle her mother.

As she swam lap after lap, she imagined her parents together as they were thirty years before, walking home from church or sharing a drink on the wide front porch. Her mother was so young, her hair golden and her eyes clear and bright. She was innocent of her future as a thirty-six-year-old widow. She didn't drink then, not more than most people. Occasionally she came home from a party tottering on her heels and laughing a little too loudly. If the children were awake, her father would steer Helen into the kitchen by her elbow and instruct Paris to make coffee. He was impervious to alcohol and late nights, rising each morning at five without fail.

She stopped at the pool wall to catch her breath and take a couple glugs from her sports drink. Her vision of her father was that of an eleven-year-old. How could it be otherwise? But it didn't matter. She aspired to emulate him, to manage every situation with quiet ease. Tom wanted her to invite Helen to convalesce at their house out of filial duty, and with the hope of improving the mother-daughter relationship. She would take her mother in, not for Tom's reasons but her own. She would find a way to cope with her, and to help her. Her father would have wanted her to do no less.

Geneva glanced at the workout sheet. One more set of five hundred yards, starting slowly and building by hundreds to her fastest pace. She pushed off the wall, her arms stretched in front in a streamlined position. She executed two dolphin kicks, coasted halfway down the lane, and began her long, smooth strokes.

CHAPTER SEVEN

GENEVA

Pushing open the glass door, Geneva entered the rehabilitation center where her mother had been since her release from the hospital two days earlier. Helen waited in the reception area in a wheelchair. Her arm hung in a sling, and her right leg was encased in a brace. An orderly stood behind her, hands on the handles.

Geneva bent to kiss her mother on the cheek. "Happy Mother's Day. Ready to go?"

"You're late."

"Tom and I had a little trouble leaving Dublin's."

"What sort of trouble?"

"I'll tell you later."

"Is it really Mother's Day?"

"It is." Geneva addressed the orderly. "Do I need to sign anything?"

He handed her a clipboard. "John Hancock at the X, please."

She glanced at the release and signed it.

Helen gave a wry smile. "You just paid my bill."

The orderly laughed. "We're going to miss your spunk, Mrs. Riley." He showed Geneva how to operate the wheelchair and followed her outside. "You have a nice Mother's Day with your family."

Geneva wheeled her mother down the ramp to the curb. Tom and Dublin waited beside the open doors of the Cherokee. Tom had accompanied Geneva to L.A. in case Helen needed assistance on the way home.

"We sprung you!" Dublin shouted. "Quick! Before the cops get here!"

"One prison to another, more like," Helen mumbled.

Geneva shook her head in dismay and set the brake.

Tom helped Helen stand; then he and Dublin lifted her into the front seat.

Dublin wiped his brow in an exaggerated motion. "Good thing you still have your girlish figure, Mom."

"Same as Nancy Reagan. A perfect size six."

Geneva recognized the thinly veiled reference to her own height and athletic build, which her mother considered less than ladylike. As if she were in control of her genetic material.

She and Dublin climbed into the backseat. He pinched her knee in a horse bite. Reflexively, she elbowed him in the ribs.

He winked at her. "Just like old times, huh, Ginny?" She smiled at him.

Tom reached across and clipped Helen's seat belt. They drove the few miles to the condo to collect her things. Helen insisted on coming inside.

"We can pack for you, Mom," Geneva said.

"I don't want you all rifling through my drawers. And how could you know what I want?"

So Tom and Dublin unloaded her into the wheelchair.

She pointed to the passenger seat. "My bag, please." Dublin placed it on her lap and wheeled her inside. The one-bedroom condo was crowded with heavy furniture from the Aliceville house. The blinds were shut, and the air was stale. Geneva tilted the blinds and slid open the door that led to a small balcony overlooking a pool. Several adults lounged nearby under umbrellas while children splashed in the water. A small boy sprinted along the coping. A woman leaped from her chair, grabbed his arm, and swatted his bottom. His wailing carried into the room.

"If you leave that open," Helen said, "all you'll hear is screaming."

"What's a little screaming?" Dublin said. "Smells like a crypt in here."

He parked his mother in the bedroom, then helped Tom empty the sparse contents of the refrigerator into a box. Geneva couldn't remember having been in her mother's bedroom before. Talia must have been the one who'd helped her move in five years earlier. How sad it must be to get older, she thought. To raise your family in a beautiful house in the small town you grew up in, where every person on the street was someone you knew, then to watch your family go, one by one. And finally, to end up in a cramped condo in an enormous city, hoping your children grant you a slice of their lives.

"The suitcase is under the bed," Helen said.

Geneva bent down and recognized the red roller bag she and Tom had given Helen for her first California Christmas. "For visiting us," he had said. "Or Florence and Renaldo," Geneva added, intending to suggest her mother had options. Now she could see how she might have felt pushed away.

The bag was stuck. While Geneva attempted to free it, she heard a drawer near the bed open. She peeked over the bed. Her mother had her hand over her handbag. The drawer of the bedside table was gaping. A flash of surprise came and went on Helen's face.

"I can help you get what you need," Geneva said.

Helen pulled a zebra-striped glasses case out of her bag and showed it to her daughter. "My extra set. Just in case."

Geneva brushed away a pang of uneasiness. "Good thinking." She unzipped the suitcase and opened the closet. "Okay, what do you want? And remember it's colder there."

"Don't remind me."

When Helen finished with the closet, she directed Geneva to the dresser. Four framed photos were arranged on top. Front and center was the same photo of Dublin and his family in Santa Monica that Geneva had on her desk at work. Another was of Geneva's family, including Diesel sporting reindeer horns, from two Christmases ago. The third she had never seen. Florence and Renaldo, grinning and sweaty, arms over each other's shoulders at the finish line of a race. She thought it an odd choice for her mother.

"Is this a recent photo?"

"That? Not really. But it's the only one of the two of them I have. No decent wedding photos." Florence and Renaldo had been married by a friend in New York. All the photos of the occasion included one or more of a motley assortment of people Helen did not know. "I don't want strangers in my bedroom. Especially not New Yorkers."

The last photo, in the back, pictured the four Riley children lined up on the porch of the house in Aliceville. Geneva guessed she and Dublin were around five and six. His expression was one of concerted seriousness, as if he had been told—for the last time—to behave. Geneva's head was turned toward him. Florence and Paris were perhaps ten and twelve. Florence was half a head taller but still very much a girl, smiling awkwardly. Paris was relaxed and bored; she understood her beauty.

"Mom, do you have a recent phone number for Paris? She sent me a number for a satellite phone almost two years ago. I've tried calling, but no one picks up."

"You know I don't."

"I just thought maybe—"

"You don't need to talk to her."

I do, though, Geneva thought. But she didn't exactly know why. She didn't really know Paris, who had left home upon graduating from high school. After she received her college degree, she didn't follow her lifelong dream and attend law school, but instead joined the Peace Corps. A year in the Central African Republic turned into five. She returned to the States for two years, living in Washington, D.C., and by then Geneva was enrolled in college in California. Paris landed a job with a development organization in Sierra Leone and, aside from brief, sporadic, and unannounced appearances at the home of one of her siblings, never left Africa again. She worked in remote areas and changed location frequently. When Geneva did hear from her, Paris only spoke of her work. She had never married.

Dublin appeared in the doorway. "I give up. Where'd you hide your bank statements?"

"What do you want with those?"

"We discussed this, remember? I browbeat you into agreeing that I would make sure all your bills got paid. You can't even write a check with your shoulder tied up."

"There's a file box in the closet."

"And I'll need the PINs that go with the accounts."

"Those things are such a nuisance! I made them all the same. PayPal, eBay, savings, the pharmacy—all the same. It's '80 proof!' There's an exclamation point at the end."

Geneva shook her head. "That's not safe, Mom."

She waved it off.

"You have to admit it's memorable," Dublin said.

"I forgot," Helen said. "The ATM's different. That one's 'cash.' "

After Dublin left the room, her mother asked what had delayed them that morning. Geneva explained Jack had been upset about having to go to his brother's judo practice. He'd thrown a ball through a window, then lay down in the driveway, blocking the cars. Dublin and Talia spoke with him for a half hour before he finally got up.

"That boy is certainly a handful."

"Yes. He can be."

"They should be stricter with him. Talia especially."

Geneva stopped in the middle of folding a sweater. "I doubt it would help."

"Why not? You have to be firm. Particularly with boys. Remember how Dublin was. Never still a minute, never listened to a word."

"But Dublin wasn't autistic."

"I don't care what they want to call it. Jack needs discipline."

Geneva lifted her head. "You never had a child with a serious problem, Mom."

Her mother's eyes narrowed slightly, as if weighing her response. She studied her daughter a moment longer, then turned to the window. "No, I suppose not. You and I should both be thankful for that."

· · ·

They packed Helen's belongings into the car and dropped Dublin at his house. As he hugged Geneva, he whispered, "Don't forget to lock her cage at night."

While Tom drove, Geneva leaned her head back and stared out the window. They left the city behind, and soon sagebrush and spindly pines replaced the palms. Joining a line of cars that climbed out of the valley, they entered the Castaic Mountains.

Helen squirmed in her seat. "Geneva, hand me my pillow, please?"

"What pillow?"

"The one I asked you to take from the bed. Don't tell me you forgot."

"Well, either you didn't tell me, or I forgot."

"We need to turn around."

"We've got loads of pillows at home."

"Not like mine. It's Tempur-Pedic."

Geneva leaned forward. "Mom, if we turn around now we're going to get caught in the traffic going into the valley." She pointed at the congested lanes heading south.

"And if we don't, I won't be able to sleep."

"Maybe Dublin can send it. You'll have it in a couple days."

"It shouldn't be Dublin's problem when you're the one who forgot."

Tom said, "We did tell the kids we'd be home by nine at the latest. I'd hate to come home at eleven when they've got school tomorrow."

Helen sighed. "I suppose I won't be sleeping much anyway because of my leg." She folded up her sweater and placed it behind her shoulder. Twenty minutes later, she dozed off.

. . .

Outside Bakersfield, while Helen slept, Tom told Geneva about his latest project: a spiral staircase with a jungle motif. The client, a rain forest biologist, wanted animals and plants carved into the risers. The railing and balusters would be covered in vines and lianas in high relief. He'd presented the client with several sketches, which were immediately approved, and was keen to set to work.

She was asking about which animals the man had chosen when her mother stirred. She twisted in her seat and pulled at the shoulder strap.

Tom asked, "Should we wake her?"

Geneva leaned in between the front seats. Her mother's brow appeared untroubled and her mouth was open slightly. "I don't know. Maybe she'll . . ."

Helen cried out and flung her left arm, hitting Geneva in the face. She pulled back and put her hand to her nose.

Tom glanced in the rearview mirror. "Are you all right?"

Before she could answer, Helen's arm flew out again, colliding with the steering wheel. The car swerved and a horn blasted behind them.

He straightened the wheel and checked his side mirrors. "Jesus."

Helen sat motionless, her arm limp on the center console. Geneva took hold of her mother's shoulder and shook her.

She awoke. Disoriented, she looked from side to side. "What's going on?"

Tom let out a long breath. "I think you had a nightmare." He checked his rearview mirror again. "You're bleeding."

Geneva dug in her bag for a tissue, then dabbed her nose. "It's okay."

"I can pull over."

"Bleeding from what? Let me look." Helen turned partway around, then grimaced. "My shoulder hurts. My good one." She adjusted herself in her seat and straightened her sweater. "It was an accident. I was dreaming about an accident."

Geneva's nose stung as if she had been submerged in water without holding her breath. Tom handed Helen a water bottle and asked if she wanted to stop for a break. She shook her head, and asked him about the crops stretching for miles on either side of the freeway.

Geneva imagined her mother lying in her bed in her condo, waking in the darkness to discover she'd knocked over a glass or a lamp. Whatever nightmare had broken the paralysis of sleep would still be running at the edges of her consciousness. A cockroach escaping the light. How daunting to piece reality together, in the confusion of the night, alone. Whenever Geneva had a frightening dream, the sight of her husband beside her instantly righted her world, as did the realization that her children were lying on the far side of the bedroom wall, deep in untroubled sleep. As alienated as she often felt from them, her family provided this comfort.

Helen laughed at something Tom said and reached over to touch his forearm. Geneva blotted her nose with the tissue. The bleeding had almost stopped, but the sight of her blood triggered a memory. She was eight, and it was Mother's Day. She had decided to sing a song for her mother—she couldn't remember which one—and had run downstairs to Paris's room to ask if she would accompany her on piano. In her excitement, she burst through the door without knocking. Paris leaped out of nowhere like a jaguar and slammed the door in her face. Geneva cried out and put her hand to her nose. It came away bloody. She ran through the house in search of her mother, her father—anyone. In the upstairs bathroom, she wet a facecloth and examined herself in the mirror. Only then did it come to her that, although she hadn't seen anyone, Paris had not been alone.

CHAPTER EIGHT

❦

ELLA

Ella would never admit it, but she was looking forward to her parents coming home, even if they were bringing crazy Nana. It had been a long weekend. She and Prince Charles (and Diesel) had stayed with Uncle Ivan and Aunt Leigh and, of course, Pierce and Spencer. You'd think that was an accounting firm and not a pair of teenage boys, right? They were okay when they were little, same as the Prince, but then they'd turned into testosterone-crazed lunatics. She'd steered clear, except that (a) she had to keep tabs on the Prince's activities, as previously noted, and (b) the twins were friends with Marcus Frye (His Most Gorgeousness). To have any chance with Marcus she'd have to be chill around his friends. And for super immature and annoying guys, they weren't all that bad.

So all weekend—at least the part of it when they weren't playing baseball, watching baseball, or talking about baseball—the Prince and the Accountants were scheming. Ella wasn't eavesdropping or anything (she wasn't a creeper), but when she sat still with a book or her poetry notebook, people—especially ones with their heads up their asses like these guys—treated her like furniture. Sunday morning she was in the living room on the couch working on a poem, Diesel snoozing on the floor next to her. In came the Accountants and the Prince from the kitchen. The back of the couch hid most of her, but the boys wouldn't have noticed anyway. They were talking about how they wanted to be in the Battle of the Bands at school. All the Novaks were musical. When they got together it was like a friggin' jamboree. Pierce played drums and Spencer played electric guitar. A senior jazz junkie called Rango said he'd play bass for them. He was weird, but even the Accountants knew bass players were supposed to be. They still needed someone who could sing, and they didn't want a girl because they were Neanderthals like that.

Anyway, the Prince wanted in. The Accountants didn't think a freshman was any better than a girl. The Prince turned on his princely charm big-time.

"Let me audition. You won't regret it."

"No way."

"Yeah, no way."

"I know my talents, gentlemen. I can sing."

"I don't think so."

"Yeah, I don't think so."

And then it got interesting. Charlie reached into his pocket and pulled out a wad of cash. He peeled off twenties like some little shyster.

"How much to let me try out? Twenty? Forty?"

Pierce grabbed two bills. "Okay, let's hear it. Pick a song. If you don't suck, forty more will get you in front of the band." Like he was some fucking talent agent. And as if two-thirds of the band wasn't right there.

Ella the End Table smiled to herself. That was a lot of cash for a kid who didn't have a job. Whatever he was up to, she'd soon make it her business.

The Prince stepped back, like his brilliance might shatter them, and cleared his throat.

Pierce said, "What're you singing? In case we don't recognize it."

Spencer snorted.

Ella knew. He'd been singing it in his room for two weeks. Probably googled "Best Rock Audition Songs for Clueless Dicks."

"'Rock on You.'" The Prince put on his most authentic bad-boy rocker face, jammed an invisible mike in his face, and sang:

> Hey, baby, baby, dancin' to the beat,
> Pickin' up my rhythm, lookin' so sweet.

Spencer turned to Pierce. "It's Lousy Ferret. Great band."

"Shut up, dickhead."

The Prince climbed up the stairs behind him while he sang and got all growly for the chorus. Good thing his voice had changed all the way. Otherwise he would've sounded like a hyena trying to yodel. Diesel's ears perked up, and he cocked his head as if he couldn't decide whether Charlie was in pain and needed help.

> *Hey, baby, baby, here's what I'm gonna do:*
> *Take you home, throw you on the bed, and rock*
> *all over you.*
> *Rock on you! Rock on you!*

The singing wasn't half bad but between the fist pumping and hip thrusting, Ella didn't know whether to laugh or puke.

> *Rock on you! Take you home, throw you on the*
> *bed, and rock all over you.*

Spencer was getting into it. He bit his lower lip, stuck out his chin, and grimaced the way guys do when they want to be all tough. Even Pierce couldn't help himself. Started fist pumping along with the "Rock on you!" parts. Ella had to hand it to the Prince. He could work a room.

Halfway through the second verse, Pierce remembered he was supposed to be cool and put his hand up. "Okay. Okay, Charlie. That's enough."

Show over. Ella got up and cut across the living room. The boys noticed her for the first time.

"Hey, Smella." Charlie swayed like he was drunk on his own manliness. "Did you like it?"

"Was that you? I was on my way to the kitchen to see if the garbage disposal was stuck."

•   •   •

Later the same day they all went over to Aunt Juliana's house. She was the middle Novak. Theo was the eldest, then Anica, then Juliana, then Ivan, and finally Ella's dad. Juliana was the only one who was divorced and the only one with no kids. She did have a boyfriend, Jon, and a Doberman, Aldo. She hadn't had either of them very long, but as Granny Novak said, every single time they got together, it was a step in the right direction—the boyfriend, not the dog. Like Juliana'd invented divorce or something.

Her house was in Novato, in the older, less strip-mall part of town. It was small but it was just her and the dog. Jon, who introduced himself as "Jon without an H," still had his own place, although there was talk of them "shacking up," as Grandpa put it. Ella and the rest of them went straight through the house to the backyard. Jon without an H was at the barbecue. For a nerdy guy he looked like he'd turned a steak or two in his time, which was how you had to be if you were a guy and you wanted to hang with Novaks. That and never talk trash about anyone in the family. Which was pretty cool, if you think about it. Maybe in twos or threes they came clean with each other, but they didn't make a team sport of it.

The rule applied to pets, too. Ella and Charlie called Aldo "Adolf," but not in front of Juliana or anyone other than their parents. That dog was scary. Usually Ella's mom didn't let them use "demeaning nicknames"—"the Accountants," for instance— but when it came to that dog, she made an exception. Juliana got him as a puppy but never trained him. In fact, according to her mom, she encouraged Adolf to be aggressive. Not intentionally, but it was all the same to her mom. Ruining pets (or kids for that matter) by not laying down the law was wrong, whether you meant to do it or not. It wasn't a big deal when Adolf was small. If he jumped on you, you could just push him down. If he nipped, you could put your hand around his muzzle and he'd get the picture. But now he was way past that stage. And he had a thing for Jon without an H.

Juliana hadn't had many people over since Aldo arrived. Now she was trying to prove she fit in with the married folk, that her guy could feed everyone, too. The whole Novak horde wasn't there, but Jon without an H had this gigantic grill absolutely covered with meat, plus some tofu or whatever for Anica's daughter Kristin, who didn't eat things with eyes. Adolf parked himself under a tree near the grill, and kept watch on either the meat or Jon without an H's back. It was hard to tell which, but something was making him drool. Then Juliana went over to see how things were going, and Jon without an H started moving some sausages from the grill to this huge platter. That was Adolf's cue. He skulked toward them, his head low like a lion stalking. Ella heard a growl roll out of him like faraway thunder. Jon without an H heard it, too, and twisted his head around. Juliana had the tray with the meat. Adolf stopped in his tracks.

Jon without an H didn't take his eyes off the dog. "Did you feed him, Jules?"

"Of course I did." Her voice was really casual.

"Cause he looks hungry."

Other people started to pay attention.

Juliana said, "Maybe I should give him a sausage."

From behind Ella, Uncle Ivan said, "Probably not a good idea to encourage him."

"It's just a hot dog." Juliana handed the tray to Jon without an H. "Here. You give him one, then you'll be friends for life."

Adolf turned the volume up on his growl as Juliana gave his whole dinner to the intruder. His haunches quivered for a second; then he sprang. Jon without an H must have played video games because he threw the tray at the flying dog, hitting Adolf in the nose, then leaped sideways in a total ninja move. Adolf landed in front of Juliana and knocked her over. A bunch of people, Ella included, got hit by flying sausages. Jon without an H scrambled to his feet and crouched like a wrestler, worried the dog was coming after him. But Adolf had gotten what he wanted, at least for that day. No one was stupid enough to pick any sausages up off the grass, and Adolf scarfed them all down. Ivan helped Juliana up. Jon without an H picked up the long barbecue fork thing and kept the grill between him and the dog just in case. When Adolf was done eating, Juliana put him in the garage.

* * *

Later, after the sausage attack and after they'd all eaten, Ella's mom texted saying they'd be home in an hour, so they all piled in the car and headed to San Miguel, stopping first to pick up Diesel. It was pitch-black and foggy when Ivan and the rest of the family dropped off her and Charlie and their stuff. Ivan waited while she used her flashlight app to find the keyhole and open the door.

She remembered to turn on the driveway lights, which was nothing short of a miracle. Her mother hated to drive up in the dark, especially with fog, but Ella almost never remembered the lights. The Prince was about to leave all his crap right by the front door. She told him not to be such a complete slob, so he dragged it to his room, bitching all the way. She tossed her bag on the floor of her room. The words floated above her and she wondered whether she should tell her mom about Adolf. She'd be upset for sure and might go off on a long lecture about responsible pet ownership and all that. Maybe she'd let Charlie tell her. Bad news from him didn't seem to freak their mom out as much.

Ella visited the Build-A-Bear dispensary and took a couple hits. Then she flopped on the bed and rolled onto her stomach, looking idly at her desk. Oops. The SAT prep book. She was in such deep shit. Good thing her phone said she had time for exactly one test from the writing section before her mom came home and ordered her execution. It was nine less than she was supposed to have done, but it was better than nothing.

Twenty minutes in, she ran into the sort of question that often tripped her up. Not because she didn't know the answer, but because the five options for completing the sentence were so lame:

8. It will be hard to _____ Leonid now that you have so _____ him.

The answer was "mollify—incensed," but how boring was that? What about, "It will be hard to make an Olympian of Leonid now that you have so disabled him"? Or, "It will be hard to get a decent settlement out of Leonid now that you have so totally screwed him." She was finally enjoying herself. She moved on to the next question:

9. He was normally entirely _____, but in the embarrassing situation in which he found himself he felt compelled to _____.

Tempted as she was to get creative, she told herself just to finish the damn thing. She scanned the choices and lingered on the word *indolent*. Not the answer but it gave her a kind of déjà-vu feeling. What's that about? Then it hit her. *Indolent*. Perfect. She dug through her backpack and took out the most important object in her world—her poetry notebook. She flipped to the last marked page—a mess of crossed-out lines, bubbled ideas, doodles, and a very large "ARGH!" But it was her beautiful mess, and so close to coming together. Like one of those optical illusions where the background and the foreground can switch. First it's a vase; then it's two people facing each other. Right before you suddenly see it the other way, if you pay attention, you can feel it about to happen.

The last line was "The slumbering notions of a half-starved god." She crossed out *slumbering* and wrote *indolent*. She put her pencil down and read the line aloud. Leaning back in her chair, she laughed. The printout on her bulletin board said the date for the poetry slam in the city was May 26. Today was the thirteenth, so she'd definitely be ready.

There was a commotion at the front door, then footsteps down the hallway. She was still trancing about her poem when her mom knocked. She grunted and her mom came in.

"Hi. We just got home. Thanks for leaving the lights on."

"Sure." She closed the poetry notebook very casually. "Nana here?"

"Dad's with her in Charlie's room."

Her mom scanned the desk. Swear to God, her mom missed her calling as a cop. She pursed her lips and frowned, but didn't say anything. Normally she'd be all over Ella's case about something: not doing her SAT or her homework or cleaning the bathroom or whatever. She didn't usually yell or lecture. Not exactly. More like a concise review of the facts, the rules, the goals, and—wait for it—the Consequences. Ella was pretty sure that was one of her first words. Dada, Mama, doggie, and consequences. When she was little, the review went like this.

Fact: Toys belong in the toy box.

Rule: When you are done playing with a toy, you must put it away in the box.

Goal: To keep the house tidy so we always know where everything is.

Consequence: Toys left out will disappear for one week.

As she'd gotten older, things had become a little more complicated. Take the SAT, for example.

Fact: Higher SAT scores will help you get into the colleges you want. (Complication: She wasn't sure she wanted to go to college.)

Rule: To score higher, you must practice, then review and understand your errors. (No argument there, unfortunately.)

Goal: To complete as many practice tests as possible for the highest possible score. (Complication One: Her estimate of her highest score was lower than her mom's. Complication Two: Her sense of how many tests she could complete without going stark raving mad was lower than her mom's.)

Consequence: She was thinking of telling her mom to shove it.

But that evening her mom didn't even ask about the tests. The day was overflowing with miracles.

Then she noticed her mom's nose.

"What happened to your face?"

Her mom touched it like she didn't know she had a face. "Oh, that. Nothing. Just a little bump."

She thought about telling her about the poem but didn't want to press her luck. Her mom didn't seem to care about poetry anyway. Instead Ella checked her phone for messages.

Her mom sighed. "Come say hi to Nana. Then you can return to whatever you were doing."

CHAPTER NINE

HELEN

No one had asked Helen if she wanted to go to Geneva's. Her children made it sound as if they were asking, but the train had long since left the station. She couldn't deny they had a point about the money—the bills Dublin showed her made her head spin—and she regretted canceling the darn insurance. Put her in a position of depending on them, and that wasn't how she preferred it. First they're helping you out; then they're telling you what to do.

Not that she wasn't grateful. It wasn't every grown child who would lend a hand to her mother, not these days. She only wished it could have been her son. He was easier. Always had been. Fidgety, the way boys often are, but he couldn't hold on to a foul mood if it came with a handle and a lid. And so eager to make a person laugh. Nothing seemed to bother him, not disorder, not noise, and not flying by the seat of his pants. Helen preferred more order than that, but had learned people like Dublin were easier to drink around. They were more forgiving, or too disorganized to realize there was anything to forgive.

When she came out to California she had the notion she'd be the one helping Dublin out. Right off she'd said she'd sit with the boys. But Talia put the kibosh on that. Dublin said they'd both decided she wasn't safe with the children, but she figured it was only Talia. All because she'd put a bit of vodka in Jack's bottle when he wouldn't quit crying. Talia being Russian, Helen had reckoned it would pass for standard procedure. And now it turned out her grandson was catawampus. Could have filled his bottle with booze and it wouldn't have made any difference. Little feller was wired up wrong. It put a terrible strain on their lives, but if they wouldn't let her help, then that was that.

Now Helen was the one in need of assistance, and she was stuck with Geneva. As much as her daughter kept her feelings to herself, Helen could plainly see she had a knot in her tail about inviting her in. That girl was as similar to Dublin as vinegar is to honey. She had to have her ducks in a row, numbered in sequence, and ready to swim. Geneva must've been cornered into taking her in by that husband of hers, a family man through and through, and good-looking besides. Geneva had been lucky to land him, with her so fixated on her career and spending more time running after animals than men.

Helen was hard on Geneva—she confessed to that. Didn't help that her youngest daughter was the spitting image of Eustace.

If you took him and prettied him up a little, you'd end up with Geneva. She had the same thick dark hair, strong chin, and squared-off shoulders, and was tall to boot. Carried it well—she gave her that. Problem was, Helen didn't want reminding of Eustace. She didn't want it right after he died and she didn't want it now. It wasn't Geneva's fault, but a ghost was a ghost.

*   *   *

They'd put her in the boy's room. She'd expected the girl's room but Geneva said the other was closer to the bathroom. When they came into the house, Tom wheeled her past the girl's room. She'd caught a glimpse of all the paper hanging from the ceiling and decided she could tolerate the posters of sports cars and the musty scent of boys coming into their manhood. The boy—Charlie, she remembered now—was sent off to sleep in the den. He didn't grouse. On the face of it, he resembled Tom, but nevertheless reminded her of Dublin. She hadn't spent much time with Geneva's children, but Charlie, at least, might help these weeks pass.

*   *   *

She woke up the first morning at Geneva's with a crick in her neck. Same thing happened most mornings since the accident. Between strange beds, her arm in a sling, and her sore leg, she couldn't get comfortable. At least in the hospital and the rehab center they'd given her a healthy dose of pain meds—until they suspected she might be exaggerating her suffering. She wasn't counting on her daughter handing out pills like candy. No, she'd have her fist tight around that, same as everything else. Helen had been craving a drink since her first moment of consciousness in the hospital and couldn't see surviving at Geneva's house—or anywhere else for that matter—sober as a judge. Charlie, with that long, smooth smile, appeared the sort who could work out real quick which side the butter was on. Maybe he'd be willing to help—for a price. There was always a price.

She could see out one corner of the window without moving her head. The weather was much as she'd left it the night before: fog thicker than day-old porridge. She wished she'd brought sunshine and a palm tree with her. And it was so quiet here. No street noise, no ambulances, no miscreants yelling at children by the pool. Big trees and wide, wide quiet. Some folks would call it peaceful, but she wasn't one of them. Reminded her of Aliceville— the house she'd been born in, not Eustace's. Stuck on the edge of the woods, with all manner of critters traipsing through the yard, her daddy lifting his shotgun at them from the narrow porch, swaying with drink, as likely to kick up a clod of dirt as kill anything. The ramshackle house never looked like it meant to stay. Any moment it might get strangled by vines or sucked into the woods by a fierce wind. She had been relieved to move into Eustace's house in town, where the streetlights shone nice and bright. Of course that was before the trouble started, when her idea of scared became the things you couldn't see.

Still, her childish notions stuck. The redwoods surrounding Geneva's house made her anxious in a way L.A. never did. Sure, L.A. was full of no good—any fool could see that—but it was no good you could lock your door against, not the kind that comes sniffing under your window while you sleep.

. . .

Someone pushed open the door. The light was dim, but she couldn't mistake the dog's boxy head. What was his name? Daisy? No. Dazzle? Almost.

"Diesel," she whispered. "Come here, boy."

He cantered over like a small horse. Helen pushed herself upright, pulled the covers up, and stroked the dog's head.

"You're a fine dog. Put me in mind of the one I gave Paris."

Diesel sat and laid his snout on the bed, ready for as long a story as she wanted to tell, so long as she kept up the stroking.

"He came from a shelter, like I reckon you did, knowing Geneva. His owner had passed away unexpected. Barely a year old he was. Pure German shepherd, with feet the size of saucers and a knowing look in his eye. I got him for Paris when she was sixteen, for Christmas. Didn't mention it to anyone, not even Eustace. Especially not Eustace. But once Paris had her arms around him, there wasn't a thing to be done about it. Not a thing."

Diesel's breath was hot on her hand. Helen recalled the look her husband gave her when Paris buried her face in the dog's neck. He pulled his shoulders back, raised his eyebrows, and glared at his wife as if she was a long-shot racehorse who'd snatched the lead from him. Stared her down for an eternity until she was compelled to look away. Then he left the room without a word.

Paris didn't notice a thing. Her attention was all on the dog. "Does he have a name, Mama?"

"Argus."

The dog looked at Helen expectantly.

"That's a funny name."

"From Greek mythology. You remember me reading those stories, don't you? Once you found out there was one about Paris, you had to hear a story every night. Got real ornery when it turned out Paris wasn't a girl."

"So who's Argus?"

"A giant with a hundred eyes. Hera—you remember her, don't you?—sent him to guard Io. He did such a good job she put his eyes on the peacock's tail for all of time."

"Who was Argus guarding Io against?"

"Zeus."

CHAPTER TEN

GENEVA

Following the weekend journey to L.A., Geneva resumed her morning swim workouts. Monday's called for length after length of butterfly stroke. Normally she dreaded butterfly, but today she welcomed the absolute exhaustion. When she completed the laps and hoisted herself out of the pool, she almost fell back in. Exactly what her body—and her mind—needed after long hours in the car and with her mother.

She drove home and ate a bowl of granola at the counter with Charlie. Tom wheeled her mother out to the Cherokee while Charlie chatted amiably with her about the Battle of the Bands and said he was sure he'd get to sing in his cousins' group. She put their bowls in the dishwasher and kissed him on the cheek, a gesture he still tolerated. After shouting good-bye to Ella's closed door, she left to take Helen to physical therapy.

As they passed Pickleweed Inlet, she thought about telling her mother she often stopped there to look at birds with the binoculars her father had given her. It seemed she should be able to say it, and her mother should welcome the connection. The few times Geneva had mentioned her father had gone nowhere. She had no concrete reason to feel this way, but nevertheless felt that the path to her mother, if there was one, was through her dead father.

They crawled north with the traffic and turned off in Petaluma.

"Almost there," Geneva said.

"What are you going to do while they're putting me through my paces?"

"The animal shelter is not too far. There's always something for me to do there."

Her mother said lightly, "More caring for the wounded and abandoned."

She laughed. "I guess you could say that."

"I don't like being a nuisance."

"It's okay."

"I know how you like things orderly, and I'm, well, a fly in the ointment."

"Don't say that. I should learn to be more flexible."

She pulled up to the entrance. A man approached, pushing a wheelchair. "Curbside service," he announced.

"I'll park and see you inside, Mom."

Geneva took care of the paperwork, then drove to the shelter. Her best friend, Drea, was the director. They'd spent long hours together developing behavior assessment protocols for dogs and cats. When pets entered the shelter, either as surrendered animals or strays, the personnel evaluated their suitability for adoption. Geneva and Drea agreed it wasn't a question of yes or no, except with dangerously aggressive animals, but rather a matter of matching pets with owners. They had already trained a handful of staff and volunteers on the rigorous protocol. Geneva tried to visit the shelter once a week to train others and, if she had time, evaluate a dog or two. The shelter was perpetually crowded, and she felt gratified to move a good dog on its path to a good home.

She found Drea in her office.

"Hey, Genie. How's your mom?"

Geneva didn't appreciate nicknames, but she made two exceptions: Dublin and Drea. "So far, so good."

"You don't look as though you've pulled out all your hair yet."

"We're all on our best behavior. Long may it continue."

"You here to chitchat or can I put you to work?"

She bowed. "At your disposal."

"There's a new one in number five. I had a quick look at her and have a hunch, but she needs testing."

"What do you suspect?"

"I don't want to bias you."

"Ever the scientist."

Drea smiled. "I learned from the best." She handed Geneva a clipboard with an evaluation form. "If you have time, stop by when you're done. And maybe we can have lunch sometime."

"I'd love that."

She pushed through the double doors into the kennels. Several dogs barked. A young couple stood in front of a cage that held a pair of boxers. She waited until they left, then walked slowly to number five and pretended not to look inside. A golden retriever lay on a mat, her head on her paws. The dog got up and approached Geneva, who noted her loose walk and drooping tail. She bent over, met the dog's gaze, and held it, then crouched with her shoulder against the cage.

"You're a pretty one, aren't you? Everyone's going to want you."

The dog cocked her head and pushed her nose into the wire mesh at Geneva's shoulder.

"Lonely, huh? That's not fair." She unhooked a leash from the cage, undid the padlock, and slipped the leash on.

In the evaluation room, she removed the leash and ran the dog through the battery of tests. First she ignored the dog and kept track of how many times it made social contact with her. She petted the dog for twenty seconds and examined her teeth.

A typical amiable retriever, about three years old. She wondered why Drea wanted her to do the evaluation. Geneva performed a mock physical, running her hands down the dog's legs and under her belly. When she looked in the dog's ears, she felt the dog stiffen slightly and noted the whale eye.

The dog followed her to a container of toys. Geneva threw a ball onto the floor. The dog chased it down, mouthed it, then dropped it.

So much for the retrieving part, she thought. But hardly a concern.

Then she engaged the dog in a tug-of-war using a knotted rope. She didn't pull very hard but the dog began growling. She let go and the dog backed away with the rope in her mouth. Her tail was rigid.

"A bit possessive, are we?"

She poured some food in a bowl and placed it on the floor. The dog sniffed it and began to eat. After a minute, Geneva nudged the bowl an inch with her foot. The dog stopped midbite and moved her muzzle toward the foot.

"Mind your manners, doggie. I've got boots on."

She waited a few moments, and pushed the bowl another inch. The dog flattened her ears and let out a low growl.

Geneva stepped back and shook her head. "No little kids in your future." Without a history—and this dog had none—she couldn't know why the dog guarded the food and was possessive of the toy. But those responses could spell trouble if a child didn't understand the growl as a warning signal.

She completed the testing protocol and returned the dog to the kennel. After she slipped off the leash, she knelt and rubbed the dog's chest.

"Don't worry about a thing. Someone's going to love you, warts and all."

. . .

On her way to her car, Dublin called.

"Stuck in traffic?" she asked. It was a running joke between them that if it weren't for freeway congestion, she would never hear from him.

"No, no. Actually, Jennifer Lopez wanted to have drinks, but I said I couldn't because I had to call you."

"I'm touched."

"I wouldn't go that far. But speaking of touched, how's Mom?"

"Fine. She got me up twice last night for bathroom assistance, but if that's the worst of it, I think we'll all survive."

"Don't underestimate her, Ginny. It's probably a ploy to get you to drop your guard. Has she been drinking?"

"We hid all the alcohol, and Tom and I are abstaining while she's here. She hasn't mentioned it."

"Sounds too easy."

"I know. Tom thinks she may have turned a corner."

"His worldview is refreshing. Rose-colored glasses for everyone!"

Torn between defending her husband and agreeing that Helen's good behavior was unlikely to last, she changed the subject. "Dublin, when did Mom start drinking heavily?"

"I think we all know it was after Dad died."

"I know, but it doesn't make sense to me."

"How come?"

"Because she won't talk about Dad. She answers direct questions but never elaborates."

"Maybe it's too painful."

"Maybe. But if Tom died, God forbid, I'd want to share my memories of him with Ella and Charlie. And I'd want them to help me remember him."

"But you're not Mom. She was sixteen—a kid—when they met. She never had a life that didn't include him."

"It still doesn't add up. It never has."

"What?"

"That thirty years later she's still drinking because she lost her husband. That she never had a serious relationship since. That she doesn't want to talk about someone who was the center of her life."

"People don't make sense, Ginny. That's what makes them interesting."

"I like to think I make sense."

"Do you? A minute ago you were teetering on the edge of agreeing with Tom that Mom was on the road to recovery."

Geneva sighed. "You're right. Maybe I'm no more rational than Mom."

"Now there's a scary thought."

She laughed softly, then paused. "Promise me something, Dub."

"You got it."

"I haven't said what it is yet!"

"Oh, okay. Have it your way." He cleared his throat and lowered his voice. "Well, Geneva, that all depends."

"Promise me that whatever Mom does or doesn't do, you and I will always be friends. And that means no secrets."

"Do I have to tell you if I get my back waxed?"

"Dublin . . ."

"I've already made that promise, and I don't intend to break it."

Her throat closed. "Thanks. Me, too."

. . .

As she drove back to the rehabilitation center, she recalled Dublin's first promise to her, made when she was eleven. Geneva sat in her closet with arms wrapped around her knees. She had pulled the accordion doors shut. Thin bars of light fell through the louvers and across her body. She dropped her forehead onto her arms. Sweat trickled down the nape of her neck and beaded above her lips. She scraped her upper lip with her teeth and bit down. The salty taste of blood and sweat. The sounds of car doors opening and closing. Argus barked, again and again. From the hall, or maybe the living room, disconnected words in unfamiliar voices floated into the closet: arrangements, so sorry, her father's name.

Light footsteps approached, and a shadow fell across the louvers.

"Ginny. It's me."

If she pushed far enough into the closet, she might disappear.

"I'm coming in."

She meant to say no, but a sob came out instead.

The door creaked when Dublin opened it. He crouched under

the hanging clothes and sat cross-legged. Then he slipped two fingers between the slats and pulled the door shut.

"Paris locked herself in her room," he said.

She pushed down on the air in her chest to stop the tears and raised her head. "Why did she get to see him and we didn't?"

"I don't know. Maybe we're not old enough."

"Is he still at the hospital?"

"I think Mr. Stanton has him. I heard him tell Mama that he looks real good."

Geneva wiped her nose on her arm. "That's stupid." She tried to picture her father lying in a coffin but the image wouldn't come. Instead, she saw him walking in front of her in the woods with his rifle. When she realized she wouldn't see him that way again, it felt like a punch in the stomach, and she moaned and dropped her forehead onto her arms.

"Ginny?"

Without lifting her head, she stretched out an arm.

He took her hand. "You still have me."

The idea that she might not had never occurred to her, just as she never thought she'd lose her father. The pain mushroomed inside her until her skin was on fire. The hand her brother held felt as if she had dipped it in a swimming pool.

She lifted her head. "Promise?"

"Yeah, I promise."

•   •   •

That night at dinner, Charlie told his parents about Aldo, Juliana's dog.

"So, Jon throws the sausages at the dog and then practically jumps over the grill."

Geneva stared at him, alarmed. Helen chuckled.

Charlie turned to Helen, seated next to him. "I know, Nana, right? But then he grabs this giant barbecue fork." He picked up his fork in his fist, gritted his teeth, and pretended to fend off his grandmother, who smiled gamely.

"Charlie, that's enough." Geneva looked at her daughter. "What happened then? I assume if anyone was hurt we'd have heard."

"He ate the sausages." Ella returned her attention to her plate.

"Inhaled them, more like," Charlie said.

Tom reached for a piece of bread. "They must be getting pretty serious if Jon brought his grill over."

Charlie cocked an eyebrow and lowered his voice an octave. "I've got all four burners on high for you, baby!"

Everyone laughed.

Geneva said, "In all seriousness, Tom, there's no point in Juliana and Jon continuing their relationship if she isn't willing to control her dog."

"Aldo isn't that bad."

"I'd say lunging at someone is pretty bad. Especially given the dog's size."

Helen said, "You worry too much. And the children are probably exaggerating."

Perhaps she did worry too much. But when it came to potentially dangerous animals, she knew her concern was appropriate. Had her family forgotten this was her area of expertise? She didn't believe in good dogs and bad dogs. Behavior was more complicated than that. Given the right circumstances, a harmless puppy could be shaped into a vicious killer. She had seen it happen often enough. Genetics definitely played a role in setting the boundaries of temperament. She had seen many more aggressive pit bulls, Rottweilers, and Dobermans (like Aldo) than other breeds. But ultimately the environment—the choices and behavior of the owner—controlled the outcome. Aldo wasn't yet beyond hope, but left unchecked, Geneva knew the situation would deteriorate.

"Ella, Charlie, I'd like you to be careful around Aldo. No roughhousing and no keep-away. Don't eat near him. Can we agree on that?"

They nodded. Their acquiescence told her Charlie's story had been no exaggeration.

. . .

Geneva helped her mother get ready for bed, then joined Tom in the living room. He put down the sports section of the paper and patted the seat next to him.

"See?" he said. "Helen's no trouble at all."

She sat heavily onto the couch. "No, not today."

"The kids seem to like her. Especially Charlie."

"That's true. I could overlook a lot if my mother made an effort with them." Write off our relationship, she thought, and concentrate on the next generation. There were worse outcomes.

"Do you want me to get up with her tonight?"

"That might be awkward for her. Maybe we should dehydrate her every afternoon."

He laughed.

"By the way," she said, "did you approve Charlie's new video game?"

"I didn't know he had one."

"When I went into the den to check on him just now, he was

playing one I hadn't seen before. He said he borrowed it from a friend."

"I'm sure it's fine, but I'll look at it when he's in school tomorrow, okay?"

"There goes your morning."

"Ha-ha."

They sat in silence for a few moments. Then Geneva sat up and shuffled through the newspaper on the coffee table.

"Something on your mind—aside from your son's innocence and your mother's bladder?"

She straightened the newspaper and turned to him. "I'm thinking of talking to Juliana about her dog."

"I'm not sure she'd listen. She thinks he's great. And he is, most of the time."

"But not when Jon is around."

"You don't know that."

"Well, she and I could talk about it."

"She'd see it as interfering. If she asks you, it'd be different."

"You mean if I were a full-fledged Novak, it'd be different."

"That's not fair."

"If you remember, I offered to help her select a puppy. She turned me down and went with Theo instead. I love your brother, but he doesn't know dogs."

"So now Aldo is Theo's fault?"

"No. But we all know Juliana is a free spirit. Given that, I would have guided her toward a smaller dog with a very even temperament."

"Okay, but Aldo's her dog now."

"Do you know if he still sleeps with her?"

"Jon?"

"Very funny. No, the dog."

Tom leaned back and put his feet on the coffee table. "I make a habit of not asking who's in bed with my sister. That's thin ice. But I heard from my mother, who has no such reservations, that Juliana tried to wean Aldo off sleeping on the bed—unsuccessfully. Which is why Juliana stays at Jon's and not the other way around."

"I'm sure you can see that's not healthy, Tom. That's why I want to talk to her. And to Jon. Before things escalate."

"We're all hoping this relationship works out. We think Jon's great for her."

"Then I would assume that 'we' would prefer him with all his limbs?"

Tom scoffed. "We don't even know what went on at the barbecue. For all we know Jon might have dropped the sausages, then panicked when Aldo went after them." He rose. "Time for bed. Give that brain of yours a rest for a few hours."

She tried, but her brain would not rest. While her husband lay beside her, heavy in sleep, her thoughts refused to unwind. Watchful as a child, watchful as an adult. Over the years, her mother, her husband, and several well-meaning others had entreated her to relax her vigil on the world. But once she noticed something, she found it impossible to look away until she understood what she observed. And now the list of things she did not understand grew longer by the day. Her mother was a lifelong source of confusion, as was her sister Paris. Ella's behavior—of late, highly variable and generally sullen—presented another mystery. She also felt disconnected from Tom. They didn't agree on how to handle the kids, his family, or her mother. She knew he loved her, but did he get her? Some time ago, she couldn't say exactly when, she had been certain he did. But now doubt had emerged, like a weed pushing out of a crack in the pavement. Even Charlie, always the easiest person in the family, was making her uneasy. She couldn't put her finger on anything, but something wasn't right.

Such a long list. Logic told her the problem was therefore not them, but her. But even this deduction failed to withstand her scrutiny. What, exactly, was wrong with her, then? How could she rest when she understood so little?

Sporadically, Geneva watched, not to understand, but because she sensed something was about to occur. This first happened as a child in Aliceville, during her regular visits to the woods. Weekend and summer mornings, she would jump on her bike and head to the far side of town. Her mother would not have approved, not because the woods were dangerous but because well-brought-up girls shouldn't muddy their knees. Careful to stay clean, she'd thread her way as deep into the woods as she dared. She would sit against a tree and wait for the world she had ruffled to return to itself. Once the forest ignored her, she became part of it. With the aid of her binoculars and natural patience, she studied whatever appeared: squirrels, quail, deer—even beetles. Time passed unnoticed. When the shadows knitted together and the forest floor grew dark, she ran back to her bike, holding the binoculars against her chest with one hand. Sweat clung to her like another skin.

One summer morning she had been sitting on a log for half an hour when she detected a change in her surroundings. A moment passed; then a Cooper's hawk swooped down to snatch a warbler from the air. A month later, she was leaning against a tree and felt the forest tremble. She turned slowly to see a black bear lumber into a clearing not twenty yards away. The bear sniffed the air with sharp upward nods, then returned to become a shadow in the underbrush. At the time, she concluded that the gravity of certain events ran slightly ahead in time. If she paid close attention, she could sense the subliminal shudder preceding something dangerous, or spectacular.

Rare as the feeling had been when she was a child, it was rarer still as an adult. And her explanation for it had changed. She had given the matter a great deal of thought and concluded it was a trick of memory. The feeling of imminence seemed to precede the event but, in fact, did not. As her unconscious mind raced to make sense of the sudden fate of a warbler or the appearance of a bear, it yanked a veil across her understanding, which she experienced as an indeterminate signal to take heed. Quick as her mind was, her perception was quicker. In the grip of astonishment, the instant between seeing and knowing flooded her with portent.

On a rainy night last winter she sensed a quavering from the car in front of her. An instant later, its brake lights came on. Her foot came down hard on the brake, and she averted a collision. Geneva wondered if other people shared in this feeling but never admitted to it for fear of appearing strange. It didn't matter in the end whether she was alone. The important thing was to pay attention because warnings never came twice.

CHAPTER ELEVEN

ELLA

After school on Tuesday, Ella drove into town to run a bunch of errands for her mom. She didn't mind because she'd just gotten her license; she only hoped no one saw her driving way below the speed limit. Being taught by her mom was bad enough. She reminded her about every little thing in this super calm voice, but Ella could tell from the way her feet kept pushing into the floor it was an act. But driving alone was worse. She knew if she made a mistake, she could kill someone. Herself, for instance.

Her mom told her to use a parking lot miles from the stores because the spaces were bigger. Ella grumbled about it, out of principle, but the truth was, parking really freaked her out. She would have picked that lot anyway. Or an enormous playing field. Or the moon.

She inched into the parking spot, got out, and checked to see how she'd done. It looked like a drunken moron had parked the car, so she got in and straightened it out. Twenty minutes later, she was good to go. On her way to the post office, she glanced down a side street lined with a bunch of old shops nobody ever went into, plus an ancient gas station and liquor store. A homeless guy sat in the middle of all his stuff next to a Dumpster near the liquor store. A tall, skinny kid walked up super casual and struck up a conversation with him. Ella literally did a double take. The kid was Prince Charles. He pulled something out of his pocket and kept looking over his shoulder like a secret agent. She scooted across the road and hid in the doorway of an abandoned dry cleaner.

What the hell was he doing? One thing for sure: No way was he helping the homeless. More likely he was getting the homeless to help him. Buying booze was an obvious conclusion, except there were easier ways. Every kid who wanted booze and looked older than Justin Bieber had a fake ID. And everyone else knew someone with access to their parents' stash. So if it wasn't booze, she figured it connected somehow to the Prince's wad of cash.

A line of cars went by and blocked her view for a second. Afterward, she caught a peek of the homeless guy coming out of the store. He sat down like he was coming home from work and plopping into his favorite chair. The Prince squatted next to him, just buddies having a chat. The homeless guy might have handed something to the Prince, but she couldn't be sure because the Prince was in the way. She stepped onto the sidewalk to get a better look, but then he wheeled around and headed straight toward her. Shit! She ducked down behind this garbage can like a total idiot. When a truck rolled by, giving her cover, she sprinted around the corner, then strolled toward the post office as if she had never seen a thing.

. . .

The next day in school she started up a conversation with Trevor, the A-plus douche who had the locker under hers. Full of himself for absolutely zero reason. She had said maybe three words to him all year and one of them was "Ow!" when he hit her ankle with his locker door. Didn't even apologize. Like she said, total douche. But today Trevor would serve a purpose.

She shut her locker. Trevor knelt and stuffed books in his backpack.

"Hey, Trevor." Her cunning opening.

He didn't even look up. Douche.

"I was wondering. You know everything that's going on, right?"

"Everything worth knowing. Why?" He zipped his backpack and stood up. He had on a gangsta wannabe T-shirt with the logo of some band she'd never heard of. The skull and blood spatter said it all. His mouth twisted in a nasty sneer. She expected little snakes to wriggle out.

"Do you think my brother Charlie's in over his head? He's only a freshman, and I know it's just for fun, but . . ." Fishing expedition with zero bait. Good luck.

"Charlie's okay. Charlie's always okay."

"That's what I figured."

"Then why are you asking?"

"He's my brother. Don't worry, though. I'm not ratting on anyone."

He frowned in thought. "His prices are kinda steep."

"I agree."

"But he's got great stuff."

"I've seen it. It's the best." She had no idea what they were talking about. Bizarrely fun.

Trevor gave her a half smile. "It's kinda creepy."

"What's creepy?" *Other than you?*

"You talking to me about this." He kicked his locker shut and gave her a lascivious grin. "But if you're the kinda ho that's into porno mags, maybe we should talk again."

* * *

Once she didn't feel like puking anymore, she knew just whom to ask for the deets: cousin Spencer. In fact, she wished she'd gone to him first instead of getting drooled on by Trevor. She caught up to Spencer after history class.

Not only did he know all about the Princely enterprise—he was too trusting to question why she wanted to know. Turned out the Prince didn't sell the magazines or even charge for peeks. He rented them overnight. Gross, right? Most parents installed pornopreventers on their computers, so for a twenty-dollar deposit, a guy could have his very own handheld experience.

"If the pages come back stuck together," Spencer told her, his gaze downcast, "Charlie keeps the twenty. Otherwise it's ten."

No wonder he was loaded.

* * *

It didn't take the Prince long to start working on Nana. She got here on Sunday and by Wednesday evening they were besties. Ella was making cupcakes for her friend's birthday, basically stalling on doing her math homework. Nana and the Prince sat at the kitchen table with a deck of cards, some poker chips, and a giant bag of M&M's. Nana the card shark. Ella always thought old ladies played bridge, but Nana was showing him how to play blackjack and weird versions of poker. They played open hands first, so the Prince could see her strategy. Then he was on his own; Nana chuckled as she raked in her winnings. An hour after they started, her pile of M&M's dwarfed the Prince's.

Ella filled the last paper liner with batter. She licked the spoon just as her mom came into the kitchen. Her mom had some sort of radar that detected salmonella exposure. But she ignored Ella's flirtation with death and creeped on the card game instead. She leaned against the counter and crossed her arms over her chest. Her face seemed half happy about the Prince and Nana bonding, and half suspicious.

"Watch out, Charlie," her mom said. "She'll take you for everything you're worth."

Nana lifted her eyebrows, but she didn't look up.

The Prince might have been working on Nana, but who's to say the old lady didn't have a plan of her own? Maybe it called for getting in good with Charlie. After all, the liquor store sold more than dirty magazines. She toyed with the idea of telling her mom what Charlie was up to, but she didn't have any cold, hard evidence. What had she seen anyway? And none of the boys involved would spill the beans. Plus, with Nana there, and the Battle of the Bands approaching, it might be more entertaining just to see how it all played out.

CHAPTER TWELVE

HELEN

Tired of talk shows and the travel channel, Helen asked the girl—Ella—to bring her some books from the town library.

"What kind?"

"When I was your age I liked romances, fool that I was. Then I got a taste for mysteries."

"Murder mysteries?"

"Oh, any kind. But a murder or two doesn't hurt."

Back in Aliceville, Helen chose her first mystery by accident. Hurrying to get home before Eustace, she dashed into the library and grabbed Agatha Christie's *The Mysterious Affair at Styles*, thinking it was about a love affair. The cover showed a balding man with a red bow tie touching his forehead like he was thinking hard. She stuffed the book into her shopping bag and hoped that peculiar man would not turn out to be the love interest. That afternoon she learned he was Hercule Poirot. Helen would come to read all of Agatha's books she could get her hands on. Poirot was her favorite, despite his high-and-mighty attitude. She didn't care two beans for Miss Marple, the nosy little old gossip. Put her in mind of her mama. Once she finished all of Agatha's, she branched out to other mysteries. Did her mind good to think about something other than her family and their never-ending wants and desires.

She hadn't done much reading since she moved to California. Books were for when it was too hot to bother breathing, or when the rain ran down the windows and the wind rattled the shutters. Or when a person was laid up.

Ella brought her a half dozen books. Helen picked out a romance, for old times' sake, and read the first chapter. She laughed out loud, the first good belly laugh she'd had in ages. How did she ever fall for this nonsense?

. . .

For the first few years of married life, Eustace was on her every night like a boy with a new pogo stick. She assumed this was normal, especially as it lined up with the way folks behaved in the romances. Besides, he treated her fine, calling her "my pretty princess" and buying her dresses and shoes in the latest styles. Took him years before he trusted her to pick out her own clothes, worried most likely she'd come home with a faded housedress and never-white-again apron like her mama's. She never thought to complain about Eustace, not that she had a soul to do any complaining to. What friends she did have—all from the other side of town—went scarce as soon as she got married.

The babies came one after another, but that didn't slow Eustace down. Didn't care if they hollered away in the nursery while he sweated and grunted on top of her. The sound of her babies crying pained her. She had a book by Dr. Spock the library lady pushed on her. He said babies needed affection, and she should trust her instincts. When she informed Eustace of this, he laughed and said Dr. Spock could have as many spoiled children as he pleased, but there would be none in his house. So Helen closed her ears to the crying and waited for him to finish, roll off her, and fall asleep. The whole procedure took minutes. Then she'd sneak out, soothe the children, and slip back into bed. Finally, she slept.

By 1971, they had four children. Eustace wanted more, but Helen, at twenty-four, was done making babies. She was exhausted, despite Louisa's help. Louisa told her she ate like a bird, and a small one at that, but Helen was worried that if she lost her figure she'd lose her husband along with it. So she pushed her plate away and lit a cigarette instead. At Louisa's roundabout suggestion, she took to tracking her monthlies. When she reckoned she was ripe, she fell ill with various maladies, or, for variety, picked an argument with Eustace of sufficient ferocity that he escaped to the local watering hole or his daddy's hunting cabin. It wasn't a card she played often, though. He was too powerful a man to tolerate her yanking his chain.

Unlike Helen's, Eustace's energy—and his ambition—appeared unbounded. He was on the board of this and that, and fished, hunted, and golfed. Then, in 1972, he got it in his head to try politics. He ran for town council and won handily. Two years later, when Paris was nine and Geneva nearly three, he got himself elected mayor. Teaching that man the ways of politics was near to teaching a hog to wallow. Aliceville didn't have more than eight thousand souls, but a mayor was a mayor. The social gatherings outnumbered the meetings, if anyone could tell the difference. Eustace kept his law practice going, too, and was regularly called away to the county seat or to Columbia. Times he came home from a night away right cheerful. Helen wasn't stupid, but she knew better than to make a noise. She had her house, her children, and her help. She had the ladies' club, if she wanted it (and she generally did not), and the church group, which she tolerated. What she did not have was time to worry about everything Eustace might or mightn't be up to. She couldn't summon the enthusiasm.

But knowing is one thing and seeing is another subject entirely. One Fourth of July they asked Louisa to look after the children and drove to the country club. Eustace had taken up golf to get in on the betting and make certain he didn't miss any goings-on. The club was set on a hillside overlooking Lake Prospect. Torches lined the lakeshore, and red, white, and blue bunting hung from the roof edge and porch railings. Round the back, Japanese lanterns and more torches lit tables draped in white. Red, white, and blue bows decorated each seat. Like a spread in a magazine. Eustace steered her to some acquaintances and left to get drinks.

The bartender had a heavy hand. Helen ate a few hors d'oeuvres to soak up the liquor, but it wasn't twenty minutes before Eustace handed her another drink. Then he disappeared. She didn't realize it right off, busy as she was chatting with Reba and Suzanne from the ladies' club. Might have been the drinks, but she'd forgotten how much fun the two of them could be. When Reba did her impression of her girl—a sweet but daft thing— trying to work out how to use the new washing machine, Helen nearly spilled her julep.

She excused herself to go to the restroom, walking on her toes to keep her heels from sinking into the lawn. Been months since she was last at the club and got herself turned around, heading left instead of right through the lobby. On her way past the kitchen she heard Eustace's voice. Nearly called out to him before she saw his silhouette in the hall shadows. He was turned a little away from her and had his hands on the hip of a woman—a girl—she couldn't see well enough to place.

"Come on," Eustace said to the girl. "Give me some sugar." He pulled her toward him. She giggled loosely—she was drunk.

The girl twisted in his grasp and her skirt fanned into a slice of light from the kitchen. Yellow. Daisy yellow.

Helen stepped back and took a deep breath. Then she returned the way she'd come, found the restroom, and spent several minutes collecting herself. She put on more lipstick and took a good long look in the mirror. Skin smooth, hair blond and silky, figure trim. Not quite twenty-eight and already yesterday's news. How was that for a sermon on vanity?

When a serving boy offered her another drink, she took it and rejoined her friends. After a time, the girl in the yellow dress appeared on the lawn. Helen watched her take the arm of a hunting friend of Eustace's, and realized the man was the girl's daddy. He and his wife had been around to their house a month before, asking if they might borrow Louisa for their daughter's seventeenth birthday party.

* * *

Such recollections were among the ill effects of sobriety. Helen had had enough of it. Since the accident, the medication had taken the edge off her cravings for liquor, but now Geneva had weaned her off most of it, saying it was habit-forming. What's wrong with a habit? Gives a person something to look forward to, something to take away the ache. The first vodka of the day was the best, with the next one a close second. She recalled how it gave her another layer, a thick one. The world kept spinning, but she cared a whole lot less. If she kept adding to the layer, drink by drink, she'd disappear without a sound, like a stone headed to the bottom of a lake. No one had a right to take it from her. Geneva's determination reminded Helen of Eustace. Another inheritance from that man.

Her shoulder had improved to the point where she could use a walker. The leg she broke and the artificial knee still pained her, mostly at night. She blamed the dampness and the lack of booze. At least her nose had healed, and she could go out in public without getting strange looks.

She missed her apartment where she could do as she pleased: play bridge, go to the movies, go shopping, sit by the pool with her neighbors—the ones without loud children. More, she pined for her car, a light blue Mustang convertible, now crumpled beyond redemption. Five years ago, she had ignored her children's prophecies of doom, and driven the Mustang clear across the country. Wouldn't have minded to keep right on driving except she ran out of road. And driving, although a heck of a lot of fun, was lonely business. Nothing worse than being alone. Except being alone without a drink.

When she visited Dublin's house, she had felt more at ease, despite the unceasing commotion from the boys—especially Jack. But their lives spilled over the edges and the spotlight rarely shone on her. Nothing like busy people to make a person feel useless. If only they had a bigger house, she could've moved in with them. It occurred to her that Dublin and Talia, especially Talia, might've hung on to the little bungalow for exactly that reason.

Here at Geneva's place, tall, heavy trees surrounded the house and fog hugged the ground at night like in a horror movie. Everything a hush. Dog didn't even bark, except when deer stood in the yard. The girl kept to her room and Tom to his workshop. Geneva worked most days. When she was home, the way she studied Helen unnerved her—as if Helen had a bomb inside her. Maybe she did. One thing she knew for sure: Without a steady soaking of alcohol, whatever lay ticking inside her was primed to go off.

She couldn't very well waltz out of the house and get her own supply. She needed a conspirator, a rumrunner. Charlie had potential, but she couldn't just ask her fourteen-year-old grandson to buy alcohol for her. Not without a foolproof plan.

·   ·   ·

Charlie was standing at the kitchen counter dressed in his baseball uniform and eating the first of two enormous sandwiches when Helen clunked in with her walker.

"Hey, Nana. You're getting good with that."

"A new trick for an old dog."

"You're not old."

"I knew I liked you."

Charlie chewed and gazed into the middle distance. "Can I ask you a favor, Nana?"

Helen brightened. "Why, I'd be delighted to help."

"I want to get Dad something special for his birthday, only I don't want him to see it."

"His birthday's not for a month."

"No time like the present."

"I suppose not. So what do you need from me?"

"I want to order it online and have it delivered to my friend's house so Dad won't know."

She scooted a little closer. "May I ask what it is?"

Charlie hesitated.

"I see." She smiled at him. "Never mind. Where do I come in?"

"I don't have a credit card. But I can pay you back, no problem."

"Oh, don't worry about it." A shady deal, no question. And there was more than one way to even a score.

"Thanks, Nana. You're the best." He opened the refrigerator and took out a bottled drink. "You want one of these? It's iced tea."

"Is it flavored?"

"Yeah. There's peach, my favorite. And green tea, which only my mom drinks. Dad likes the lemon, which explains why there aren't any." He pushed a bottle aside. "And pomegranate. Mom bought that one by mistake."

"Isn't it any good?"

"Try it. If you like it, there're a few more in the garage."

"Which kind does Ella drink?"

"I don't think she likes any of them."

The stars had aligned. "I'll be brave and try the pomegranate, thank you." She motioned to the nearby couch. "And let's sit here a minute. I have a proposition for you."

CHAPTER THIRTEEN

❧

GENEVA

Geneva tied off the last suture on the cat she had spayed and changed out of her scrubs. On the way to her office she ran into Rosa the intern, who said the Kahnemanns were in the waiting room with Trixie, their cocker spaniel.

A thin, dark blanket of dread fell over her. "Please tell them I need five minutes."

"Room Two is open."

"Okay. I'll meet them there."

She continued to her office and opened Trixie's file on the computer. Seven months ago, Geneva had removed a section of the dog's small intestine because of an obstructive tumor. She scanned the pathology report to remind herself of what she already knew: The growth had been malignant. At the time, she estimated Trixie might survive a year. And now the Kahnemanns had returned. She closed the file.

Trixie lifted her head when Geneva entered the room but stayed at the Kahnemanns' feet. The couple, in their early fifties, described the dog's symptoms. The woman's voice trembled. Geneva spoke to Trixie in a low voice and gently examined her. When she palpated the abdomen, the dog flinched.

"From what you've described and what I can tell from my exam, I'm afraid there's been a recurrence. It's blocking the bowel."

Mr. Kahnemann said, "That's what we figured. What can we do?"

"First I'll want to confirm my suspicions with an X-ray and maybe an ultrasound." She went on to explain their treatment options, which included another surgery and an experimental chemotherapy drug. "But this type of cancer almost always recurs, even after aggressive treatment."

"And if we do nothing?" he asked.

His wife turned to him. "She's in pain. We can't do nothing." She bent to stroke the dog.

"I'm just making sure we consider everything."

Geneva nodded and said they could treat the pain but the obstruction would still be there.

Mrs. Kahnemann sat up. "What do you recommend, then? We want to do the right thing. Trixie's been such a good dog."

Geneva had long ago come to terms with her inability to save every pet. But she struggled when asked her opinion on such decisions because most people didn't reason the way she did.

"I can't make the decision for you. I can only give you the best information I have."

"But what if Trixie were your dog?"

She knew exactly what she would do. The dog was suffering and the odds of any treatment adding more than a few months to her life were minuscule. She would put the dog to sleep immediately. But she would not lead the Kahnemanns down that path. Early in her career, she voiced her opinions more openly. She was shocked at the lengths to which owners would go to forestall the inevitable, with too little concern for the animal's quality of life. But her colleagues, Stan in particular, cautioned her to allow clients control over treatment decisions. On bad days Geneva viewed this stance as less philosophical than mercenary, as delaying euthanasia always increased the bottom line of the veterinary practice.

"I could guess what I would do, but I can't give you a definitive answer because Trixie's not my dog. That changes everything." Mr. Kahnemann gave her a look of frustration. Geneva suspected he had already decided the dog should be put down and hoped for her support. "I would only encourage you to think about this from Trixie's point of view."

Tears fell down Mrs. Kahnemann's cheeks. "I don't want her to suffer."

"Of course not. She's had a wonderful life with you. You've taken such good care of her." She bent down and scratched Trixie behind the ears. "I'll take her for an X-ray. Please take some time to talk it over."

She encouraged the dog to its feet and led it into the treatment room. As she prepped Trixie for the procedure, she mused that dogs rarely knew what people had planned for them. And that, when it came to death, counted as a mercy.

The laughter of her husband and son met Geneva at the front door. When she entered the house, Diesel bounded over and sat, his haunches twitching with the thrill of her homecoming. Charlie's books lay open on the counter in front of him, but his body was twisted toward the television in the living room. Tom stood in front of the television and shaped a disc of ground meat with his hands.

"Hey, there."

"Hi. Sounds like a celebration."

"Hey, Momster. Giants just scored on an error. The outfielder did the funniest dance under a pop fly. Then the ball landed on his head."

Humiliation plus pain equals delight for the home team. Humans are strange animals. "Did you two have a good day?"

"Yeah, we're great." Tom picked up another ball of meat. Diesel's gaze followed Tom's movements, and he whined softly.

"Diesel . . ." Geneva said.

The dog looked over his shoulder at her, walked slowly to his mat by the door, and collapsed onto it like a bag of rocks.

"Good boy." She turned to her husband. "Where's Mom?"

"Sleeping, I think."

"At six thirty?"

"Said she had a hard physio session. I didn't see much of her this afternoon because the rain forest guy was here."

"Should I check on her?"

Charlie leaned over his books and rested his forehead on one hand. "She was fine when I came home from school. Pretty happy, actually."

Happy? Something in her son's tone struck her as odd, but she couldn't see his face.

"I've got an idea," Tom said. "Since our patient is resting, let's have a glass of wine from the secret stash."

Geneva opened her mouth to protest, but then realized a glass of wine sounded perfect. "Good thought. And while I'm getting it, perhaps you, Charlie, could take Diesel for a short walk, then give him a biscuit. The hamburger is torturing him."

"But what about the game?"

Tom washed his hands. "Hit record on your way out."

•   •   •

Geneva carried a tray into the backyard and set the table. The bright yellow and orange place mats set off the turquoise-rimmed plates beautifully. She laid yellow napkins on top of the plates and lined up the bottom edges of the forks and knives. As she tossed the salad, Tom took the burgers off the grill, then went inside to call the children to dinner. Geneva sipped the last of her wine, an earthy Sonoma Pinot, and sat down. The evening air was fresh. She relaxed into the chair. A jay squawked and she tipped back her head to follow its flight from the roof to a tree.

As she straightened her neck again, the movement reminded her of riding on her father's shoulders when she was small. If she was tired of walking, or simply bored, she would stand in front of him, her arms stretched high, and he would swing her up onto his shoulders. She remembered wondering if adults were thrilled every second of their lives seeing the world from such heights. Sometimes she would arch her back and look to the sky. He would tighten his grip on her ankles, and she would arch farther and farther, until the world was upside down and receding, and no longer boring.

The back door slammed and startled her.

Ella stomped down the steps and threw herself into a chair. She pulled the cuffs of her long-sleeve gray T-shirt over her hands and tucked them between her legs. "It's freezing out here!"

"Maybe you need a sweater."

"Maybe I'll eat inside."

"I'd like us all to eat together. I haven't seen you all day."

Ella shivered theatrically.

"What've you been up to?"

Her daughter ignored her.

Charlie threw open the door, which Tom caught before it hit the side of the house. "Easy, easy. You're like a gorilla."

Charlie gave a gorilla grunt, sat down, grabbed a burger from the platter, and put it to his mouth.

"Charlie . . ." Geneva warned.

Tom tapped him on the head. "Wait for everyone, okay?"

"Pig." Ella pulled her knees to her chest and yanked her shirt over them. "It's freezing!"

Charlie said, "Want Marcus to come warm you up?"

Geneva selected a burger and passed the plate to Ella, who made no move to accept it. Geneva put it on the table in front of her. "Who's Marcus?"

"No one!"

Geneva looked at Tom, who shrugged. "Ella, aren't you going to eat?"

Two fingers emerged from the shirt cuff and lifted the edge of the bun. "It's burnt."

Tom lifted his plate. "Trade?"

"Or you can have mine," her brother said around an enormous mouthful. He pointed to a nearly empty plate.

Ella scowled at him and switched plates with her father. She applied copious quantities of ketchup, mustard, and relish, pushed up her sleeves, and ate.

The jay squawked again from a nearby branch. Geneva watched as it held an acorn in its feet and hammered it to pieces.

Ella finished her burger. "Okay, I ate. Can I go now?"

Geneva didn't look up. "Sure. Please take your plate in."

"Like I'd forget after years of boot camp."

Perhaps this was what had happened between her mother and Paris. It didn't matter that their personalities were different from Geneva's and Ella's. A teenager pushing hard enough and a mother too baffled and hurt to know how to respond could conceivably add up to a lifelong estrangement. Look at how distant she herself felt from her mother, twenty-five years after becoming a teenager. She'd always attributed that to her mother's drinking and the disastrous consequences, but maybe the drinking was a red herring. Maybe one day your children are teenagers who won't talk to you, and the next they are adults who don't want you in their home.

The situation with Ella wasn't catastrophic; she knew other parents had dealt with far worse. Drea's son had been suspended for being stoned at school—and neither Drea nor her husband had any idea their child smoked at all, much less during school. But although her problems with Ella didn't appear serious, Geneva worried about where they were headed. She didn't want things to spiral out of control, to get blindsided and realize too late she could have prevented a serious problem if only she had intervened earlier. Tom said she worried too much, but his reassurances had come to mean little to her.

She admitted her pride was at stake. Geneva thought she knew her daughter and believed she understood her. Hadn't she held her in her arms countless times after some mishap, listened to her fears and anxieties, and counseled her in her relationships with her friends, teachers, and family? Geneva knew when Ella wanted a hug (the tiniest of pouts gave it away) and when she only wanted to vent (her hands twitched at her sides). To other people, Ella probably appeared the same when she was tired, bored, or nursing an emotional hurt, but Geneva could readily discriminate these states. She had been a conscientious student of her daughter's behavior for sixteen years. It was at the core of being a good mother. Or so she thought. Trying to understand Ella's behavior now was like trying to listen to a recording of a symphony whose volume vacillated unpredictably from barely audible to deafening. She couldn't hear the music, and all she wanted to do was leave the room.

Wasn't that what Paris had done, moving to another continent? And maybe that's what her mother's drinking did, transport her to another room where there was no music at all. Geneva didn't recall Paris and her mother fighting often, but conflict could stop well short of mudslinging and fisticuffs and still cause damage. Over the years she'd asked Dublin several times about why Paris had excommunicated herself. He didn't know any more than she did. He was, after all, only a year older than Geneva, and perhaps, as a young boy, was not tuned in to the wavelengths of female discord. Florence ought to know more. Geneva had little history of discussing emotional matters with her, but resolved to ask her about their mother's relationship with Paris—and with her. And if she could get Paris on the phone, she might ask her directly. In the past, Paris had been clear that any discussion of their mother was off-limits. But Geneva wasn't prepared to let the issue rest, not with her mother under her roof and the fear of losing her own daughter prickling under her skin.

CHAPTER FOURTEEN

ELLA

Fresh air is grossly overrated. And "fresh" is apparently synonymous with "arctic." Dinner was two hours ago and Ella's hands were still numb. And she hadn't come close to finishing her homework. She spent some time fooling around on the guitar, then dug in a pile of clothes for something clean to wear to school tomorrow, and thought it would be really helpful if her mom did her laundry like she used to. Afterward, she wrote a half-assed outline for her paper on *Pride and Prejudice* and did the problem set for math. Not a single stupid answer matched the ones in the back of the book. How did she ever end up in the second-hardest math track? Oh, wait, let's take a wild guess. Her mom. Well, she was way too tired to figure out where she went wrong in those problems. She'd just do what she always did: Wait for Mr. Ryan to go through them in class.

Everything would be so crystal-fucking-clear she'd wonder how the hell she hadn't breezed through them the first time. Then she'd go home, start another set, and discover the symbols were, in fact, hierofuckingglyphics and she wasn't a goddamn Egyptian scribe.

Her mood was tanking, so she lay on the floor and watched the words float on the ocean for a while. Sometimes they energized her and other times they put her to sleep. Today she just hoped they'd stop her from screaming out loud. Maybe she was PMSing. What day was it? If it wasn't PMS, then she was having a nervous breakdown.

Her stomach felt gross from mainlining that burger. Family dinner. As if everyone was thrilled to hang out together. The whole thing was so contrived, like her mom read a magazine article: "Teenagers from families that sit down to eat dinner together at least four times weekly are 56 percent less likely to use illegal drugs and 62 percent less likely to have an unwanted pregnancy." What it doesn't mention is that teenagers who eat with their families are so convinced their parents are completely batshit, they'd do anything not to become parents themselves, including never having sex.

Her mom was the most annoying, for sure, but Prince Charles was second place and gunning for the lead. Who the hell did he think he was, yanking her chain about Marcus? Wait until she found the right moment to tell their parents the Prince wasn't such a prince. And not just the porno mags, although she still couldn't get over how nasty that was. After school yesterday she'd run into Charlie at the bagel shop in town. He was with Spencer and two seniors she knew were not just stoners but did meth and E and God knew what else. Nice friends. And guess what. The Prince was totally out of it. Spencer was practically propping him up. When he saw her he tried to be super cool, but couldn't pull it off because, for one thing, his eyes wouldn't focus. One of these days, when Ella didn't feel like killing him, she'd give him a sisterly lecture about how druggies always turn out to be big failures and that he shouldn't be such a moron. A little discreet weed was one thing, but pills? And meth? And lots of cool kids didn't do drugs at all. Like Marcus. At least that's what she'd heard.

Ella rolled onto her side and curled into a ball. Marcus. As if he would ever be interested in her. Dream on, loser. Maybe if she got a boob job and a personality transplant. Honored guest at her pity party, for one.

Hold on a sec. How the hell did the Prince know about Marcus? It wasn't like she walked around with a giant torch emblazoned with his name. The only person in the entire world who knew was Megan, and she knew for a fact Megan would never tell anyone. Ella wasn't sure of many things these days, but she and Megan had each other's back 100 percent. So how the fuck did Prince Charlie find out about Marcus? Was she that obvious with her nonobvious stares at him? Did everyone at school know?

The thought made her want to puke. And smash something. Maybe smash something, then puke on it.

A knock at the door.

"Ella?"

Her mom.

No, no, no. "I'm really busy."

"This'll only take a sec."

She got up and yanked the door open. Her mom had her planner open. Who the hell uses a planner anymore?

"I wanted to remind you that your last SAT prep class is on Saturday at two."

"I'm not going."

"But it's your last one."

"And now we know the last one was my last one."

Her mom looked like she was going to stomp her feet. "It's important, Ella."

"To you. So you go."

"That's not helpful."

"Here." She picked a prep book from her desk and thrust it at her mom. "I'm sure you'll think it's a beach read."

Her mom did that yoga thing with her shoulders that drove Ella nuts. "Do you have a specific reason for not wanting to attend the class?"

"I have a conflict."

"But I gave you these dates ages ago. Remember the stickie?"

Fuck the stickie. "I'm not going."

"Can we sit and talk about it?"

"No." She started to close the door. "Bye, Mom."

"Ella, really. Please be reasonable." She put her hand on the door handle.

"I've got a poetry slam. That's my conflict."

"Poetry doesn't trump SAT prep."

Ella pushed on the door. Her mom, who was super strong, resisted. Ella's face got hot and her head nearly exploded. Her mom was all cool and collected, which made her more furious. She pulled on the door to give it a good slam, but her mom saw it coming and took a step in.

"What's wrong?"

Ella backed away. Her skin prickled and her lungs shrank up until she thought she would pass out. Instead of getting out of her fucking room, her fucking life, her mom took a couple more steps toward her. It was too goddamn much.

"Get out! Get out of my room!"

"Please don't shout."

"Stop it! Just stop it!"

"Stop what? What am I doing?"

"Telling me what to do! I'm not a baby! I don't want you telling me what to do!"

Her mom stepped back and held the planner up like she could ward off evil forces with it. "I'm only trying . . ."

"I don't give a shit what you're trying to do! Just leave me alone! Leave me alone! I hate you!" She ran at her mom battering-ram style but at the last second threw herself on the floor.

"What's going on?" Her dad's voice.

Tears came out of nowhere. She buried her head in her arms to block out everything. "Dad, make her leave. Please make her leave."

The door closed. When she opened her eyes, the wordstorm was blurry and spinning.

. . .

It took forever to calm down. She listened to some music but crying had given her bad hiccups and they hurt. She didn't normally risk getting high when her parents were home, but she was desperate. A couple of tokes later, her hiccups had stopped and she didn't give a shit about her mother anymore. She doodled in her poetry notebook while she waited for the orange spray to get less intense, then went to have a shower. She was running the water to heat it up when a loud thud came from the Prince's room, where Nana was staying.

She turned off the water. "Nana?"

Footsteps down the hall from her parents' room. Her mom's

voice came from the Prince's room. "Tom! Can you give me a hand?"

Ella wrapped a towel around herself and stuck her head out the door. She heard Nana say what sounded like "I'm fine. I'm fine."

Her dad whooshed by.

"Is Nana . . . ?"

Too late. He was already in the room with Nana and her mom. Low voices, shuffling, then Nana said, loud and clear, "I'm fine!"

She closed the door. A minute later, her parents passed by.

"Tom, I swear to God she's been drinking."

"Now, Geneva, just because she slipped . . ."

"Because she's drunk! I don't know how, but she is."

"Did you smell alcohol?"

"No, but . . ."

"And, what? She's got a still in her room?"

"Don't put it past her."

They kept arguing and yelling in the kitchen. Her mom sounded like a paranoid freak. Ella could see why her dad didn't buy her story. But she also knew the Prince and Nana were up to something—and her mom might be right. If her mom wasn't such a tool, she could almost feel sorry for her.

CHAPTER FIFTEEN

GENEVA

Tom, Geneva, and Helen stopped at Juliana's on their way to yet another Novak family celebration—Tom's father's birthday. Tom had offered to fix his sister's sticky kitchen door. Helen said she'd stay in the car if it was only going be a short while.

When they pulled in, Juliana was making room under the hood of her VW Bug for party food. She always made an array of side dishes to balance the barbecue fetish of the Novak men.

"Jon went for a run so he's showering," she said. "He should be ready in a minute."

Tom lifted his toolbox out of the rear of the car. "So long as we're there on time. You know Mom."

"I know, I know. Says she's Czech, but I swear to God she's Swiss."

Geneva followed Tom into the kitchen. "Where's Aldo?"

"In the backyard, I guess."

She moved containers from the refrigerator to the counter, in preparation for carrying them out to the car, and watched her husband work. He opened and closed the kitchen door a few times and examined the problem spots, running his hand over the wood as if the remedy were written upon it in Braille. The sight of his efficient, graceful movements and the serene look on his face amazed her. She would be afraid to take tools to an object as permanent as a door. He would find this amusing, given her willingness to cut open and repair living bodies, but it was nevertheless true.

He said, "Ella seemed okay this morning about going to the prep class."

"Yes, she did. I'm just grateful for the absence of screaming."

"That was almost a week ago."

"Feels like only yesterday."

"I'm pretty sure some conflict's perfectly normal. From what I can remember, Juliana did battle with my mom nearly every day."

"Maybe you're right." But Geneva wasn't convinced. Fighting with Ella didn't feel normal. It felt terrible, like fighting with herself. Whatever was going on, there had to be a better way to cope. She didn't understand how such a quiet, easy child had morphed into a volatile young woman. As a medical professional, she knew hormones were potent chemicals, and that Ella's control over her actions might be limited. As a mother, and as a person, she wasn't looking forward to years of unpredictable behavior and conflict. It hurt too much.

She watched Tom dig through his toolbox. "Missing something?"

"A hammer, of all things."

"I can check the garage."

"Great. I'll spray the pins in the meantime."

She thought about Ella as she headed through the living room and into the garage, dark except for a strip of light at the bottom of the garage door. She reached for the light switch on the wall to her left. A loud bark startled her. Before she could back up and shut the door, Aldo appeared from around the corner. In a single bound, he flew through the doorway as she stepped aside. The dog's shoulder hit her thigh, knocking her over.

"Tom!" she shouted, and scrambled to her feet.

But Aldo veered away from the kitchen and bounded down the short hall that led to the bedrooms.

Hearing the commotion, Juliana rushed through the front door. "Aldo!"

Tom appeared from the kitchen, glanced at Geneva, and ran down the hall after the dog. Juliana and Geneva followed.

Geneva gasped. The bedroom door was ajar. The dog plowed into the room without slowing.

"Jon! Watch out!" Juliana shouted.

As Tom reached the open door, Geneva heard Aldo snarl. Jon shouted for help. Geneva stepped into the bedroom in time to see the dog knock Jon backward onto the bed. Jon, shirtless, threw his arm in front of his face and lifted his legs to kick, but Aldo lunged forward, jaws wide, and bit down on his arm. Jon cried out and tried to pull his arm away, but the dog's jaw had locked. With his hind legs braced against the floor, Aldo pinned Jon to the bed.

Juliana screamed, "Aldo! Stop!"

Tom stepped forward and made a grab for Aldo's collar.

Geneva cried, "No! Don't!"

In one lightning movement, Aldo released Jon's arm, whipped his head around, and snapped. Tom jumped away and grabbed his forearm, swearing. Jon rolled quickly onto his side, smearing blood across the bed, and covered his head with his arms. The dog, wild-eyed and snarling, pulled back for an instant, then pounced on Jon again, ripping into his shoulder.

Jon cried out in pain. "Get him off me!"

Tom lifted his hand from his forearm. Blood from two long gashes dripped to the floor.

Geneva, heart racing, scanned the room. A broom, a lamp, anything. Her eyes fell on the small deck beyond sliding glass doors to her left. She rushed over and yanked sideways on the door handle. Locked. She flipped the lever below the handle and flung the door open. A quick sprint across the deck; then she jumped onto the lawn and found what she hoped for—a hose. She picked up the nozzle and opened the faucet. As she ran toward the bedroom, the hose caught on the edge of the deck. She grabbed a loop, whipped it in an arc and jerked it free.

She reached the doorway. Aldo still had Jon's shoulder in his jaws, oblivious to Tom's kicks to his haunches. Through the open door, Geneva shot a stream of water at Aldo's head.

The dog yelped and leaped off the bed. She kept the hose trained on his head. Aldo stumbled against Tom's legs and snarled. Water bounced off him in all directions. He flung his head from side to side and snapped at the spray.

"Get away from the door!" Geneva yelled.

Tom vaulted sideways past the end of the bed and Juliana quickly backed away, leaving a clear path to the hallway.

Geneva stepped from the deck into the bedroom and hoped she would not run out of hose. Aldo stood broadside to her, unwilling to give up ground even though he could not turn his face into the water. He no longer snarled, but his tail was rigid and his hackles were raised. She turned the hose onto his flank. The dog yelped and lurched away, bouncing off the doorframe. His paws slipped on the wet wood floor; then he regained his balance and skittered down the hall. Geneva released the lever, stopping the stream, and dropped the hose on the floor.

Tom ran across the sodden carpet and slammed the bedroom door. "Jesus Christ."

Juliana stood frozen against the wall. On the bed, Jon moaned and peeked out from under his arm. "Is he gone?"

"Yes. It's okay now." Geneva knelt on the bed and tried to gauge the seriousness of his shoulder wound. Several deep puncture wounds and plenty of blood, but not enough to suggest a major artery. "Let me see your arm, okay?"

He gingerly turned onto his back. His face was ashen, and splattered red. Blood poured out from under a six-inch flap of skin on his forearm. Geneva yanked a pillowcase off a pillow, wrapped it around Jon's arm and held it firmly to stem the bleeding. "Who's got a cell phone? Someone call nine-one-one. Juliana, any first-aid supplies in this bathroom?"

Her voice trembled. "I think so."

"Go get them." Juliana didn't move. "Now!" Geneva reached for the edge of the comforter and pulled it over Jon's legs, then looked up at Tom, who watched her minister to Jon. "Are you okay? Can you put pressure on it? There's a towel over there."

"It's not too bad." He wrapped the towel around his left arm and pressed it against his stomach. "The hospital's only a couple of miles away. It'd be faster just to take him. Unless you don't think it's a good idea for us to move him."

She put her hand on Jon's neck to take his pulse. "I don't think he's shocky. Jon, we're going to take you to the car, okay?"

He raised his head a little and nodded. "Okay. But isn't that fucking dog loose in the house?"

Juliana came in and handed Geneva an emergency kit. "This is all I've got. Should I go find Aldo and put him in the garage?"

Out on the street, a car horn blared three times. A bolt of fear shot through Geneva.

"Tom! That's Mom! The front door is open!"

He threw the bedroom door open and ran out. Juliana followed. A minute later, he returned, panting.

"She was leaning on the horn because she's pissed off we left her alone. She saw Aldo take off down the street. Juliana went to find him."

"Tom, can you let Jon lean against you so I can bandage him?" With practiced movements, Geneva wrapped gauze around the wounds. Blood oozed through the layers. Together, she and Tom helped him up and headed down the hall.

"Watch the wet floor," she said.

. . .

Geneva drove.

Tom pulled out his phone. "What should I say to Charlie and Ella?" After her prep class, Ella was picking her brother up from batting practice and then going to the party.

"Just say we'll be late. That way your parents will have the kids there anyway. We can explain everything later."

"Sounds good." He sent the message, then read aloud a text from Juliana saying she'd found Aldo.

"She needs to put that dog down," Helen said.

Jon said, "I'd help."

"Once they taste human flesh, that's it."

A grim silence hung in the air.

Geneva felt Tom's eyes on her. "What's the law say, Geneva?"

"I'm obliged to file a report, as is the doctor who will treat you. And the dog must be quarantined for thirty days."

"Even if it's had its shots?"

"Yes."

"Anything required after that?"

"The right decision."

•   •   •

Geneva waited with Helen in the waiting room of the Novato Community Hospital while the men received treatment. Her mother repeatedly asked her how long it would take and whether they might still make the party. The prospect of access to alcohol made Helen dogged.

"Mom, I know why you want to go. Even if I condoned it, I'm not about to leave here before Tom and Jon are ready."

"Maybe Ella could swing by. It must be on her way."

"Not really. And I'm not comfortable with her driving unfamiliar routes."

"You're too protective."

And she had been overly concerned about Aldo. "I haven't been able to reach Ella anyway. She's not answering my texts."

"Because she's driving! Let me text Charlie."

"For God's sake, Mom! Leave it alone!"

Several people in the waiting room turned to look at them.

Helen leaned over and lowered her voice. "You've got no cause to shout at me and attract attention. It's embarrassing."

Geneva hadn't meant to raise her voice. But before she could apologize, Helen said, loudly enough for everyone to hear, "And it's perfectly reasonable for me to want to get out and socialize. You've kept me cooped up for too long." She gestured at her walker and her leg. "You think it's easy being laid up like this?"

An elderly woman seated nearby leaned forward and scowled at Geneva.

She pictured walking out of the hospital, leaving her mother behind. She would get in her car and drive away. Perhaps she'd stop by the house, pick up Diesel, and go for a quiet walk at the marsh. Afterward she'd sit outside her favorite café and read a book, Diesel at her feet.

Her mother's voice pulled her out of her reverie. "Are you ignoring me?"

"Not intentionally, Mom. It's been a very stressful day."

Helen smiled but her eyes did not. "Well, you didn't get bit, did you?"

* * *

After they took Jon home and made sure he had everything he needed, Geneva hoped Tom would want to go home, as she did. But his father had never had a birthday without all of his children present, and Tom refused to be the first to break tradition.

"My arm is fine," he told her. "I'm fine."

She acquiesced, mostly because she lacked the energy to disagree. She also wanted to see her children. As terrible as Aldo's attack on Jon had been, at least Ella and Charlie had been far from the action, unlike during the sausage incident. Geneva counted on her children to return her attention to normal things, such as batting practice and the uselessness of SAT prep class. A crisis like today's certainly put things in perspective.

Their decision to attend the party delighted Helen. And Geneva decided she didn't care if her mother had a drink or two that evening. She had had enough of fending off disaster for one day.

CHAPTER SIXTEEN

ELLA

She was in such deep shit. The poetry slam lasted way longer than it was supposed to; then she got lost trying to find 101 North. She'd brought her friend Megan along as her personal GPS device, but it turned out not even the combination of Megan's iPhone, the Google map Ella had printed out, and the Jurassic-era unrefoldable map from the car could deal with the massive construction detour. Didn't help that she was nervous as hell driving in San Francisco. One-way streets, crazy-ass drivers, and way too many pedestrians. The only bad thing that didn't happen was taking one of the peds out. Of course she wasn't exactly home yet.

Then there was that little issue in the parking garage. Who would put a ginormous pole right next to a parking space too small for a smart car, much less her dad's Toyota truck? Megan wanted to get out and direct her, but she'd parked so close to the wall the door wouldn't open. Luckily, it was more of a scrape than a crunch. An extended scrape. But that could have happened anywhere. And this particular scrape most certainly did not happen in San Francisco.

Forget the driving-related disasters, though. The slam was awesome. Must have been a hundred people there. When her turn came around, she was so nervous she was sure no words would make it out of her mouth. Her first line squeaked out as if she was on helium, and she almost ran off the stage. But then she spotted Megan grinning at her like an idiot, and after that, well, it just flowed. Her last line, the one inspired by the wordstorm, got her some applause. That's right. Applause. So cutting out all those pieces of paper and staying up late agonizing over words and rhythm and ideas, and dealing with the whole SAT practice crap had all been worth it. Ella didn't make it into the next round of the slam—she didn't expect to—but a bunch of people came up to her afterward and told her how cool her poem was. Someone even said it was chill. Her poem was chill. Oh yeah.

She had Megan text Prince Charlie that she'd be late—using Ella's phone because, technically, her permit didn't allow her to drive anyone under twenty-five who wasn't in her family. "Technically," because everyone broke that rule—not that her mom would care about that excuse. The Prince was pissed about waiting and threatened to rat on her to their mom, which would have officially made the day a champion-level fuckup (not counting the slam). But Ella got Megan to text him back that she'd make it up to him if he could not freak just this once. He must've been okay with it because her mom hadn't sent the FBI out to track her down yet.

By the time she found the right road, dropped off Megan, and got to the field, the Prince had been cooling his heels for an hour. His face was all pissy, but when she pulled up to the curb, it changed to shocked.

"Holy shit! What happened to the truck?"

That obvious? Not good. "Oh, the little scratch? It'll come off."

He laughed. "Yeah, right."

"It's not my fault someone hit me while I was parked."

He threw his stuff in the rear, got in, and slammed the door. "How come you're so late?"

"The prep class ran late."

"An hour?"

"Not quite. There was traffic."

"It's like two miles away." He reached for a piece of paper on the dashboard. "What's this?"

Ella moved to snatch it from him, but he was too quick. "Give it to me."

"Sutter Street garage? That's in the city! You drove to the city?"

Her stomach tightened. "Must be from a meeting Dad had."

"It's dated today, you liar. What were you doing there?"

She sighed. Game over. "The poetry slam. It was so cool." She looked him in the eye. "You won't tell, will you?"

"I don't know. What's it worth to you?"

Why couldn't he ever act without some sort of payback? This time it didn't matter, though, because she had the goods on him.

"How about this? You keep quiet about my trip to the city and I'll keep quiet about your porno enterprise."

The Prince barely skipped a beat. "That? It's history. Besides, where's your evidence?" He waved the parking slip. "I've got this."

"You think Mom and Dad wouldn't believe me? You want to take that chance?"

"Maybe not. Maybe I'll let it go this time. But you owe me."

Little prick. "Thanks."

"Are you gonna drive now? I'm ready for some barbecue." He slouched down and put his stinky feet on the dash.

She put the truck in gear and pulled away.

The Prince said, "You coming to the Battle of the Bands on Tuesday, Smella?"

"Everyone goes. You have your songs picked out?" Every band did one cover and one original. The originals were always less like music and more like stand-up comedy.

"Yup. We're going with 'Rock on You.' But the other one is a surprise."

"An air of mystery . . ."

"Yup. I'm not singing that one. A girl is."

"Spencer and Pierce agreed?"

"I can be very persuasive."

No shit. "Who's the girl?"

"Rosa Contreras. You know the one that works at the vet with Mom. She's got mad pipes. And she's totally hot."

Ella had to admit the girl was cute.

The Prince put on this big-time announcer voice. "It's gonna be the performance of a lifetime."

She laughed. Their relationship was twisted, but it worked for them.

•   •   •

They rolled into the party, excuses ready to go, but no one paid any attention to them. Uncle Ivan, Aunt Leigh, the Accountants, and the rest of the gang were all gathered around Juliana. She was pretty freaked-out, telling everyone Adolf had gone all Cujo on

Jon without an H, and attacked her dad, too. When Ella heard that, she was ready to freak out herself, but it turned out her dad wasn't hurt badly. But Jon without an H almost became Jon without an Arm. He had a couple dozen stitches in his arm and shoulder. Juliana must've changed her shirt, but there were spatters of blood on the seat of her shorts.

Ella could tell Juliana wanted to keep talking about it, but Granny Novak tried to change the subject because she didn't want Granpa's birthday spoiled. Not even a rabid-dog attack had clinched that. Plus it was a Novak rule that Novaks weren't to blame if someone else could take the fall. Was Adolf a Novak? Ella was pretty sure he was. At least compared to Jon without an H.

Juliana said, "Aldo was probably upset because Jon was on the bed. He thinks it's his."

Upset? Upset usually doesn't equal stitches.

"And Geneva let Aldo out of the garage. Nothing would have happened if she hadn't let him out."

Granny Novak was determined to move on. "So is everyone coming here from the hospital? It's nearly four o'clock. And what about Geneva and her mother? They weren't hurt. There's no reason they can't come. We've got so much food."

Juliana shrugged her shoulders. "I haven't heard."

The Prince piped up. "I'm guessing we won't see Jon."

The Accountants laughed, but Granny sent them a look that cut them off at the knees.

• • •

Ella texted her dad to make sure he was okay and found out they were on their way. The boys headed outside to circle around the barbecue like lions at a kill. She went, too, because it was either that or listen to Juliana, whom she decided was certifiable. Actually made her mom seem totally rational in comparison. No wonder she had trouble in the boyfriend department. Jon without an H would be reactivating his Match.com account if he had any sense at all.

Granny and Granpa Novak had a cool backyard, set up for fun and games. In addition to the largest barbecue known to humanity and lots of places to sit and eat, there was a bocce ball court, a grassy place for badminton or volleyball or whatever, and a swing hanging from an oak tree. Whether there was a specific occasion or not, the outside refrigerator always had drinks and snacks. Party Central.

The boys were up to their elbows in a Doritos bag, talking about the dog attack and all the extremely cool and brave things they'd have done if they were there. Jackie Chan Animal Control. Ella dug around in the fridge for a drink and heard Spencer tell the Prince the amplifier had arrived at Rango's house. The Prince told him to shut up.

"Why? It's so cool you bought it!"

Ella peeked around the side of the fridge. The Prince socked Spencer on the arm; then Pierce hit him, too.

She straightened up, popped the top of the soda can, and cleared her throat. "What's this about an amplifier?"

Spencer rubbed his arm. "Sorry. I forgot it was a secret."

"I can't believe I'm related to you," Pierce said.

For once the Prince didn't have a snappy comeback and looked at her sheepishly. She winked at him. Gotcha, big boy. Why he bought the amplifier was obvious. It was his ticket into the band. That's the problem with flashing your wad at guys like the Accountants. They know how to up the ante. How the Prince managed to buy the amp was a bit trickier. She didn't know how much something like that cost, but it had to be more than what a stack of sticky porno mags would bring in. And she suspected he'd already bought other stuff with the money, like those video games he said belonged to a friend. Plus she'd seen him at school last week with an iPhone. He'd been bugging their parents about getting one since Apple fell off the tree, but they'd been 100 percent sure he didn't need one. Of course, when she asked him about the iPhone, he said it was someone else's. But she wasn't drinking that Kool-Aid.

The big sister in her said she should tell her parents before Charlie got into trouble he couldn't charm his way out of. But this wasn't the time to play the big sister. This was the time to stay cool. Because however he was lining his pockets, she was onto him, and he knew it. Her excursion into the city would stay their little secret. Not only that, her sources informed her Marcus would be at a party later at the house of a sketchy senior. Her mom would never approve, so she planned to sneak out. It was going to be so much simpler now that the Prince was in her pocket.

CHAPTER SEVENTEEN

HELEN

Helen knew the exact moment she became a woman. It wasn't when Eustace married her, that was certain, though her sympathy for her sixteen-year-old self was considerable. She didn't become a woman on her honeymoon, either, as much as that week opened her eyes to a host of things—good and bad—she'd only weakly imagined: the way money made everything smoother, how the ocean pushed against the shoulder of the beach, the sweet listlessness of her first oyster, and how a man lying on top of her felt twice as heavy as he ought.

Neither did bearing and suckling children make her a woman—not in her heart. When she was pregnant, women she met, even ones she didn't know from Adam, felt obliged to give her advice. Must've been because she resembled a child herself, one hiding a prizewinning watermelon under her shirtfront. They told her the pain of bringing a child into the world would change her forever, but it didn't. It was only pain. And like most things, good or bad, it didn't last forever. The birthing didn't make her a woman and neither did her babies. They were more like siblings to her. Sometimes when she walked them in the night, her feet dragging as if the rug was a pool of molasses, she got befuddled and thought they belonged to her mama. The babies seemed as confused as she was about why God had placed all of them on this earth, leaving them to cope through long days that shone too bright and through nights that stretched too dark. Helen wished someone would hold her and sing to her until the questions answered themselves or disappeared.

Through ten years of marriage Helen held on to her childhood. Looking back, she appreciated what a monumental feat of ignorance that had been. Day in and day out, she held on to the notion that because she was married, she had love, and because she had love, she was lucky—even blessed. So many girls never drew the attention of a responsible, hardworking man from a good family. Heck, a lot of them never found anything better than one who didn't get drunk every single night. And despite Eustace's determination to have his own way, he never ignored her and he most certainly never laid a hand on her. He was, by and large, still the romantic swashbuckling pirate who had weakened her knees at sixteen. And, as a child of twenty-seven, Helen figured that meant she owed him plenty: her body, her loyalty, and a whole bucketful of gratitude.

But watching Eustace cozy up to the girl in the daisy-colored dress was the beginning of the end of that. Helen took her first step to becoming a woman when, instead of strutting over and smacking him across the face, she went straight to the restroom and fixed up her lipstick. Her next step down that road came three minutes later when the waiter offered her a drink and she said, "Why, I think I will," and whisked one off the tray. Soon as he left, she drank it straight down. And when Eustace came up to her some time later, snaked his arm around her waist and kissed her on the mouth right in front of those two from the ladies' club, she pushed him off like he was an overeager puppy and wiped her lipstick from his mouth with her thumb, shining her eyes up at him. That was when Helen Riley became a woman.

Only a fool would suppose her husband's fondness for the girl in the daisy-yellow dress was a singular event, and Helen was no fool—not now. As she had never to that day been successful at getting Eustace to do anything other than what he'd made up his mind to do already, she didn't even attempt to shift him directly. What would have been the use of that? He would have laughed at her. So she did what she could to remove temptation. Of course she kept herself pretty and youthful, and made herself available to him without complaint, leastways when she wasn't likely to get in the family way. If Louisa couldn't look after the children, Helen found an elderly woman or, failing that, chose one who'd taken a long dip in the ugly pond. If she caught a whiff of her husband's interest in a girl, she'd do her best to sour him on her, tactfully, of course. Didn't take a law degree to figure out he preferred them innocent, so she'd drop hints about the girl's reputation. And Eustace had his own reputation to look after, so if Helen could manage it, she'd insinuate that the girl's daddy had suspicions that a man of questionable character was sniffing around his precious baby. It was nearly a full-time job. The sad truth was the county was chock-full of girls dumber than a sack of wet mice and standing in need of a prayer. She ought to know.

At the time, she thought of Eustace's taste for girls as an affliction—a hurtful one, and distasteful, too—but an affliction nevertheless. It didn't necessarily change everything between them. Helen was his wife and the mother of his four children, and no purring kitten in a daisy-yellow dress would ever change that.

*   *   *

Once the children moved out of diapers and could mind their manners, Eustace took more of an interest in them. Paris, being the eldest, snared his attention first, but Helen was certain that would have transpired no matter when she came into this world. For starters, she resembled Helen in every detail, right down to the mole on the second smallest toe of her right foot. The two of them couldn't walk down a street without receiving commentary on it. It was a strange species of admiration, as if the blue of Helen's eyes and the angle of her cheekbone had won a breeding challenge against Eustace's features. How was she supposed to take pride in what she had not had a hand in? Still, the girl was uncommonly pretty, so Helen was only too happy to absorb the compliments. She thought of it as partial compensation for the injury caused by her husband's tomcatting.

Paris was a compliant child, which made it easy for Eustace to take her places. She learned right off when she should speak and when she should rely on her own thoughts for entertainment. In comparison, Florence, younger by two years, appeared willful, but Helen knew that next to Paris, every child was. Florence's feelings might have been hurt because her daddy preferred Paris's company, except she didn't care for being trapped in a booth while Eustace had lunch with his friends or sitting stock-still in a bass boat for hours on end. Stopping for an ice cream on the way back from a meeting or after a round of golf would have been right up Florence's alley, except Eustace didn't tolerate children who expected things, so he never told them ahead of time whether that day would be an ice cream day or not. If she wasn't sure to get a cone, Florence would rather stay home. Paris didn't mind either way.

Paris and Florence shared a room upstairs until Dublin arrived. The baby slept in a room between his parents and his sisters. Paris was a light sleeper and woke whenever her brother cried. And when he was hungry or wet, that boy was never shy to let the house, and half the neighborhood, know about it. Though she was not yet six years old, Paris asked if she could have the downstairs bedroom, at the rear of the house, designed for the live-in help. Helen wasn't partial to a midge of a girl sleeping so far from her parents—and so near to the back door—but in the end agreed with Eustace that one part of the house was as safe as the rest. Besides, he said, the room would get use sooner or later with more children on the way.

When Geneva was born a year after Dublin, the little ones stayed together in the nursery. No amount of commotion created by Dublin ever bothered Geneva. If he hollered, she'd sit up in her crib, looking for all the world like an owl baby, brown eyes wide and watchful. If he was making mischief—the normal state of affairs—she'd watch that, too, with a smile pulling at the corners of her mouth. Once Dublin started school, Helen and Eustace tried to shuffle things around, as a boy of that age ought not share a room with his sister. Dublin went down in the help's room, and

Paris moved in upstairs again with Florence. But Geneva wouldn't have it. After Helen had made sure all the children were asleep, Geneva would climb out of her bed, dragging her stuffed monkey and blanket, and tiptoe through the dark house. Come morning, Helen would find her with her brother, sleeping head to toe like shoes in a shoe box. No amount of cajoling, bribery, or out-and-out insisting would stop her. When they locked her bedroom door, she lay down behind it and sobbed until the sound of it broke Helen's heart. Eustace went so far as to spank Geneva, but the next night she was out of her bed and off visiting Dublin again.

So Paris returned to the help's room, and Florence got the nursery, as it was the smaller of the upstairs rooms. Paris and Florence didn't get along too well, so it was all for the best. There wasn't a single thing they could agree on, and it vexed Helen to no end. While Louisa stayed home with the little ones, Helen walked the older girls to school in the mornings, and collected them every afternoon, unless it was raining pitchforks and hammer handles, in which case she drove. Paris and Florence argued about who would hold which of Helen's hands, whether they would stop to pat Mr. Thurston's hound, and how many steps it took to cross from Main Street to Marshall Street, where the school was. The way back presented further difficulties because Paris invariably desired to visit her daddy in the mayor's office, and Florence insisted on going straight home to a slice of Louisa's fruit pie and the freedom of bare feet. Eager to separate the pair, Helen would leave Paris with her father, assuming his secretary gave the green light.

"She's always an angel, Mrs. Riley. And the mayor will be ever so pleased."

"Well, send her straight home if she gets underfoot."

Helen looked forward to those afternoons. Geneva and Dublin would be waking from their naps when she came home. Florence would kick off her shoes, then race out the back door, with the little ones chasing after her like foxes after a rabbit. Louisa brought a tray with lemonade and a pie or a cake. Helen sat under the sycamore and listened to her children's squeals of laughter. Oh, there might be a beesting or a skinned knee to tend to, but it was, all things considered, a peaceful time. But when Paris came home with them, the mood was different. Paris would play, but with a purpose that set the others on edge.

"Too many rules," Dublin would say, throwing the ball away in disgust.

"I'm telling Daddy you're a bad sport."

The invocation of Eustace was Paris's privilege, as the eldest and his favorite, but Helen regarded it as an intrusion. She didn't find any harm in shifting the rules toward leniency when her husband didn't know about it. Did it really matter if Dublin used the side of the garage as a backboard for his kickball? And why couldn't the entire house, not just the children's rooms, be used for hide-and-seek? Paris, however, was keen to uphold her daddy's view of things. Helen suspected the girl spoke to Eustace about her behavior as well. How else had he known she sometimes invited Louisa to sit with her under the tree of an afternoon? So when Paris spent an afternoon at the mayor's office, everyone was happier.

Same as most men, Eustace saw in his son an opportunity to create a man in his own image. Such an enterprise was likely more successful when starting from scratch, as the Lord had done. Eustace attempted to school Dublin in what he took as proper activities for a Southern man: fishing, hunting, and golf. He might've added football except Eustace got winded collecting the paper from the sidewalk in the morning. They did play catch once or twice, and Dublin was no worse nor no better at it than most boys, but the activity made Eustace perspire like a whore in church, and he took to a chair after a few throws. As the remainder of Eustace's chosen activities required patience, the boy was doomed from the start. While Eustace didn't hide his disappointment from his son, neither did he reject him altogether. Dublin was too likeable by half, and Eustace was as susceptible to his charms as anyone else who lived and breathed.

Geneva got all the patience that ought to have been Dublin's, and another helping besides. Eustace took her hunting and said she never once spooked an animal—except him, when he forgot she was behind him. But she didn't pander to him the way Paris did, and her lack of discourse bothered him when the activity didn't necessarily call for silence. For her own part, Helen found the girl unnaturally quiet, but it never worried her. Dublin seemed to get along with her fine, and Helen took it as a sign her youngest daughter was in her own way a good companion and would not grow old alone.

When Paris moved into the help's room the second time, Geneva was five and Dublin was six. The plan called for Geneva and Dublin to share the bigger upstairs room until they grew out of their attachment, or until their parents decided enough was enough. That point had about arrived when Dublin turned twelve. But then Eustace died, and there was no way on God's green earth anyone—least of all Helen—was going to force them apart then. When Florence went to college two years later, Geneva moved into the old nursery and took over Florence's desk and closet, but there were mornings, right up until they left the house for good, when the wall between those two rooms got in the way, and Geneva would be back in her bed across the room from Dublin. She put her pillow on the end of the bed opposite his feet to make it easier to see his face.

For months after Dublin left home, Geneva hardly said a word, not that Helen would have had a lot to say in return. Luckily it was only a year before Geneva set off herself. She might have appeared to be content with her own company, but Helen knew better. She was like a child on a teeter-totter, with her end stuck on the ground and the other end in the air, empty.

CHAPTER EIGHTEEN

❧

GENEVA

Juliana called Geneva on Sunday morning, the day after her dog attacked Jon, and asked her not to file a bite report. Geneva said her hands were tied. Aside from her professional and legal obligation, the doctor would be filing his own report.

"I expect you'll hear from Animal Control," Geneva added, "as will I."

"Why will they call you?"

"I'm a certified Animal Behaviorist. They've consulted me on several cases in the last few years. When they realize I was a witness, they'll want to talk to me."

"So you're going to decide what happens with my dog?"

Geneva ignored her sister-in-law's indignant tone. "No. I'll just tell them what happened, and my professional opinion, if they ask."

"Which is what?"

"I know you love your dog, and I'm sorry. But he's become vicious. Can you control him? Can you guarantee he won't attack someone again?"

Juliana exhaled loudly. "I thought that because we're family, Aldo and I would get special consideration."

The subtext wasn't subtle: Are you a Novak or aren't you? "This isn't about allegiances—it's about safety."

"You're the one who let him out of the garage!"

So that's how she'd spin the story. Geneva had created the problem, so she should fix it. Already she could feel the warm Novak cocoon splintering open. It didn't matter that Juliana should have let them know Aldo was in the garage, or that Geneva's actions were irrelevant because Aldo had it in for Jon and would have found another opportunity to rip him apart. If Jon and Juliana broke up over this incident—caused by Geneva—the Novaks, starting at the top with Granny, would lay the blame at her feet. She guessed how Tom's allegiances would fall, and was saddened.

"Juliana, what if it had been Tom who let Aldo loose? It wouldn't change what happened to Jon. How is he, anyway?"

"He won't answer my calls."

"If you don't hear from his lawyer, think of it as special consideration."

• • •

She had barely put the phone down when Florence called. They hadn't spoken since Helen moved in two weeks earlier, but neither had Geneva expected to hear from her sister. Typically, they didn't speak more than once a month.

Florence said, "I heard you were the hero with the hose."

"Who told you that?"

"Mom. She called me from the party. Sounded tipsy."

"She was. I shouldn't have allowed it."

"She is a grown woman."

"In what sense?"

"I've said this before, but I really think that if Mom got more exercise and drank more water, she'd feel better. And feeling better is the first step toward shaking off addiction."

Geneva suppressed a laugh. Florence thought every problem could be alleviated by exercise and proper hydration. "Maybe, but her exercise options are a bit limited right now."

"Okay, but I'll email you some things she can do with her walker. You'd be surprised."

They spoke for a while about Florence and Renaldo's personal training business, and Florence dutifully asked about Charlie and Ella. Geneva cast about for an anecdote that might appeal to someone with no interest in children.

"The other day Ella returned Tom's truck with a massive scrape down the side."

"Is she okay?"

"Oh, yes. It happened while she was parked."

"Can I tell you again how wonderful it is not to have a car?"

Or children? She enjoyed Florence, but their lives overlapped in few places. "Be my guest. Luckily, Tom's ego isn't bound up with his vehicle. Ella was contrite and offered to help wash it off."

Florence laughed. "Were we ever that naive?"

"Worse, I'm guessing." She saw her opening. "Listen. I really think Paris ought to know what's going on with Mom. She can't keep her head in the sand forever."

"I think she can if she chooses to. Anyway, I wouldn't know how to find her. Why does it matter that she knows?"

Geneva paused. She wasn't used to such a direct conversation with Florence. "She's my sister. Same as you."

"Except—"

"Why is Paris an exception? Why can no one tell me why Paris is different?"

"She was always different. Always." Despite Geneva's interruption, Florence's tone was even. The older-sister role. "Dad loved her best, of course."

There was no rancor in her voice, but Geneva felt the sting. Perhaps she was a close second. Perhaps, if he had lived, her father would have come to appreciate the woman she had become. Was that why she wanted to find Paris, to evaluate the competition?

Florence went on. "And Mom was so jealous of Paris, she couldn't see straight."

"Jealous?"

"You were little, but you've seen the photos. She was just like Mom, but prettier, if that was possible. Nothing else mattered."

Geneva knew Florence was referring to the lack of attention her athletic ability had garnered from their parents, particularly their father. "So you were jealous of her, too?"

"I sure was. Until I figured out there was more to life than being the prettiest princess."

She had heard her sister moving around while they spoke—as she always did—but now Florence was still. Tension filled the pause. "What is it?"

"One thing I never figured out is why Mom pushed me into sports so hard. Sure, I had ability, but she was the one who insisted I play year-round. Didn't seem to matter to her what the sport was, as long as I was playing nonstop."

"Was that bad?"

"No. But neither of them ever came to watch me play. Do you remember coming to a basketball game or a race with them? And then when Dad died, all of a sudden Mom didn't give a damn whether I made the team or not. I guess I understand the shock of losing your husband, but she didn't even want to pay for uniforms or shoes or anything anymore. More than ever, I needed an outlet for my energy. And I needed my teammates."

"I don't remember you stopping."

"I didn't. I stole the money from Mom's purse sometimes just so I could stay on the teams."

This was news to Geneva. "It doesn't make sense for Mom to do that."

"No, it sure doesn't." Florence let out a long breath. "But when you find something about her that does, you call me, okay?"

"Don't wait by the phone." And they both laughed.

Geneva could tell Florence was ready to say good-bye, but she had one more question. "So, if Paris was so close to Dad—and that's what I remember, too—then why did she move to Columbia for the internship when she graduated? And why go to a college so far away?"

"Daddy got her that internship. It was a law office, after all, and Paris wanted to be just like him. But he was devastated when she left."

"I remember."

"Drowned his sorrows in bourbon. I wanted to kick him. No one except Paris mattered at all."

Florence's candor surprised Geneva. "I suppose a lot of things went on I didn't know about. Were things between Paris and Mom that bad?"

"Geneva, you're the one with a teenage daughter. You tell me."

After they hung up, she went to the bookshelf in the living room and retrieved an old photo album. She flipped through the pages, searching for the last pictures of Paris in Aliceville. She hadn't looked at the photos for several years. There was a rare one of Paris and Florence, sitting side by side on the bed in Paris's room—the narrow maid's quarters. Florence gazed at the photographer, presumably Eustace. The naked window was behind her, casting a shadow over her face, but Geneva could see her smile was tentative. Paris leaned back, her torso twisted toward the window. Light fell across her face, accentuating her cheekbones and the natural pout of her lips. Paris could not have been more than sixteen, yet she appeared more mature than their mother had in her wedding photos, or even in ones taken years after. Maybe it was the times; Paris grew up in the late sixties, after all. But then again, so did Florence.

She bent closer to study the room and noticed for the first time the top of Argus's head in the shadows next to Paris's legs. Geneva had trouble summoning details of her sister, but her memory of the dog's despondency after Paris left home was vivid. Everyone showered Argus with attention—except Eustace—but the dog stalked through Paris's room, up the stairs and down the halls, looking for her. At night he gently turned the knob on her door with his mouth and slept beside her empty bed. Florence offered to move in to give the dog company, but Helen wouldn't have it. Instead she stripped the bed, discarded the linens, and scrubbed the floors and walls with disinfectant so strong, humans couldn't approach the room, much less a dog. Eventually Argus took to sleeping by the front door. Whether he was waiting for Paris or had taken up a more general policing role, Geneva wasn't sure.

She turned the page. Her father sat in a lounge chair under an umbrella at the club, drink in hand. He was dressed in white slacks and a pale blue button-down shirt, open at the collar. She remembered taking the photo. He had brought the camera to photograph Paris before a family supper on the eve of her departure for Columbia and the internship. The cocktails had conspired with the heat to tire him, and Geneva followed him to the shade. Beads of sweat ran from his hairline and the color was high in his cheeks. He lifted his drink and rolled the perspiring glass against his forehead.

"Can I take your picture, Daddy?"

"Not now, sugar. I'm hardly at my best."

She rarely asked him for anything, and never twice. That day, she asked again. "Please?"

"Why do you want my picture?"

She shrugged. But she did know, even if she couldn't verbalize it. Initially she had assumed Paris's departure meant she would get more of her father's attention, and had anticipated it eagerly. She also thought the tension between her parents, which she intuited had to do with Paris, would ease. But now she wasn't sure. A week ago, she was staring at herself in the mirror and entertained, for the first time, the idea that there was something wrong with her. She was missing a key trait, and it made her boring or even unlovable. Maybe it was as simple as not being as pretty as Paris. She didn't even know if she was prettier than Florence. It was hard for her to compare eleven to fifteen and seventeen. But whether the reason was looks or personality or birth order or some other ineffable quality, Geneva knew she would not have any more of her daddy than before.

He gave her a long look. "Go ahead then." He drained his drink.

She held the camera steady and twisted the focus ring until she had it right. Holding her breath, she pushed the button. The photo came out a little blurry anyway, because during the instant before the shutter clicked, she shivered. Like the moment before the bear stepped out of the shadows and lumbered into the meadow in front of her, time did a tiny backflip, and she felt an infinitesimal shock wave. She was sad not to be Eustace's favorite, and jealous of Florence, whom she supposed would gain ascendancy. But the ripple that entered her when she took her father's photograph gave her a puzzling feeling of relief.

CHAPTER NINETEEN

ELLA

At Grandpa Novak's party, there had been so much excitement over Adolf's attack she'd forgotten to tell her parents about the ding on the truck. Okay, maybe it was less like forgetting and more like postponing. It didn't matter anyway because when they left the party and walked out to the cars, the damage was pretty hard to miss from thirty yards away, even though it was getting dark. For a split second she considered claiming total ignorance, but then she remembered the Prince knew all about it.

Her dad inhaled sharply. "What happened here?"

"I forgot to tell you."

"I guess you did."

Ella's mom stood there looking like she just got sideswiped. Of course the Prince was grinning like a moron.

"It happened while I was in the class. People are so irresponsible. Aren't you supposed to leave a note?"

"Yes, that's the rule—and the right thing to do," said her mom.

Her dad ran his hand along the damaged part. "Do you remember the car parked next to you?"

This was the kind of question that convinced Ella adults were a different species. "No."

"Appears to be white paint."

"It's in a weird place," her mom, the forensic expert, said. Then she sighed and pulled out her keys. "I'll see you guys at home. Anyone want to ride with me?"

.   .   .

That marked the beginning of Ella's weeklong guilt trip, including a stop at the Cathedral of Expedient Lies, where she paid her respects at the Tomb of the Unknown Hit-and-Run Driver. All week she hit the prep books hard and more than made up for the class she ditched the Saturday before. After school on Friday—a day when no one worked—she finished two more practice sections, then closed the books and stacked them neatly on the floor. She would have preferred to burn them in the backyard and dance around the fire, but she'd been a little too close to other flames recently. She celebrated with a visit to the bear dispensary—her first all week.

The next morning her phone alarm woke her at a criminal hour. But she was as ready for the SAT as she was ever going to be, and eager to get it over with, so she got up and dressed, remembering to put on her lucky gray sweatshirt. By the time she was ready to go, her stomach was in a sour knot. Her mom tried to get her to eat this enormous breakfast she'd made—eggs, toast, juice—but just the thought of it made her want to puke.

Her mom headed for the door. "I've got to go or else we'll be late for the game. Charlie and Dad are waiting outside. Promise me you'll at least take a piece of toast with you?"

"Okay, Mom. Don't stress out."

Her mom stood with her hand on the doorjamb. Ella could tell she wanted to say something profound, or hug her, or get in some last-minute vocabulary review. Instead, she backed out the door. "Good luck. And don't *you* stress out."

"I'm good."

She took a bite of toast, then realized she was dying of thirst. She opened the fridge, hoping for a Coke—Breakfast of Champions!—but there wasn't any. She moved things around for a while, then spied two iced teas in the back. Caffeine. She twisted them around so she could read the labels. Peach and pomegranate. She remembered vaguely that pomegranate was good for you—anti-inflammatory or antioxidizing or whatever—and took it. Then she saw she was late and flew out the door.

Crossing the driveway, she unscrewed the top from the bottle and paused to swig down half the contents. Super cold from being at the back of the fridge—her throat went numb—and super disgusting. Maybe her toothpaste made it taste like cough medicine. Whatever it was, it was vile. She wiped her mouth with her sleeve, put the top on, climbed into the truck and headed to school.

By the time she got her room assignment and sat down, she felt dizzy. Was that a normal part of being nervous? She couldn't seem to focus on the question. Scanning the room, she tried to see whether the other kids looked like she felt, and decided they seemed pretty normal, considering it was early and they had a five-hour test ahead of them. Ella remembered she needed stuff from her bag under her chair. When she bent down, her brain sloshed, and she nearly fell. Somehow she managed to get her pencils and lucky eraser onto her desk.

The proctor handed out the packets and told them not to open them until he said so. He paced back and forth while he went over the instructions. Why did he have to move? It made what he said so vague, like he was inside a giant block of ice. He was blabbering about the different sections, but Ella was way past listening. She held on to the sides of her desk and watched the room sway. Maybe she was allergic to pomegranate? Maybe the anti-whatevers had anti-ed too many whatevers, and now she was on her way to permanent brain damage. So much for acing the SAT.

A girl next to her said, "Are you okay?"

Ella swiveled her head toward the sound. The movement sent the room into a tailspin. She gripped the desk harder but her foot lifted off the ground, shifting her weight, and the whole blurry space that was either the room or just the inside of her head jerked away and she slipped out of her chair and landed on the cold tile floor.

CHAPTER TWENTY

GENEVA

Geneva received a call from the school and left the game immediately to pick up Ella and bring her home. Now she sat on the edge of the couch and placed a cold washcloth on Ella's forehead. Her daughter's eyes were closed and her cheeks were pale.

"Feeling any better yet?"

"Ish."

"And you were fine when you woke up?"

"A little nervous, but not sick."

Geneva wondered how much anxiety Ella would own up to. Maybe she had caused this by encouraging—pressuring—her to practice as much as possible. Her only goal had been for Ella to do her best and not have to take the test more than once. But she may have completely misjudged her daughter's level of stress.

"Ella, do you remember your heart racing, or feeling sweaty?"

"No."

Not likely a panic attack. She studied her daughter's face and thought about her symptoms. Dizziness, nausea, imbalance. And slurred speech, which was not a symptom of stress. A stomach bug? That didn't fit either.

She was missing something. She stood quickly and walked the few steps to the kitchen. Ella's breakfast was on the counter where Geneva had left it, a bite gone from the toast.

"Did you have anything else this morning other than a little toast?"

"Mom . . ." Ella groaned.

"I'm not upset. I'm trying to figure out what's wrong with you."

"An iced tea. I was really thirsty."

"Did you finish it?"

She shook her head.

"Where is it?"

"Where? I dunno." She looked at her mother. "It tasted really gross. I think it's in the car."

The clanking of the walker on the wood floor of the hallway heralded Helen's appearance. She wore a robe and slippers, but her hair was tidy.

"So much coming and going so early in the day! Don't you people ever take a Saturday morning off?"

Geneva ignored her and hurried out the door. She jogged over to the truck, opened the door, and grabbed the bottle from the center console. The bottle was half-empty and the liquid much paler than it should have been. As she unscrewed the cap, she knew what she would find and a wave of anger rose inside her. She sniffed the tea, then took a small sip. Now that the liquid was tepid, the taste of vodka was unmistakable. Geneva recapped the bottle and leaned against the truck.

Judging from the color and taste, about half the tea had been replaced with vodka, so Ella had drunk four ounces of vodka on an empty stomach. In someone unaccustomed to drinking, and she was certain that was true of Ella, it was enough to account for her symptoms. And while Geneva knew in her heart who had spiked the tea, she forced herself to consider every option. If nothing else, the exercise would give her time to calm down. She considered them in reverse order of probability.

Tom. They'd hidden all the alcohol, but if he wanted a drink he could have one. He had no reason for subterfuge.

Charlie. Teens drink. Geneva didn't think her son drank with his friends—not yet—and the family refrigerator would be a strange place to store it. And didn't boys gravitate toward beer? Still, she resolved to be more vigilant, especially as he had acted oddly on a couple of occasions.

Ella. She had resisted studying for the test and it was conceivable she had made herself sick in order to avoid taking it. If that were the case, she believed her daughter would simply have faked an illness rather than risk getting in more serious trouble for being drunk at school. Also, she had been studying hard all week and seemed eager to have it behind her. It wasn't Ella.

Her mother. She had already suspected Helen was sneaking drinks. Between early bedtimes, walker mishaps, and the dearth of complaints, Geneva had lacked only hard evidence. And now she had it in her hand.

But she was too angry to confront her mother now. Instead,

she would tend to her daughter and wait for Tom to come home. She was mad at him, too, and wanted him present when she revealed what an utter mistake it had been to help Helen.

*   *   *

Helen was reading in the backyard and Ella was asleep in her room when Tom and Charlie came home. Geneva sat in the kitchen with the newspaper in front of her.

"Hey, Momster. How's Ella?"

"Asleep."

Tom asked, "Is she okay?"

She nodded. Charlie grabbed an apple from the bowl on the counter, then headed to his room.

Tom pulled up a stool across from his wife. "So does she have a stomach flu?"

"She's drunk."

"What? How?"

"Accidental. There was an iced tea in the fridge that was half vodka."

"Who did that?"

"Who else?"

He frowned. "How do you know?"

"I like the odds."

"Did you talk to her yet?"

"No. I was too angry."

"Good call." He ran his hand through his hair and shook his head. "Maybe we made a mistake cutting her off. Maybe it would have been smarter to regulate her drinking."

Geneva couldn't believe what she was hearing. "Yes, Tom. It was our fault. Mismanagement."

"That's not what I said."

"Because the way I see it, she violated our trust. And how do you think Ella will feel? She was ready to have the SAT behind her."

"I'm not sure what we should say to Ella."

"How about the truth?"

He sighed and looked her in the eye. "I know this is a setback, but don't you think, overall, having your mother here has been positive? Seems like you've been getting along fine."

"Only because I absorb every criticism. Then we get along perfectly."

"Geneva . . ."

The back door opened and they fell silent as Helen made her way into the kitchen. Tom raised his eyebrows at Geneva, imploring her to remain calm. She flipped to the next section of the paper.

Helen brightened when she saw Tom. "Oh, you're back. How'd the game go?"

Not once in three weeks had Helen asked a question about Geneva's life. She supposed her mother saw no point in pandering to her.

"Fine, Helen. Charlie had an RBI."

"That's great! He's a fine boy. So friendly and helpful."

Geneva's mind snagged on the word *helpful*. Helpful how? Maybe she was reading too much into everything. After all, her mother did need a lot of help.

"Helen," Tom said. "I'm going to be blunt with you. We found an iced tea in the fridge that had vodka in it. Was that you?"

Helen turned toward the refrigerator as if reminding herself what it was. Geneva studied her mother's posture and face to gauge her reaction. Before she could conclude anything, Helen smiled thinly at Tom.

"You caught me red-handed. I was having so much fun at your dad's party that I put a little vodka in a water bottle and stuck it in my purse." She shrugged as if to say these things happen. Geneva gave her a stern look. Helen continued. "Of course I was worried one of your kids might drink it, so I put it in the iced tea. That particular one's been in there since I got here."

"You're very observant," Geneva said.

"Runs in the family."

"Well," Tom said. "At least we have an explanation."

Helen asked, "Did one of you drink it?"

"Ella did. Right before the SATs."

"That can't be why she feels sick. Why, there wasn't enough in there to get a fly drunk! Maybe she's got the flu. Kids bring all sorts of illnesses home from school, don't they, Tom?"

"They do, Helen, but . . ."

Geneva turned to Tom. "Why are you agreeing with her?"

"Only about kids spreading bugs."

"That's irrelevant!"

Helen shifted her weight from one foot to the other. "You need to calm down, and I need to sit down. My knee's aching."

Tom helped her to the couch.

Geneva, restless with anger, rose from her stool and stood in front of her mother. "Mom, I want you to admit that you acted wrongly, that you endangered our children."

Helen stared at Geneva's knees. "I do wish I'd finished it off."

"Oh, this is absurd! I can't listen to this!" She swung around to face her husband. "Thanks for backing me up!" She stormed out of the room with every intention of throwing her mother's belongings into a suitcase and putting her on the next plane to LAX.

Halfway down the hall, she paused at Ella's door, which she

had left ajar. Resting her hand on the doorknob, she tried to steady her breath and slow her racing heart, but failed. She inched the door open until she could see Ella, lying on her side, her shoulder rising and falling slightly with each breath. Geneva watched for a moment, then entered, and quietly closed the door behind her. The only chair stood opposite the bed and was piled high with clothing, so she sat on the braided rug and leaned against the chair.

She didn't know what to do about her mother. She didn't know whether she could, in fact, send her back to L.A. Helen couldn't yet make it up the steps to her condo, put on her shoes, or even reach the controls on the microwave, and she couldn't afford the weeks of help she would still need. And Geneva didn't know how much she cared anymore about her mother's problems. Three weeks ago, she had cared enough to bring her here, but now Geneva questioned her motivation for that decision. Had she been trying to demonstrate to Tom that she was a good person, that after eighteen years of soaking up the Novak family spirit she was finally primed to open her home, and her heart, to her mother? What if she had refused? Would Tom have been disappointed in her, and, if that was the case, what did it say about their marriage and how he felt about her? She had done what Tom had convinced her was right, and now she didn't know where she stood with him, her mother, or herself.

She needed to reason this out. The decision to help her mother was in the past. What mattered now were her decisions from here. What was she going to tell her daughter when she woke up? That she got her first hangover courtesy of her grandmother? Geneva told Tom she didn't want to lie to Ella, out of principle, but she wondered whether it would help her to know the truth. Sitting cross-legged on her daughter's floor, the late morning sun angling onto the rug in front of her, Geneva felt trapped in a net of poor options. If she could only see clearly which road would lead to the least harm for her family. But that, right there, was the sticking point, because if she could simply cleave her mother from her notion of family, the way forward would become clear. Wasn't clarity what she was after? What had her mother done to deserve any more consideration than she'd already had?

Geneva's throat closed. She bit down on her lip, pulled her knees to her chest and rocked. She glanced at her daughter, her mouth a perfect bow, her golden bangs touching the ends of her eyelashes. Geneva's nose stung and her vision blurred. Tucking her head into the cradle of her arms, she cried, silently, so as not to wake her child.

CHAPTER TWENTY-ONE

HELEN

The interesting thing about being caught red-handed, Helen surmised, was you could throw your red hands in the air like you were surrendering, and paint a painfully remorseful look on your face, but without punishment to fit the crime, what's to stop a person from carrying on the same as before? Geneva was mad as a wet hen about the iced tea—didn't bother to hide her feelings, neither—and Helen figured she was likely as not to be sent packing, cripple or no cripple. But she didn't care. If she had to hire help, she'd hire help, and if she ran out of money, she ran out of money. One thing for certain, whether she was up here in the fog or down south in the sunshine, she planned to live the way she pleased. She was sorry the girl got tipsy and missed her test, but it wasn't exactly the end of the world. At sixteen she'd been drunk a dozen times or more and the only unfortunate circumstance was that one of those times hadn't been her wedding night.

She and Charlie would devise a different plan. He'd helped himself to some fancy new toys on her nickel, so he owed her that. One hand washes the other. So long as her credit card held up, she knew she'd get her drink. Keeping Geneva off her back was another matter. Maybe, just maybe, that girl would give up the fight. If not, Helen had an emergency supply of pain pills. Every time someone had left a bottle nearby, she'd taken one for safekeeping. She had a dozen in reserve. She would never look forward to one of them as much as a good, stiff vodka, but when it came right down to it, forgetting was forgetting.

Afraid of misremembering where she'd stashed the pills, Helen put them with the last letter she got from Paris more than twenty years ago. No way on God's green earth she'd ever forget where she'd hidden that. Crumpled it up and threw it away on more than one occasion, but always dug it out of the trash. The letter was like a piece of herself she despised. Even lying on the bottom of the trash can, it still belonged to her. If throwing it away didn't change anything, she reckoned, might as well hold on to it.

The letter, now soft as a puppy's ear, was in her quilted makeup bag, zipped inside an inner pocket. She usually kept the bag in her purse. She wanted to be reminded of it, and also the pills, so she kept it close. The letter and the pills went together, she now realized, although she hadn't planned it that way. Pain and pain relief. If Geneva understood—and after thirty years of silence on the subject, Helen had no intention of educating her daughter now—she'd realize why Helen didn't give a damn about getting caught sneaking alcohol. Her hands were red all right, but not for the reasons Geneva supposed, and in any case, she was long past caring.

. . .

Helen kept out of the way for the rest of the day, although she was sorely tempted to discover whether Geneva had thrown out the rest of the iced tea. Before supper she fiddled with the radio in her room, and chanced upon a station that played old tunes. Dancing music, they used to call it: Benny Goodman, Glenn Miller, the Andrews Sisters. The lighthearted songs cheered her some, until one came on she'd rather not have ever heard again: "Blue Moon." She reached over and switched off the radio, but it was too late. The song kept on in her head.

Every summer the club in Aliceville hosted a number of events, including the father-daughter dance, held in mid-July. Paris had been itching to go for years, but Eustace made her wait until she turned fifteen. Eustace was keener on dancing than the majority of men and suggested to Paris they practice their steps. Of course Paris said yes.

So after supper one night they cleared a space in the living room, and Eustace shuffled through the records. Paris looked pretty and grown-up in her sundress with the sweetheart neckline and her hair arranged on top of her head, showing off her long neck. She wore the attitude of a dancer before she took a single step. The other children lined up on the couch and watched for a time, expecting a show, but soon drifted off when they realized it was only some stepping and a twirl or two. Humming to the music that drifted through the house, Helen tidied the kitchen, then went outside to catch what breeze might be caught and see that Dublin didn't get filthy before bed. When Geneva began to rub her eyes, and Dublin and Florence started to argue over who had kicked the ball the farthest, Helen pushed the younger ones inside and up the stairs to bed, and Florence went to watch TV in the den. On her way past the living room, Helen noticed Paris was getting the hang of the steps.

She thought her children were settled, but Geneva had forgotten that monkey of hers on the back porch, and wouldn't contemplate putting her head on the pillow without it. Helen reprimanded her for her carelessness, then headed downstairs.

The staircase took a corner halfway down, and when Helen reached the landing, she paused without knowing why. The sad, sultry notes of "Blue Moon" floated up to her. She proceeded, but was careful of where she placed her feet lest the stairs creak. Eustace had neglected to cut the lamps on, so the only light came from the stairwell, falling short of where he and Paris were dancing. Nevertheless, Helen could see enough to tell they were slow dancing. He had one hand around Paris's waist and the other held her hand against his shoulder.

All the dances had to be practiced, she supposed. And Geneva would be up out of her bed in a minute if she didn't get her monkey. Helen's foot was hovering above the last step when she froze. Eustace brought Paris's hand to his lips and held it there for a long moment before returning it to his shoulder. Helen's insides twisted, and her hands went cold as ice. She shook her head as if she could make the image settle differently in her mind.

Can't a man kiss his daughter's hand?

She strained to see their faces, hoping for a sign that everything was as it should be. They made a slow quarter turn. Eustace's back was now to her and she couldn't see her daughter at all. But then he bent his head and Helen could only surmise he'd planted another kiss, this one on the crown of Paris's head.

Helen turned and crept up the stairs. At the top, she held a hand to her chest and willed the air to return to her lungs. When she could breathe again, she walked to the linen closet, opened the door, then closed it firmly.

"Don't get up. I'll be right there," she called to Geneva, loudly enough for everyone in the house to hear.

. . .

After Eustace had gone to sleep, she stared at the ceiling as if it was a movie screen that was about to show her what to make of her husband and her eldest daughter. Or Eustace and her, because in her mind there most certainly was a connection. When was it she had gone from being grateful that he'd taken an interest in one of the children to feeling it had maybe gone too far? She couldn't put her finger on it, not even near it, because all that time she'd been too busy thinking about how nice it was to have one out from underfoot. And who could blame her? Four children was a handful and a half.

Lying there, she made a conscious decision not to take it personal. Pure foolishness, it was, to on the one hand be happy to have Eustace's attention settle elsewhere, and on the other be jealous of it. And it was only attention. He was a big man who liked the light shining all over him. Helen didn't think she could muster up the energy for that job anymore, even with a gun to her head. Heck, she couldn't even remember being young enough to entertain the notion. If Paris was content to stoke that man's pride, then Helen should step out of the way. Jealous feelings would do none of them a lick of good. She'd be forced to do away with those concerning Eustace. It only required practice.

Helen thought it natural a woman would come to look upon her own daughter with envy. She'd seen it clear enough in the face of her own mama when she came to visit, and probably she'd have seen it earlier—before Eustace—if she'd known to look for it. How could a woman not look at a girl, fresh as a rosebud, hair shining, eyes bright, her breasts perched high on her chest, and not think of herself as coming up a bit short? And when the daughter's looks were a pure gift from her mother, as Paris's were, that made it all the worse. At times Helen imagined her youth and beauty pulled out of her and soaked up by Paris. If she was a sweet girl, or deferential to her mother, Helen might have swallowed it better. But Paris took her looks as her right, and Helen couldn't help but be niggled, just a bit.

It was the course of nature, and the way of life. Even a woman like Helen could see that, at the ripe old age of thirty-three.

CHAPTER TWENTY-TWO

GENEVA

On the Monday after Geneva's confrontation with her mother, she drove into Mill Valley to meet Drea for lunch. She bought a salad at the café counter, found her friend at a table by the window, and apologized for being late.

"Forget about it. It's my day off." Drea smiled broadly. "I could sit here all day."

The café bordered a park. Dappled light played across the cheerfully painted wooden tables. Geneva wondered if she or Drea had ever whiled away an entire day in a café.

"But you won't. Knowing you, you've got a list of errands as long as your arm."

"Longer. But a girl can dream."

They started on their lunches. Drea filled her in on shelter news, and said she had placed the retriever Geneva had evaluated with a childless couple with a large backyard.

"I love happy endings," Geneva said.

"Hey, what happened with your sister-in-law's Dobie?"

Geneva put down her fork. "Not a happy ending. Juliana asked me not to file a report. What was I supposed to do? Plus, the doctor filed one."

"She shouldn't have put you on the spot."

"Oh, she did better than that. It was my fault because I opened the garage door."

"Yeah, that was irresponsible of you."

"Wasn't it? And if she and Jon break up, I may lose my honorary status as a Novak."

"I'm guessing the dog had to be put down."

"Sadly, yes."

"Where's Tom in all of this?"

"Officially neutral. But he witnessed the whole thing, and was bitten, too, so as much as he would have liked to sweep the snarling Doberman under the rug, he couldn't. But I was hoping for more than neutrality."

"Poor you."

Geneva nodded, grateful for her friend's acknowledgment. What a relief not to have to explain she was trying to behave with integrity. She'd been doing a lot of explaining lately. Her chest tightened with emotion.

"You okay?"

"Yes. There's just a lot going on." She told her about Ella drinking the vodka-laced iced tea, and about her ambivalence around allowing her mother to continue to stay with her.

Drea listened, then said, "Neither of your options sound very good. You'd feel guilty if you dumped her. But it's not as if your mother meant harm, and you've put her on notice. How much longer does she need?"

"I don't know. Three weeks, maybe longer. She wasn't strong to begin with, which doesn't help."

"She's already been here three weeks, hasn't she?"

"Four."

"So you're probably more than halfway."

"You're right." Geneva picked at her salad, then stared out the window.

Drea put her hand on Geneva's arm. "What else is going on?"

Geneva turned to face her. "When Josh got suspended, did you and Bill really have no clue? Not the slightest hunch?"

"Yeah, we had a hunch, but doesn't every parent? I mean, you hear stories all the time about kids doing dumb things and their parents being completely in the dark. How can every parent not think it could happen to them?"

"But nothing specific."

"No. We thought he was squeaky clean. Thank God it was only a little weed."

"And he's okay now?"

Drea laughed. "According to the clueless parent, yes. He's earned back some privileges, so we'll see." She paused. "You got a hunch?"

Geneva nodded.

"Charlie?"

"Yes. Well, maybe both."

"Both?"

"I'm probably wrong, and it's probably because of my mother. I'm seeing conniving addicts everywhere."

"Maybe. And maybe you're a teensy bit stressed."

"You think?"

They both laughed.

"Then again," Drea said, "a hunch is more than we had."

.   .   .

On her way back to the clinic, Geneva stopped at Ella's favorite bakery and picked up an assortment of cookies and muffins. Ella deserved some recognition of what she'd been put through. Geneva planned to talk with her that evening about Helen's role in making her ill. Yesterday she had asked her mother to be part of the discussion—the first words she spoke to her after their argument—but Helen refused, just as she refused to admit anything of consequence had happened.

She was carrying the bakery box to the car when Dublin called.

"Hey! Guess what."

"What?"

"No, really. Guess."

"No hints?"

"Nope."

From his tone, this was more than a typical Dublin joke. He had news. But Geneva, buoyed from seeing her friend, played along. "Mom got drunk and crashed her car."

"You're almost as funny as I am. Guess again. Think improbable."

"You won the lottery and will pay for a nurse so Mom can go home."

"Nope. Something that hasn't happened in ten years."

Geneva got behind the wheel and glanced at the dashboard clock. "As much fun as this is, I've got to go to work."

"Okay, okay. You're such a good sport, you get a hint. Say it's June, which it is, and you want to go to Europe's most famous city, but instead it comes to you. Or, rather, me."

She was sliding the key into the ignition and froze. "Dub, you're kidding, right?"

"Nope. She's in town for some aid conference. Called me an hour ago and said she's got time midday tomorrow."

"How did she sound?"

"Remote. Awkward. You know, the same."

The same. A decade had passed and Paris hadn't changed. Neither had she changed during whatever interval had passed between visits before then. Five years? But in that moment, Geneva realized that while Paris may not have changed, she had. She was no longer content to be the baby sister who watched everything and understood nothing.

Her brother was still talking. "I'm taking the kids out of school. They've never met her. They think I've made her up."

"That's understandable. Sometimes I don't think she's real. And you do have a casual relationship with the truth."

"I prefer to think of it as a fertile imagination. But if I was making up a sister, I'd pick a more interesting name. Aunt Helsinki. Aunt Budapest. Aunt . . ."

"I'm coming to see her."

"You are?"

"Yes. Is she staying with you?"

"No way. A hotel and a couple of hours of family time, tops."

"I'll only be there for the day."

"Pity! You know how I love sleepovers."

"I'll email you the details."

"It'll be a party."

. . .

It was only a short drive from the bakery to the clinic, but in that time Geneva made two decisions. First, she was not going to tell Tom she was flying to L.A. tomorrow to see Paris. Although reluctant to keep secrets from him, she felt distanced recently. His fence-sitting concerning the behavior of both Juliana and Helen smacked of disloyalty to her. Not taking sides was his default stance, but she was nevertheless hurt. And the last thing she wanted was to defend her motives for the trip to him—or to anyone. She wasn't certain of her motives herself, but knew she had to go. She'd be there and back before anyone missed her.

The second decision was to ask Paris the hard questions and not let her off the hook. Geneva hadn't seen her sister in ten years. Who knew how long it would be until she saw her again? Ten years ago, Helen was still in South Carolina, and Geneva was buffered by distance from her mother's behavior. Most of the drunken phone calls went to Florence and Dublin, and all Geneva had been required to do was show up periodically at holidays and limit the damage. But now Helen was too close. And although her siblings seemed to accept Paris's decision to opt out, Geneva did not. She wasn't willing to give up a sister—even one she barely knew—without a reasonable explanation any more than she would accept that her mother's drinking was without cause. She had gone out on a limb to do the right thing by her mother and, in return, she hoped to get some straight answers.

. . .

Geneva thought her talk with her daughter went well. She'd kept it short, not wanting it to devolve into a lecture, and tried not to be overly critical of her mother. Ella didn't say much, but she seemed to be listening. The pastries were a hit.

After dinner, while Tom finished up some work in the barn, Geneva retrieved the old photo album and leafed through it while sitting on her bed. She compared features, expressions and postures at various ages, and tried to reconstruct how she and her siblings had related to one another. Florence told her Paris had always been different. Geneva had her memories of Paris as aloof and detached, but did not trust them. She knew that people often remembered what they wanted to believe, and she'd had little chance to gather new data over the last three decades. The photos were hard evidence, if she could study them dispassionately.

She understood genetic recombination, and knew siblings could get any mixture of traits from their parents. She could see, for instance, that she was a version of Florence, with a lighter build, wider eyes, and a more reflective, less competitive nature. She and Dublin were also versions of each other, but mirror reflections, opposites that nevertheless betrayed a common origin. Dublin and Florence also shared features, and their smiles were identical. As Geneva studied the photos more closely, the familiar backdrops of backyards, swimming pools, and holiday tables receded, leaving only disembodied figures. Paris was obviously the only blond, the only petite one, but other than that, she looked like one of four siblings. Her eyes, though blue, were the same shape as Geneva's, and the look of surprise captured in one grade-school photo was pure Dublin. Photos didn't lie. In group photographs, Paris stood, perhaps, a little farther away from her siblings. Then again, Geneva herself could also be singled out for directing her gaze at the others, rather than at the camera. A stranger shown this album and asked, "Who's different?" would not, she wagered, have necessarily selected Paris. Only the last several photos, particularly the one of Florence and Paris sitting on Paris's bed, would have drawn comment, due to the contrast in their poses, and Paris's solemn, almost regal, poise.

"What's so captivating?"

Startled, Geneva fumbled the album in her lap and raised her head. Her mother stood at the end of the bed.

"I didn't hear you come in."

Helen stared at the open album. "Walking down memory lane?"

"I suppose." Geneva thought of her trip the next day. "How many years has it been since you've seen Paris?"

Her mother didn't hesitate. "Just gone twenty-seven years."

"And you don't want to see her?"

"I never said that. It's her that wants nothing to do with me. Although by now I've laid it to rest."

She examined her mother's face to see if this could possibly be true. Her blue eyes gave nothing away. "Mom, what if you stopped drinking, if you tried a program? Do you think Paris would be more amenable to mending bridges then?"

Helen laughed. "It's you that would please, not Paris."

"But the reason Paris won't see you . . ."

"Isn't drinking."

"But if she thought you were making changes . . ."

"She wouldn't care." Helen sighed as if she hated air. "Honestly, I can't blame her."

The room darkened around the edges. Geneva's head felt light. She rested a hand on the bed to steady herself.

"Mom," she said, her voice a whisper. "What did you do?"

Helen looked straight through her. "Not enough and too much, all at the same time."

She swung the walker around a quarter turn, then another, and left.

CHAPTER TWENTY-THREE

ELLA

When Ella saw the pink box from Brioche, she knew her mom was prepping her for A Talk. She came through big-time. Turns out she's the only teenager in history to get drunk for the first time this way: accidentally, on the morning of the SAT, and at the hands of her grandmother. Her mom was all apologetic and told her it was okay to be angry with Nana, which she guessed she was. But it's not like everyone didn't know Nana was an alcoholic. Did they all think she'd just lie there and detox quietly? That obviously wasn't her style.

Her mom said Nana brought the vodka home from Grandpa Novak's party, but Ella knew damn well she didn't. She thought about telling her mom about what she almost knew for certain about the Prince—that he was Nana's connection—but decided against it. First, her evidence was all—what was that *Law & Order* word?—circumstantial. Her mom wasn't going to believe the Prince was up to no good without cold, hard facts. Second, from what she could see, one more piece of bad news and her mom was going to need to be fitted for a straitjacket. Nana should be spiking *her* drinks to chill her out a little. So because the mother-daughter heart-to-heart seemed to be making her happy, Ella left it alone. It was all ammo for another day, when the hammer would finally come down on the Prince. Or not. He'd gotten away with a lot so far.

While her mom talked, Ella stayed quiet. Because if you can't say anything nice, don't say anything at all, right? Even though Nana was the alcoholic and the one who messed up her SATs, it was her mom who invited her to their house in the first place. So, if her mom asked, which she didn't, Ella would say it was her mom who messed up. Just saying.

CHAPTER TWENTY-FOUR

HELEN

Helen knew something was wrong as soon as she picked up her handbag. It was too light. She'd gone to get one of the pills she'd stashed in there, after getting—temporarily, she hoped—cut off from her vodka supply. Saturday Ella had drunk her iced tea, and Sunday Helen finished off the emergency vodka she hid in the closet inside Charlie's rain boot. She did feel sorry about the girl getting sick and missing her test, although she considered it the unfortunate consequence of making an elderly woman who ought to be treated with respect sneak around like a low-life junkie. Here it was Monday and she was left with pills.

She hobbled over to her nightstand for some water to get the pill down with. Maybe once the medicine took hold she could think straight and remember where she'd put the confounded gun. She could see it now—triangular hard case, pale blue. For the life of her, she couldn't recall ever taking it out of her bag. But she must have done it, because it wasn't there.

She prided herself in being careful with the weapon. All her life, she'd been around guns. She knew what to do and what not to do, not that her daddy had been a paragon of safety. Helen bought the predecessor to the missing gun shortly after Geneva went to college and left her alone in that big house. But it wasn't the house that got to her; it was the nightmares. How she thought a gun could protect her from the inside of her own head, she didn't know, but the gun did provide a measure of comfort. In case the dreams turned real, she supposed. Before she moved to California, she'd treated herself to a new one, with a blue pearled handle and matching case. She cleaned it from time to time, but otherwise it stayed in her bedside drawer—until she was dragged up here. Good thing she managed to sneak it into her purse while Geneva was getting the suitcase from under the bed. And it stayed a good thing right up until it went missing.

A gun was a darn sight more dangerous than an iced tea and vodka, but what could Helen do? Say to Geneva, "Have you seen my gun anywhere? It's light blue and loaded"? Maybe in L.A. she'd have some sympathy, but not up here with the granola people. The way she saw it, a gun in your purse was no different from a pack of tissues. You don't often need one, but if you do, it comes in handy. Helen imagined Geneva and the rest of them would just as soon carry a rattlesnake around. No, it was a nuisance she'd misplaced the gun, but she'd have to figure out where it wandered off to herself. She'd probably taken it out when she'd had a drink or two, just to feel the cool of the metal in her hand. Then she'd hidden it somewhere better than her purse. The only question was where that might be.

. . .

That night she was feeling lower than a doodlebug, on account of the gun, the iced tea, and those lousy pills. The kids were in their rooms with their homework and their gadgets, and she could hear Tom sawing away in the barn. The dog wasn't talking either, so she went hunting for Geneva. Should've stayed where she was, as it turned out, because that girl started asking questions about Paris again. Helen could see how she'd wonder about a long-lost sister, but this was yesterday's news. Been thirty years, give or take. But Geneva was Geneva. Once she got an idea in her head, she was dug in like an Appalachian tick.

Not that Helen spilled any beans. Thirty years of stonewalling and deflecting had given her plenty of practice. The only unfortunate happenstance was that once she was in her room again, all she could think about was Eustace and Paris.

Paris turned sixteen in October of 1981. Eustace wanted to throw her a big party at the club, but she wasn't keen on it. Truth was, the girl didn't have any friends her age, only admirers, meaning they'd just as soon stab her in the back as say how do you do. She wasn't the socializing type, and at a party in her honor she would've been obliged to shine her light on everyone. Instead, Helen arranged a special supper at home, with her best linens and silver, and the wedding china. Louisa made Paris's favorites, ribs and banana cream pie, and even though Helen didn't think ribs belonged on her wedding china, she held her tongue.

Everyone was in a fine mood that evening, once Dublin got over having his hair slicked down. Paris managed to be gracious about her gifts, right down to the hummingbird's nest Geneva gave her. Using two fingers, Paris lifted it out of the box by the stick it was attached to. Helen thought it was some tiny dead thing and gasped. Paris was dumbstruck until Geneva, usually quiet as a church mouse, explained in elaborate detail where she'd found it, and how carefully the birds had constructed it—covering the outside with lichen for camouflage—and how many eggs fit into it and so on. She believed, God love her, she'd chosen her gift wisely and no one, not even Paris, had the heart to set her straight.

The last gift was from her father, a small blue box wrapped in white ribbon that Helen and the rest of the civilized world recognized as Tiffany.

"For my princess," Eustace said, bowing as he handed Paris the box.

She pulled on the bow slowly, like she was teasing a kitten, then opened the lid and held up a gold necklace with an open heart pendant.

"Oh, Daddy!"

"May I?" He took the necklace from her and placed it around her neck from behind.

When Paris lifted her hair off her neck so he could do up the clasp, Helen turned away.

After Florence and Geneva helped Helen tidy up from dinner, the girls went to find their brother for a board game, and she went to lock the back door. Halfway down the hall she heard laughter emanating from Paris's room. The door was closed, but she went right in.

Paris sat up against the pillows, the covers over her legs. Her nightgown was open at the neck, the heart necklace on display. Eustace sat on the bed facing her. Paris let go another giggle, then covered her mouth with her hand. Her cheeks were red, and her breath came quick.

Eustace turned his head like an eagle. He smiled, but his eyes were black ice. "What is it, Helen?"

"I heard laughing. Why on earth was the door closed?"

"Wind must have blown it."

Paris broke out in a fit of giggles. Eustace laughed, too.

"Daddy was tickling me."

He made a grab for her waist and she shrieked and fell sideways.

Helen could see she had nothing but a camisole under her nightgown. "Paris is too old for tickling, Eustace."

"Oh, no, she isn't." He lunged at her again and wriggled his fingers into her armpit.

"Eustace!"

He leaned over his daughter, one hand on either side of her, his face inches from her lips, full and parted, releasing small gasps. Then he sat up and ran both hands over his hair. Paris righted herself and caught her breath. She gave her mother an appraising look.

"There's only one of us that's too old for tickling, Mama."

Eustace smiled, his gaze locked on his daughter.

Helen felt blood rush to her face. She turned on her heels, leaving the door open and forgetting entirely to lock the back door.

•　•　•

Over the next few days, she endeavored to sort out her feelings about what she had witnessed. They never did settle out. She was angry, that was certain, at Eustace in particular, but Paris, too, for making her feel like yesterday's news—or last year's. She was hurt, because she couldn't think of anything she'd done to either Eustace or Paris to deserve it, except maybe being as vain and self-centered as the both of them. And she was scared. Boy, was she scared. Because sure as eggs is eggs Paris had not the foggiest idea what she was getting herself into. And worse—much worse— Eustace most certainly did.

Naturally, it was her duty to warn her daughter, to educate her on the desires of men. She'd had a talk with Paris two years before, when she'd started her monthlies, and had laid out—pretty clearly, she thought—what the whole mess was about. Paris had sat with her hands in her lap, like she was in church, and let her mother talk her way through it.

"That all, Mama?"

"I believe it is. In a nutshell."

"Can I go now?"

"Sure you can. Unless you want to ask me a question."

"Not really. I learned all that in school, and from general talk."

Helen's eyes widened. "General talk?"

"It's 1979, Mama."

"Yes, but . . ." She stopped, suddenly embarrassed. "Well, why'd you let me go on about it then?"

A sly smile played on her daughter's lips. "I wanted to hear you tell it."

Young girls were mouthy back then, same as now, but she wasn't fooled. Naive as she had been, even sixteen-year-old Helen had knowledge of the facts of life, and had nevertheless been swept off her feet by a man's charms. She didn't know exactly what Eustace was up to, or how far he meant to go, but she did know that, whatever it was, Paris wasn't prepared for it.

So a few weeks after Paris's birthday, Helen sat her down for another talk. Not about her father in particular, but about men generally, and made sure to impress upon the girl that men were more alike than not when it came to their base natures. It was a woman's responsibility to stop advances before things got out of hand because, after a certain point, a man had to wrestle with the devil to stay in control. The devil almost always won, so a smart girl didn't allow herself to be led down the garden path. Paris put on her church face, and when Helen asked if she understood, she said she did, and got up and left.

Helen had been careful with her words, but Paris must've reported back to her father. He came into bed that night, his skin burning through his pajamas with rage, and forced himself on her like he aimed to kill her with it. When she cried afterward, he slapped her cheek and told her to shut up.

"And if you ever insinuate again that my daughter is a whore, you can expect far worse."

. . .

Helen began to keep a closer eye on Paris and, without getting caught at it, tried to interfere with the time she spent with her father. But as Eustace did and went as he pleased, and Paris wanted to be with him, her efforts amounted mostly to worry with no reward. She stood at the window, waiting for Paris to come up the walk, smiling and unharmed, while her other children went short of attention. That's the way it had to be. If Dublin broke his arm falling out of a tree, it could be fixed. You couldn't put a splint on what might happen to Paris. As far as Helen could tell, there had been no more tickling sessions. She agonized day and night what might be going on elsewhere, but in their house, she hoped her watchful eye was keeping Eustace's mischief at bay.

Louisa still worked for the family, though she was getting on in years and didn't come but once a week. Helen had a young girl come in to do the heavy cleaning, so all that was left for Louisa was a bit of dusting, linen-changing, and cooking. Helen couldn't do without Louisa's cooking. Everything she made tasted better than what Helen could produce, even using Louisa's recipes. Louisa teased her and said it was because Helen always added lazy to everything, and it soured the taste. That made them both laugh.

Louisa came three days in a row in the second week of December to get ready for the Christmas party Eustace had decided to throw. He had invited all the local mucky-mucks, his buddies from the club, and his entire family. It was enough to make Helen a nervous wreck. But Louisa took it all in hand and together they checked off each item on a list running four pages. Luckily, Eustace wasn't bothered about the expense, so Helen hired folks to string the lights, decorate the house, set up the tables and chairs, and run the bar. She and Louisa did most of the cooking, and at the end of the three days the refrigerator would not have accommodated another meatball.

The evening before the party, Helen came downstairs to find Louisa rushing for the door, her coat and bag in hand. When she saw Louisa's face, she put her hand on the woman's arm.

"What ever is the matter?"

"I've got to leave."

"What for? We've still got things to do."

Louisa looked at her feet. "Mr. Riley has let me go."

"Let you go! That can't be right."

Louisa put her hand on the doorknob. "I need to be going, Helen."

She stood in front of her. "What's the hurry? Come in the kitchen a minute and talk to me. I'll sort it out with Eustace. You know I will."

"There's nothing to sort out. Not after . . ." Louisa's voice trailed off. She glanced across the room, toward the hall leading to the back door.

"What? You've got to tell me."

Louisa's face was a hodgepodge of fear and sympathy. "I can't tell you anything."

"Paris?" It was more of a plea than a question.

Louisa's eyes brimmed with tears. Her jaw was set, like she was acting against her nature but about to do it all the same. Whatever Eustace said to her had made an impression, because Louisa opened the door and ran down the steps, not bothering to put on her coat against the cold. Helen called after her, yelling her name and not caring who heard, but Louisa put her head down and hurried around the corner as if someone was chasing her.

*   *   *

Neither Eustace nor Paris seemed any different from usual at supper that night. Paris talked about her new dress for the party and offered to help Florence with her hair. Dublin lobbied his father for special dispensation to stay up late the next night on account of the party. Everything was so normal, in fact, that Helen felt disoriented. So she pleaded exhaustion, asked Florence and Paris to take care of the supper dishes, and excused herself. She went upstairs to her bedroom and sat by the window, considering what to say to Eustace. Of course she wished she knew the particulars of what Louisa had seen. Was it a kiss? Or something more? A wave of nausea reached up her throat at the thought. She fought it off—she shouldn't let her imagination run off with her sense— and resolved to call Louisa the next day. After a night's reflection, she might be more amenable to talk. And Helen wanted to talk to her because Louisa was the nearest thing to a friend she had.

When Eustace came upstairs, she told him flat-out he had no right to fire Louisa.

"No right? I am her employer."

"But she's been with us for so long!"

"Too long. You don't pay any attention, but she's been snooping around where she doesn't belong."

"Snooping? Snooping where?"

In two steps he crossed the room and loomed over her. "Who are you to question me? You'd be wise to check the silver and your jewelry."

She opened her mouth to protest, but closed it right quick. Eustace didn't need a reason to fire Louisa. He could pull one out of thin air. No one would ever take the word of a black housekeeper over that of the mayor. It might have been 1981 other places, but in Aliceville it was pretty near 1951.

Helen took a deep breath. "Eustace, if you believe Louisa saw something and got the wrong impression . . ."

He set his jaw. "Wrong impression? Of what, exactly?"

"Well, I only thought she might be mistaken."

"About what, Helen?"

She turned from him and stared out the window. Three illuminated reindeer with red bows around their necks stood in the front yard.

"Never mind."

*   *   *

The next day she called Louisa but she didn't answer. She tried again the next day, and the next. Just before Christmas, she drove across town to Louisa's house and knocked on the door. A dog barked inside. Helen stood shivering on the porch for a long time. Finally, she put the poinsettia and the wrapped present on the doormat and drove home.

She saw Louisa at a distance from time to time, and ran into her once at the grocery store. Louisa said, "I'm sorry," spun around, and wheeled her cart down the aisle.

CHAPTER TWENTY-FIVE

GENEVA

Geneva's cab drove past the La Brea Tar Pits and deposited her in front of the Page Museum. At the edge of the main pit, a pair of fiberglass mastodons faced a fiberglass mammoth sinking into the bubbling tar. The mammoth's trunk was curled up against its forehead, and its mouth lay open in mid-scream. Geneva paid the driver and entered the museum.

She had met Dublin here before. It was his son Jack's favorite place. Jack could be entertained for an hour or two by the fishbowl—a glass-walled paleontology lab where he could watch scientists clean and prepare Ice Age fossils. He was less interested in the reconstructed skeletons on display than in the process of unearthing bones and teeth from the hardened asphalt. The tedium of the work fascinated him. Jack also loved the display of thousands of dire wolf skulls along one wall of the museum. This was Geneva's favorite exhibit, as well, and where they had arranged to meet.

Dublin stood in front of the skulls, shoulder to shoulder with his older son, Whit. Jack crouched next to Whit, his face almost touching the glass. The amber backlighting from the display shone on all three faces. Geneva admired them for a moment and savored the realization that these were members of her family with whom she felt no conflict.

She touched Dublin on the shoulder. "Studying the dire situation?"

He grinned and gave her a hug. She waved hello to her nephews, knowing one was at the awkward age for hugs and the other had always been.

"This one," Jack said, pointing at the skull in front of him, "has smaller canines than average."

Geneva bent down next to him. "Show me."

Dublin said, "You've probably noticed Paris isn't here yet."

"She doesn't exist," Whit said.

"There's no proof," Jack added.

"You're right about the tooth, Jack." She stood up. "Haven't you boys seen pictures of Paris?"

"Dad totally Photoshopped those," Whit said.

"Using whose face?"

He thought about this. "Nana's. When she was young."

"That would probably work." She turned to her brother. "Is there money riding on this?"

"You have to ask? If she doesn't show, I'm out big bucks."

Over his shoulder, Geneva watched a woman cross the room

toward them. The woman caught her eye and lifted a hand, then dropped it, as if she had had a question, then decided not to ask.

"You boys better get ready to pay up," Geneva said.

Paris, now forty-six, still resembled Helen but could never have been mistaken for her. Her hair was no longer blond, but light brown and graying, and cut bluntly at chin length. She wore a navy T-shirt, a couple of sizes too large, tan cargo pants, and running shoes stained with red African clay. Her hands were stuffed into her pockets, with her elbows turned in, a posture both defiant and awkward. Last night Geneva had examined photos of her sister's youthful face. The face before her was lined and dull, the lips no longer full, the cheeks without a trace of pink. The transformation was unsettling. Nevertheless, Helen's blue eyes stared out at her.

"Hello, everyone," Paris said.

Dublin stepped forward and put his arms around her. She patted his shoulder. Geneva placed her hand on her sister's arm and quickly kissed her cheek. She smelled of hotel soap. As she stepped back, Geneva noticed Paris's only jewelry—the Tiffany heart necklace their father had given her for her sixteenth birthday. Had she always worn it?

Dublin made a sweeping gesture with his arm. "Whit, Jack, may I present to you, Ms. Paris Riley!"

Whit stood with his mouth open. Dublin kicked him lightly in the shin. Whit stuck out his hand and said, "Nice to meet you."

Jack glanced at Paris, then resumed studying the wolves.

She frowned.

"Jack," Dublin said, "let's check out the fishbowl. You can watch the scientists."

"I'm not very good with kids," Paris said. "Especially not American ones."

They found a place to sit while the boys went to see the lab. Geneva asked Paris about the conference she was attending. She explained her involvement with a variety of foundations that provided funding for basic sanitation systems in remote portions of East Africa. She acted both as a liaison between the foundations and local groups, and as a watchdog to ensure the money ended up in the right place.

"Sounds dangerous," Dublin said.

"I suppose. But there's no point in fighting for clean water and basic hygiene and then watching the money siphoned off for useless luxuries for the tribal chief."

"Can't argue with that," Geneva said.

She had long admired her sister's dedication to difficult goals, and felt guilty she had never been motivated to improve basic human conditions in the same way. Instead, she provided medical services and behavioral therapy to pampered pets. The work at the shelter was her only contribution to the community, unless one counted the enlightened self-interest of helping in the schools. Listening to her sister talk, she realized even the shelter animals lived under better conditions than the people Paris assisted.

Yet, as Paris answered their questions about her work, her tone became increasingly strident and preachy. She had her cause—a righteous one—and that was all that mattered to her. Geneva saw for the first time how black-and-white the world appeared to her sister, how she stubbornly, albeit valiantly, pursued her work goals. And, as far as Geneva could tell, there was nothing else in her life other than work. No husband, no boyfriend, no relationships beyond those necessitated by her position. She hadn't traveled except as her job required, and she had no hobbies. She was beyond single-minded. She was obsessive.

Why hadn't Geneva noticed this before? The last time they had seen each other was in New York. Dublin hadn't been able to come because Whit had been born a few days before. Geneva wasn't going to travel across the country for a three-hour visit, but Tom found a cheap flight and insisted she go. The three sisters had coffee, then walked through Central Park as snow fell lightly around them. Once the small talk expired, Florence asked Paris whether she planned to return for her wedding, in eight months' time.

"Not if our mother will be there."

An argument had ensued, in which Florence told Paris to "get over herself." Paris retorted that Florence's preoccupation with sports and her body revealed she had never left behind the adolescent persona of high school jock. She was buying in to the same Cinderella complex their mother had perfected, only glorifying muscle instead of breast tissue. A different sort of vanity, but vanity nevertheless. Geneva didn't say a word. At the time, she thought each sister had a point. Moreover, they had squabbled constantly growing up, so why would they relent now? The episode saddened her though, as she had hoped they could have moved on from their childhoods. She was sorry she'd come.

Sitting on a bench in the Page museum, Geneva saw her eldest sister in a new light. Until now, Paris had always been the girl their father adored, who had for some mysterious reason broken off from the rest of the family to help the people of Africa. That girl had been beautiful and captivating and selfless. Now, as Geneva listened to her lecture Dublin on how Hollywood—his industry—corrupted the wealthy by entertaining them instead of opening their hearts to the plight of the downtrodden, she thought her sister was simply strange.

. . .

Dublin's boys complained of hunger, so while he shepherded them to the cafeteria, Geneva and Paris went outside to the Pleistocene Garden. As they walked the crushed gravel paths, the midday sun pulled the musky scent of sage into the air. The crowded plantings of sedges, buckwheat, and wormwood spilled over the borders and grew in between small pools of tar, nearly hiding them. Whether in modern L.A. or in the Pleistocene, Geneva thought, you had to be careful where you stepped.

"Did Dublin mention that Mom has been staying with me?"

"No. He knows better than to bring her up." Paris slowed her step. "I thought you didn't get along with her. Or has that changed?"

"Not really. She had a car accident and needed a place to mend. I only mention it because having her around has made me think about our childhood."

"Geneva, don't spoil this."

She stopped in the shade of a sycamore and firmed her resolve. "Mom may be unstable and unreasonable, but I'm not. You've chosen not to interact with her. But you called Dublin and let him know you were in town, and you knew he'd call me. So if you're not willing to write all of us off, you're going to have to give a little."

Her sister's expression was wary. "Give a little what?"

"Of yourself. Help me understand."

"What exactly?"

"Us. Our family. Look, I was eleven when Dad died. You were

already gone. But things between you and Mom had been tense for a while before you left, right?"

She let out a little snort. "You could say that."

"Ella is sixteen. Believe me when I say I have firsthand experience of what that developmental period is like."

"Developmental period? You think I had some version of your suburban teenager's rebellion?"

Geneva brushed off the slight with a shrug. "How should I know? That's my point. My daughter's anger feels very real to her—and justified. I'm certain of it." As soon as she said this, she realized she'd never acknowledged this to Ella, and winced inwardly at her own insensitivity. How could she have ignored this essential fact?

Paris stared at her, as if waiting for her to talk about something more compelling than her daughter's feelings.

Geneva was determined to make good on her promise not to let her sister off the hook. "Your anger at Mom seems real to me, too, Paris. I don't know you at all well, but you're my sister. I won't give up on what I don't understand. I'm not designed like that."

"And I assume Mom won't tell you anything."

"No."

"What does that say? Because the only reason I'm not telling you is because you and Dublin and Florence seem to have some connection with her."

"So it's her secret, not yours?"

She laughed bitterly. "Funny enough, it's the only thing we share."

Frustration grew inside Geneva. Why did Paris have to speak in riddles? She could tell Paris had reached her limit and was about to clam up. Geneva was sorting through the jumble of questions in her mind when her sister spoke.

"When I left for UNC, I didn't think Daddy would come apart the way he did."

"Didn't you?" She had no idea where Paris was headed.

"Florence was impossible, of course. Always had been. And I suppose, if I'd thought it through, I'd have realized you were far too young." She fingered the heart pendant at her throat and gazed dreamily into the middle distance. "You loved Daddy, didn't you?"

"Yes, of course I loved him."

Her sister gave her an appraising look and smiled. In that moment, the years fell away and Paris became again the girl at sixteen—regal, contained, self-assured. "Not like I did."

CHAPTER TWENTY-SIX

HELEN

Tuesday morning, coming home from physical therapy, Tom informed Helen he had to visit the rain forest man to show him the handrail he'd finished and to take more measurements. When he said he'd be gone a few hours, she saw her chance. The kids were in school and Geneva was at work, so she'd finally be on her own. Time to go hunting.

She was getting around better. She still had to be careful not to put too much weight on her bad leg, but the pain would remind her when she'd done too much. The physical therapist told her at every visit it was important not to favor it more than she had to, as that would make trouble on the other side, and the bad knee would never get better unless it got stronger. But for today she'd hobble around however she could and worry about the consequences another time. Come hell or high water, she was going to find the stash of booze.

Here it was Tuesday and she hadn't had a drink since Friday. Friday! Might have been her imagination, but it appeared Charlie was avoiding her. Probably afraid of getting caught now that his parents had the measure of her motivation. She'd covered for him by making up the story about sneaking vodka from the party, but he wasn't showing his appreciation. Or maybe he was busy with that band of his, with the contest coming up tomorrow. Whatever the reason, she was left to fend for herself.

She waited a half an hour after Tom left, in case he forgot something and came back, and used the time to formulate a hunting plan. Ella's bedroom and the den, where Charlie was sleeping, were out, and so was the kitchen since she'd already searched it, except the cabinets at the tippy top. Her daughter would've counted on her exploring the easy places anyway. Helen started with Geneva and Tom's bedroom. When she opened the door, Diesel got up from his mat to see what she was up to.

She patted the top of his head. "Don't you tell on me, boy."

She found her way to the closet. She might've felt sorry for invading their privacy, except this counted as an emergency. Geneva's neatness worked against her in this instance, as it was easy for Helen to see where a few bottles might hide among the tidy piles of sweaters and row of storage boxes. She didn't have to open anything, just pushed the boxes and bins to see if they were heavier than they ought to be. Sadly, they weren't. She made sure everything was good and straight before she left.

Diesel followed her around to the last few places she'd thought of in the house. That left the garage and the barn. She figured the barn was more likely, as it was farther away. And Tom probably did the carrying, and that's where he'd put it. He had a habit of locking the barn whenever he left, but she'd seen Ella take a key from the kitchen drawer when she wanted to sit in her chair out there. Helen found the key and headed outside. Diesel wanted to come, too, but she wasn't going to have him running off, so she made him sit on his mat.

Tom's workshop wasn't as neat as the house, but it wasn't a mess either. There were three tall cabinets on one wall and another set under a long counter on the other side. She stumped her walker toward the low cabinets but, in her enthusiasm, missed seeing a metal knob sticking out from a piece of equipment. It caught her hip and she cried out. She wiggled her hip around a little to see if it still worked. It did. There'd be a big old bruise, but she figured she'd live, so she kept on with her search.

Good thing, too, because in the second cabinet, under an old blanket, she struck gold. Tempted as she was to take a swig then and there, she didn't want to be falling down in the driveway and held off. After inspecting a few bottles, she selected the vodka and the gin, each more than half full, and blessed her daughter for buying top-shelf brands. She put the bottles into the grocery bag she'd brought, locked up the barn, and returned to the house to scare up some mixers.

Helen had a drink in the kitchen, because no one was there to see, other than Diesel. She didn't like drinking alone, never had, but it beat not drinking by a mile. She missed her friends in L.A.— the bridge ladies, the neighbors she sat with at the pool, even the doddery old coots at the senior center. They weren't bosom buddies, but they were better to drink with than a dog. Worse, Diesel kept reminding her of Argus, Paris's shepherd, and that naturally led to thinking about Eustace and Paris. Once she started down that road, it was hard to stop, so she poured another inch of vodka.

*   *   *

She didn't have a clear idea of what Eustace was up to with Paris, but if he fired Louisa for seeing it, it was more than nothing. But Louisa wasn't inclined to talk, and without ever having seen anything herself, Helen had no cause to go running to the police. What would she tell them? Her husband tickled her daughter? Even if she had seen an untoward act with her own eyes, she doubted anyone would believe her. Her husband was the mayor and from an influential family, and she was, and always would be, the girl from the other side of the tracks who had been lucky to snag him. If only Paris had the sense God gave her, but Helen could see Eustace had the girl under a spell. Her daughter might've listened to her if they'd ever been close, but they hadn't, and it was too late for that now.

Still, Paris was her flesh and blood, and Helen wasn't the type to give up easy. The idea of getting the girl a dog came to her after she had read about a German shepherd in a book. A killer was on the loose in a small town, and the dog figured out who it was before anyone else. The shepherd protected its owner, a young woman living on her own, from ending up dead same as the rest of them. That was only a story, but she figured a guard dog might teach Eustace to keep his hands to himself. Because even a dog can sniff out when things are dead wrong.

Helen had never so much as twitched her nose without consulting her husband, so when she came through the door on Christmas Eve with Argus, she was as nervous as a cat in a room full of rocking chairs. But what could he do? Paris took to the dog right away and, for the first time in ages, smiled at her mother sincerely. Eustace was steamed, that was plain, and quit the room directly. Geneva was nearly as bothered as her father, seeing as she'd been asking for a dog since she could talk, but Helen had her priorities. Wouldn't be long before Paris was off to college, and if Geneva wanted Argus to be hers then, Helen wouldn't mind a bit.

The dog slept on the floor beside Paris, just as Helen had planned. By the time Christmas break was over, he was following her around the house, sitting behind her seat at the table and lying by the door with his head on his paws when she was out. Helen relaxed a little.

She should've known better. Eustace didn't roll over easy. A few days before Easter, she came down the walk with her arms full of groceries and nearly got run over by Argus, pulling Geneva to the curb.

"Sorry, Mama," she called over her shoulder.

"Where in heaven's name are you going with that dog?"

"Argus!" The dog let up. "Daddy asked me to walk him."

"Why doesn't Paris do it?"

"He said she's busy. I don't mind." And off she went.

Helen didn't know whether she wanted to go in the house at all. But the ice cream was melting, so she did, making more noise than she needed to. She put the ice cream away, then called down the hall for Paris to help her with the rest. Took her a couple minutes, but she came.

Not long after, the dog didn't finish his supper three evenings running. She couldn't see anything wrong with him, and went so far as to investigate his stools after Paris took him out to do his business.

"What are you doing, Mama?"

"Argus hasn't been finishing his kibble." She pointed to the lump on the grass. "And doesn't this look darker than his usual?"

Paris made a face. "I'm not looking at that. And I don't need to. It's probably because Daddy's giving him steak."

"Steak?"

"Yup. He wants to be better friends with Argus. Isn't that sweet?"

Helen shook her head, then went to get a shovel from the shed to clear up the mess.

Paris called after her, "There's nothing Daddy can do that's all right with you, is there? You're so pathetic, you get jealous of a dog!"

. . .

That summer the heat broke records. Nearly every day, Helen left Argus in the shady backyard with plenty of water and drove the children to the club pool. She secretly hoped one of the young men might strike Paris's fancy. The girl was a flower full of nectar with boys buzzing around her. She ignored the furtive glances of the shy ones, which was most of them. A handful of the braver ones squatted in the grass by her lounge chair, trying to fire up a conversation, but she only yawned and peered lazily over their shoulders, as if expecting someone more interesting, so they drifted off.

Eustace joined the family occasionally. He'd pull a chair up next to Paris's and chat with her and read the newspaper. Not a soul approached her then, and he stared down those foolish enough to look twice.

One day, Florence stood in the shallow end and threw coins in the deeper water for Dublin and Geneva to fish off the bottom. Eustace put down his newspaper and watched her throwing and running through the water.

"Florence is getting to look like a prizefighter."

Helen shielded her eyes from the sun and appraised her daughter. At fifteen, she was five-foot-eight, long-legged, and still growing. She wore a bikini, same as all the girls, and her brown hair was pulled into a low ponytail. The muscles in her arms and legs stood out some, but the way the girl exercised, she wasn't surprised. And maybe her hipbones and ribs poked out more than Paris's did, but nothing was wrong with her appetite. Florence had played varsity basketball all winter and varsity soccer in the spring. She loved running, even in the heat. Helen thought she looked just fine and said so.

"Fine? Helen, too many muscles on a girl isn't fine. And she's flat as a pancake on top. She needs to eat more and run less. Otherwise, no man but a blind one will have her."

She looked from her daughter to her husband and back again. Prizefighter, he reckoned? Not yet, but she'd see what she could do. She didn't figure on Florence being Eustace's type, but she wasn't taking any chances.

CHAPTER TWENTY-SEVEN

ELLA

Question: What's gray and brown and lies on the floor?
Answer: Ella, because she feels like a shit.

When she found out Nana put the vodka in the iced tea, Ella pretty much blamed her mom. But a few days floated by, and she did a little thinking about the situation, taking a look at it from more than just her point of view. Radical, huh? Like the word-storm, where things could line up in unexpected ways, where a word took on a surprising meaning just because it drifted past at the right time. Yup, it happened.

Ella grew a conscience.

Let's face it. She knew there was shady business between Charlie and Nana because he had an iPhone and new video games and, oh yeah, a big spanky amplifier. And she saw him at the liquor store, buying porno mags, but only a moron wouldn't think he used that connection to get booze for Nana later. So she could totally have stopped all of this from raining down on her head if she'd done the right thing and told her parents about it. But she didn't, because she had broken a few rules herself—including sneaking out to that party where kids were so wasted it wasn't funny. (And she still wasn't feeling so great about driving into the city and denting the truck. Guilt didn't seem to wither with time the way she'd hoped. Was that the purpose of fessing up? If only her family were Catholic!)

But the main reason her conscience was ballooning inside her and threatening to choke out her last gasp of I-don't-give-a-rat's-ass was because she hadn't taken care of her brother. He sold porno, bought booze, cheated in school, smoked weed, and probably charged a lot more to Nana's credit card than she ever knew, and what had Ella done about it? What? Nothing? No, worse? Used it to cover her own tracks? Yeah.

Then the icing on the cake. At lunch yesterday, her friend Megan tells her she saw Charlie in the park near the community center with two older guys she didn't know. Megan was playing hide-and-seek with the kids she was babysitting, and neither Charlie nor the other guys knew she was under the picnic table when they walked by. She heard Charlie working his magic to get a better price on some skittles. Ella didn't know what that was.

Megan said, "Me neither. I googled it. It's Ecstasy."

Ella asked her three times if she was sure she heard it right. Megan said she was, and looked really sad and scared. Ella's skin went all prickly and she couldn't finish her sandwich.

The Prince was her brother. He'd been there, in her life, for as long as she could remember. He made her laugh more than anyone else, except maybe Diesel, and he wasn't that bad a kid. At least not until recently. High school wasn't designed to bring out the best in people, that was for sure, and because she wasn't looking out for him, he was on a slide.

So she made a resolution, because that's what people with consciences do. She resolved to tell her parents everything she knew or suspected about Charlie. She hadn't quite decided whether she would come clean about her own little slipups. There was no point in planning these things out too carefully. She'd play that one by ear.

And because Charlie was her brother, she was going to cut him one last break. Tomorrow was the Battle of the Bands, so she'd wait until that was over to spill the beans. Her mom wasn't home anyway, even though it was ten o'clock, and she really wanted to tell her parents at the same time. That way if one of them went ballistic—say, her mom—she could duck behind the other one.

So tomorrow Charlie would get to use his amp and be a rock star and stand next to Rosa the Hottie before his world came crashing down. For his own good. For real.

❧

CHAPTER TWENTY-EIGHT

GENEVA

Geneva read the monitor a second time, hoping her flight's status had miraculously changed from "delayed" back to "on time." It hadn't. She walked briskly to the gate counter and asked the attendant if there was an alternate flight that might get her to San Francisco around the time of the scheduled arrival.

"Not a chance. It's fogged in up there. Welcome to summer."

The new arrival time would put her in the thick of commuter traffic, but there was nothing she could do. She found a seat, pulled her phone out of her bag and was surprised to see two missed calls from Tom. She'd silenced her phone at the museum and hadn't expected his calls since she was supposedly at work. As she debated whether to call him, the phone warbled. Dublin.

"Hi. Were your boys impressed with Paris?"

"Distinctly underwhelmed. Whit said it was better when she was a myth."

"I don't remember her being so . . ."

"Imperious? Self-important? Obnoxious?"

She laughed. "Yes. And she had some pretty strange answers to my questions about Mom and her. I felt like Bilbo Baggins talking to Gollum."

"Do tell."

"Hmm. I'm going to think about it first, okay?"

"You're the boss. Listen, I called about something else. Does Mom have a new iPhone?"

"I don't think so. Why?"

"I picked up her mail on the way home and there was a credit card statement showing that, plus some other weird charges."

"Like what?"

"A few Amazon purchases for forty or fifty bucks. Doesn't say what for. And an eight-hundred-dollar one to an electronics warehouse."

"Electronics? Do you think we should contact the fraud department?"

"Yup. But can you talk to her first?"

"Sure."

"Could be she's building a bomb or preparing to hack into the State Department."

Geneva's gaze fell on the sports bar across the concourse. "Any liquor store purchases?"

"Nope. That was the first thing I checked."

"Okay, I'll ask her. And Dub?"

"Yeah?"

"Thanks for being normal."

He laughed. "If I'm the normal one, you are so screwed."

*   *   *

She couldn't remember why she'd been reluctant to tell Tom about wanting to see Paris. After all, he'd been the one who'd encouraged her to fly to New York last time. How much explaining would it have taken? My sister's in L.A., so I'm taking off work and going to see her, just for the day. It dawned on her that perhaps she was engaging in her own teenage rebellion by making a move without consulting a soul, just because she could.

Tom picked up right away. "You okay?"

"Yes, I'm fine. I'm in L.A. waiting for a plane home."

"What? What's going on?"

"Paris is here and I needed to talk to her."

"Wow. Okay."

"And I don't know why I didn't tell you."

He was quiet a long moment. "Things have been pretty tense, but we've got to stay on the same page."

"You're right." But she wasn't sure they were in the same chapter. "Anyway, did you call about anything in particular?"

"Maybe we should discuss it when you get home."

That didn't sound like news to look forward to. "I'm going to be a while. SFO's fogged in."

"All right. Ivan called to tell me his boys have been smoking dope. They were high right after the band was rehearsing at Rango's house, so he was giving me a heads-up."

What had Drea said? *Trust your hunches.* "Did you talk to Charlie yet?"

"No. I wanted to talk to you first." His tone was slightly admonishing. She hadn't been available. "And he's not home until late tonight. He has practice. Then there's a study session for his history final."

"I had a hunch about this." Immediately she regretted admitting it.

"You did? Jesus, Geneva, do you think you might have told me?"

"It was pretty nonspecific. Haven't you felt as if something's up with him?"

"No. And maybe nothing is. Let's keep a level head."

And put on some rosy glasses and skip through the daisies. He might be right, but she didn't think so. Her antennae had been twitching for a while. "Have you ever known me not to have a level head?"

"I don't know. Lately you've been sensing disaster around every corner. It's pretty wearing."

His voice was strained, as if she were a bloodhound pulling him down every rabbit trail. And, in truth, that was close to how she felt. But she couldn't ignore her intuition about her son any more than those concerning her mother and Paris. If only she understood.

There was nothing to be done about Charlie at the moment. If it wasn't too late when she got home, they'd talk to him then. And she'd ask her mom about the credit card charges. Her mind circled back to her conversation with Dublin. An iPhone and expensive electronics. Add a skateboard and you'd have a teenage boy's wish list. Another hunch, or a logical deduction? In either case, too much to speculate about on the phone.

"You're right, Tom. We haven't got all the facts. I'll let you know my arrival time when I get it."

"Okay. And don't worry about Charlie. If he were in any kind of trouble, Ella would have told us about it. I was the youngest and my siblings never let me get away with anything. Ever."

The flight was delayed another hour, so she bought a sandwich and a bottle of water. While she ate, she thought about what Paris had said about their father "coming apart" after she left home. Florence said he'd turned to drinking, but Geneva didn't have a firm recollection of it. She did remember he'd broken his arm, or maybe his collarbone, falling into a bunker playing golf, and now she realized a drink or two could have made that more probable. The accident must have happened in October because she had an image of him carrying a pumpkin onto the front porch, his arm in a sling. As she watched from the window, the pumpkin tumbled from the crook of his good arm and exploded all over the clean white porch. He swore loudly enough for her to hear through the window. When he bent to pick up the pieces, he slipped on the in- nards and fell hard onto his backside. She ran away then, unused to seeing him compromised.

Even now she found it hard to accept that a broken bone marked the beginning of her father's demise. If it weren't for his injury, he would not have been taking Tylenol several times a day. Maybe a couple of tablets for bourbon-induced headaches, but no more. And if he had not primed his system with heavy daily doses, then the amount he accidentally took a week before he died prob- ably wouldn't have killed him. By the time anyone figured out what was wrong with him, it was too late.

Maybe what Paris meant was that if Geneva had been old enough to take Paris's role as the apple of their father's eye, he wouldn't have turned to the bourbon the way he did. Because that, too, as they later learned, contributed to the disastrous effect of Tylenol on his liver. But Geneva, at eleven, was not Paris. Her legs were too long for the rest of her, and she hadn't yet dropped her habit of sucking on her hair. She didn't talk when she had nothing to say and didn't laugh unless something was funny. She knew what charm was—her mother and Paris had it in spades—but didn't believe she needed it. At the museum, Paris hadn't sounded as if she blamed her. How could you blame someone for being eleven? And both then and now, she knew that as much as she loved her father, the last person she wanted to be was Paris.

*　*　*

By the time she got home, it was nearly midnight and everyone was asleep except Tom. He was waiting in bed for her. She was relieved he didn't want to talk about drugs and credit cards and long-lost sisters. He didn't want to talk at all. He watched her undress, then pulled back the covers and opened his arms. "This is my idea of getting on the same page."

She climbed into bed. Sex wasn't agreeing. It wasn't understanding, or even listening, but she welcomed it all the same.

CHAPTER TWENTY-NINE

❧

ELLA

The Battle of the Bands was right after seventh period. The whole school was there, even the teachers, the rest of the staff, and, of course, the parents who show up at everything because they don't have a life. She was grateful her parents weren't the type to stalk her at school.

They'd set up the stage between the gym and the cafeteria. Everyone was hanging out wherever: on the benches, leaning against the walls, sitting on the concrete. She was with Megan, of course, near a bunch of other junior girls who they knew but didn't like. Not that it would occur to those girls that anyone might not be dying to trade places with them. Ella was pretty sure if a freak accident took out half her brain she'd still not be as dumb as the four of them put together.

The first band didn't completely suck, meaning a decade of piano lessons finally paid off for the guy on the keyboard, and the singer was cute enough that the fact that he couldn't hit any high notes didn't matter. For their cover they'd picked a song Ella supposed was popular in a very small circle—the other three guys in the band. Not very smart. It goes without saying their original song was a disaster. The next band was better because it was a bunch of the drama and band kids. They knew what they were doing, but there were so many of them it was like the Jackson Twenty-five.

Next up was the Accountants, the Prince, Rango and the Hottie, only their actual name was There's an Amp for That. They made a huge deal about hooking up their snazzy amplifier, making sure everyone got that it was Big and New and Expensive and Cool. She couldn't wait to find out how much that set Nana back. Anyway, they launched into "Rock on You." Rosa the Hottie was next to the drums with a tambourine, which was hilarious. When the Prince took the mike a lot of kids booed him, just for being a freshman, but it didn't faze him. He did a good job getting the crowd jacked up and the music was loud, for sure. The cover was a hit.

Megan asked, "What're they doing next?"

"Supposedly a big surprise."

Megan rolled her eyes.

Hottie came to the front. "Confession. We wrote the music, but the lyrics are by Ella Novak. Big shout-out to Ella!"

She couldn't believe it. What lyrics?

Because she's so popular, a bunch of kids said, "Who's Ella?" Then all these heads turned toward her.

Megan said, "What's going on?"

She was too confused—and worried—to even shrug. Then the Accountants and the Prince started strumming their guitars. Slow and open notes, like a ballad. She stared at the Prince, searching for some clue, but he was concentrating on his fingers.

Hottie shook her hair away from her face, leaned over the mike and sang low and throaty:

> *If I stare, at the boy over there,*
> *Will he feel my eyes on him?*
> *If I dare to say: You take my breath away,*
> *Will he care how I feel about him?*

Ella was sure she wasn't hearing what she was hearing. How the hell? Her entire body went numb.

Megan put a hand on her shoulder. "You wrote this?"

She knew the next line and the worst part was she couldn't stop it being sung. Hottie's voice, now higher and clearer:

> *I say "Marco," you say "Polo,"*
> *You're sounding so far away.*
> *I'm looking for you, Marco,*
> *Polo's all you've got to say.*
> *I'm over my head here, Marco.*
> *Swimming with my eyes shut tight.*
> *If I reach for you, across the pool,*
> *Will I find you in my arms tonight?*
> *Marco.*

Ella's face was on fire. If only she could have melted straight into the concrete. Megan was shaking her shoulder to get her attention, but all she could do was stare at Hottie's mouth. Ella's words kept pouring out of it, like a volcano spewing lava.

One of the girls next to her saw her face and squealed, loud enough for the universe to hear, "Oh my God. Is this about Marcus?"

And Ella's life was officially over.

. . .

She pushed her way out of the crowd. News traveled fast. Everyone was hooting and pointing and laughing and, unbelievably, the song was still playing, like sinister background music in her own personal horror flick. She could barely see through her tears and white-hot anger.

The only minuscule good thing was that she'd driven to school because she was supposed to take The Absolute Fucking Traitor to the dentist after the Battle of the Bands was over. If she didn't have her dad's truck, she'd have to take the bus, and the problem with the bus was that it had people on it. High school people. The ones who listened and watched her starring role in Life's Most Embarrassing Moments.

She found the truck right away because she always parked in the same place. She threw her backpack on the ground, squatted down, and rummaged through the pockets for the keys. Megan caught up and squatted beside her.

"You okay?"

She couldn't open her mouth, because if she did, she'd start screaming and never stop.

"Not everybody thinks the song has anything to do with Marcus."

Damage control.

"It's a really great song. I mean, poem."

That did it. She collapsed against her friend. Megan put her arms around her and they stayed in a huddled, mewling ball for a long time.

"I hate him!"

"Me, too. How could he think that was okay to do?"

She imagined her brother going through her stuff in her room, finding her poetry journals, flipping through the pages with his disgusting, thieving fingers. Taking her work, her art, and using it to make himself look good and—oh, yeah—destroy her.

She found the keys, got up, and opened the truck. There on the front seat was Charlie's backpack. He'd gotten the keys from her earlier so he could leave it there. Just looking at it made her want to kill him.

She reached across and grabbed it and threw it out of the truck as if it were his head. Splat on the ground.

Turns out it wasn't zipped up all the way because his crap flew everywhere.

Megan said, "Whoa . . ."

"Shit."

Megan looked at her, wondering what came next.

"I don't care about his stuff."

"I don't blame you."

Some other kids were headed to their part of the parking lot. Megan and Ella stared at the books, paper, wrappers, pens, shorts (shorts?), water bottle, playing cards, and tons of other garbage scattered around the truck and under the other cars.

Megan pointed at a light blue triangular case at her feet, like she didn't know whether picking up stuff belonging to The Absolute Fucking Traitor was good form or not. "What's this?"

Ella shrugged and picked it up. It was weirdly heavy. She turned it over, then laid it flat in one hand and unzipped it.

Megan leaned over to see. "What the . . . ?"

Ella nearly dropped it. She couldn't fucking believe it. Why did Charlie have this? She looked at Megan in case maybe she knew. Nope.

She'd never held a gun before. The closest she'd been to one was standing near a policeman. Of course, the policeman's gun wasn't pale blue.

A senior whose name she didn't know was a few yards away, kicking at Charlie's stuff. "What's up with all this?"

She shut the case. She was holding a weapon on school property. Holy crap! Was it loaded? How could she tell? Okay, okay, assume it's loaded. Assume the worst. Because that's today.

Megan said, "It was an accident." She glanced at Ella. "We were just going to pick it up."

Frozen to the spot, Ella nodded and her friend started shoving stuff into the backpack. The senior went to his car.

Her hands shaking, she slowly zipped up the gun case. Then she didn't know what to do with it. Tears stung in her nose and she bit her lip so she wouldn't whimper like a freaking baby.

"Megan," she said softly, "can you do something with this?"

Megan looked at her as if she wasn't sure any friendship, even theirs, should include weapons handling. But then she held open the backpack. "Let's put it back in here."

She slid it in carefully and Megan zipped the backpack closed and put it in the truck. They both stared at it like it might jump at them, or explode. Ella pulled her phone from her pocket. Her sweaty fingers slid across the screen as she dialed.

"Mom? Yeah, it's me. What? No, I'm okay." Tears clogged

her throat. "Maybe not so okay." Now her nose was running and she really couldn't help the fact that she was coming unglued. Totally unglued. "Can you come get me? Please? I'm so sorry. I'm really, really sorry. There's a bad mess and it's my fault. Can you please come get me? Please?"

CHAPTER THIRTY

GENEVA

Geneva struggled to stay under the speed limit as she drove the ten miles to the high school. On the way, she called Tom on the hands-free, and told him about Ella's phone call.

"And you have no idea what's going on?"

"None. I'll bring her home as soon as I can."

She found her sitting in the truck with Megan, her head resting on the steering wheel, her back shaking with each sob. When Geneva opened the door, Ella threw her arms around her neck. Geneva cupped Ella's head as she had done when she was a baby.

"Can you tell me what's happening?"

"I just want to go home."

"Okay. But do you need a doctor? Megan, are you all right?"

The girl nodded.

Ella straightened and looked at her mother. "Let's go home. Let's get Charlie and go home."

In her panic, Geneva had forgotten about Charlie. And an aspect of her daughter's tone bothered her. "Does this have to do with Charlie in some way?"

Megan gave Ella a furtive glance. Ella said, "Yes," and began to cry again.

* * *

Tom was waiting when they pulled into the drive. As they got out of the car, he gave Geneva a questioning look over the top of Ella's head. She shrugged and shook her head. Tom took Ella's backpack from her and put his arm around her shoulders. Charlie was already at the door, scowling.

"Charlie, how'd the Battle go?"

"How should I know? Mom made me leave before they announced the winner."

They went inside and Charlie headed toward the den.

Ella said, "Don't let him take his backpack in there!"

Tom asked, "Why not?"

"I'll tell you everything in a minute! Just don't!"

"Charlie, let's sit down now."

He didn't turn around. "I'll be there in a minute!"

Geneva exchanged glances with Tom. "Charles, leave it now!"

He dropped his backpack in the middle of the room and threw himself on the couch. "Does it have to be a family emergency every time Ella has PMS?"

"Shut up!" Ella said.

"Okay, you two," Tom said and sat down next to Geneva. "Ella, maybe you could start at the beginning."

She slid her hands between her knees and stared at the coffee table. "I'm not sure where the beginning is."

"Great," said Charlie.

Geneva put a hand on his arm and gave him a stern look.

Ella exhaled loudly. "Okay, so there's a lot of stuff going on you guys don't know about."

Geneva glanced at her son, whose expression had changed from annoyed to worried.

Tom said, "For example . . ."

"For example, the truck. It didn't happen in a parking lot."

"It didn't?"

"No. It was in a parking garage. I hit a pole."

Geneva said, "Well, that's not very serious. Of course we would've preferred if you'd been honest with us. Where was this parking garage?"

"Um . . . In the city?"

"San Francisco?"

"Uh-huh."

"You drove to San Francisco after your SAT class?"

Charlie snorted.

"No, Mom." She pulled the cuffs of her sweatshirt over her hands, and addressed the coffee table. "I didn't go to the class at all."

"What? Ella . . ."

"Let me tell it! I drove to the city for the poetry slam. And because I was worried about getting lost, Megan came with me. And the parking space was really tight and I hit the pole. Then there was construction, and we got lost on the detour, so I was really late picking up Charlie. But you didn't notice because you were at the hospital with Jon and Dad." Exhausted by the confession, she dropped her head onto her arms.

"Wow," Tom said.

"Wow, indeed." Geneva felt a small surge of gratitude that all that had been damaged was the truck, then returned to the reality that there was more of the story left to be told. "But what does that have to do with today?"

"Nothing," Charlie said. "Ella's just freaking out over a song we did." He got up. "Can I go now?"

Ella jumped up and pointed at him. "You're not going anywhere! You think I'm telling them everything because you're a conniving thief who doesn't give a shit about anyone's feelings? I'm not. I'm telling them everything because you're too stupid to know how you're fucking up your life!"

Geneva quickly glanced at Tom and saw her fear mirrored in his face. "Both of you sit down. Please. Ella's told us about the car. Charles, do you want to tell us anything?"

"Like what?"

Ella said, "Like where you got the money to buy an iPhone and new video games and a huge freaking amplifier!"

"What?" said Tom. "Charlie, how . . ."

The sound of Helen's walker clanking loudly in the hallway silenced him. She came around the corner, gripping the walker tightly and swaying a little. "This is a very loud discussion."

"Sorry, Helen. If you want to go back to your room, we'll keep it down."

"I think Nana should stay," Ella said.

"I agree." Geneva pointed to the empty chair next to Tom and watched her mother maneuver unsteadily into place. She saw Tom's puzzled look. "I haven't had a chance to tell you—Dublin told me last night—but my mother has had some unusual charges on her credit card. I thought it was probably fraud."

Helen said, "Oh, is that what the commotion is about? Can't I buy my grandson a few things without causing a stir?"

"An eight-hundred-dollar amplifier?"

"Well, I didn't know about that." She turned to Charlie. "Really! You might have asked."

He shrugged. "You said anything I wanted."

"That's true. I did."

Geneva said to her mother, "I don't suppose Charlie did anything in return for your generosity?"

"I can't imagine what."

Tom turned to Geneva. "Where are you going with this?"

"I know my mother."

Ella nodded. "I think Charlie's been buying booze from that place on First Street."

"No, I haven't." He looked at his sister uncertainly. "And anyway, how could I do that? It's not like I'm twenty-one."

"I saw you. Not buying booze, but you gave money to that homeless guy."

"That's not a crime. That's charity."

Geneva said, "What homeless guy? What is going on here?"

Charlie waved it away. "Don't listen to her, Mom. She's crazy."

Ella crossed her arms over her chest. "You're not very smart, Charlie. You're forcing me to tell them everything."

Tom and Geneva said, "There's more?"

"Nobody likes a tattletale," Helen said, wagging her finger at her granddaughter.

Ella sighed. "Charlie gave money to Pierce and Spencer to let him in the band. He got the money from buying porno magazines at the liquor store and renting them to boys at school. Disgusting, right?"

Tom's face darkened as he stared at his son.

"Renting them?" Geneva asked.

"You don't want to know," Ella said.

"Prove it," Charlie said.

"Spencer told me."

"The guy's an idiot."

"Smarter than you, apparently."

Geneva put up her hand. "Let me guess the next part. Mom, you asked Charlie to buy liquor for you at the store through this same man. You hid it in plain sight in the iced tea in the fridge. In return, Charlie got access to your credit card. Is that about right?" She glared at her mother, but she would not meet her gaze.

Tom leaned forward. "Helen, you actually used my son this way?"

She pursed her lips and nodded at Ella. "It's her word against his, isn't it?"

"Plus the credit card statement."

"Which only says I'm guilty of favoritism."

Geneva said, "Oh, for God's sake, Mom! How about some honesty!"

Helen raised an eyebrow as if considering the suggestion, then returned to appearing somewhat bored.

Geneva asked Charlie, "Do you still have nothing to say?" He lowered his chin and turned his palms up in resignation. Tom shook his head and his jaw muscles contracted into a hard lump. Part of her was dying to ask him to find the silver lining to this cloud, but the pain on his face moved her. If he was guilty of naïveté, so was she. He must be thinking the same thing she was: How had all this transpired under their watch?

She studied her mother, and noticed her blue eyes were glassy.

As she weighed the likelihood of getting a straight answer to a direct question about whether she had been drinking today, Ella shifted in her seat and spoke.

"Yeah, honesty. About that. So, you know how the bands had to do an original song? Charlie actually went into my room and dug through my stuff and stole one of my very private poems."

Geneva wasn't sure who the person sitting in the chair across from her was, but he seemed less and less like her son. At that moment he would not look at her.

"And then he takes this poem, which, as long as we're being honest, was about a boy I had a crush on, and gets Rosa to sing it to the whole school, so that every freaking person knows everything about my entire private life!" She threw herself against the chair back, pulled her knees to her chest, dropped her head and sobbed.

"I'm sorry, sweetheart," Geneva said. "I'm so sorry."

"I guess that was a pretty sucky thing to do," Charlie said. "But it was a really good song. I kinda thought she'd enjoy the fame."

Ella ignored him. "The poem is only part of why I'm so upset."

"Oh, Christ," Tom said.

The hair stood up on the back of Geneva's neck.

"So, I run to the truck to get away from the song, and Megan follows me. Charlie's backpack is inside and I'm so furious with him that I throw it out. Only it isn't zipped up, so all his stuff flies everywhere."

Charlie started to get up.

"Sit down now!" Tom shouted.

"Dad," Ella said. "Can you get his backpack? I don't want to go near it."

"Ella, you are such a loser. Dad, I can explain. I wasn't going to do anything with it."

"With what?" Geneva watched Tom carry the backpack to the couch and pull out a book and a couple of notebooks.

"What am I looking for? Oh, wait." He lifted out the gun case.

Helen said, "So that's where it went!"

"I can't believe this." Tom unzipped it and Geneva gasped.

Ella said, "That's yours, Nana?! It scared the living crap out of me."

Geneva's eyes were locked on the gun. "Mom, tell me it's not loaded."

"Of course it's loaded. It's about as useful as tits on a boar otherwise."

Tom glared at his son. "Talk. Now."

Charlie cleared his throat. "Well, it was pretty much an accident. See, I wanted to order something using Nana's credit card, like she said I could—"

Ella interrupted. "What now? A Maserati?"

"—and I lost the piece of paper where I'd written the number. So I thought that instead of bugging Nana about it, I'd just look in her purse."

Helen clucked her tongue. "You need to learn to respect people's privacy, young man!"

"Okay, okay. But I saw this case in there and opened it to see what it was."

"And how is it, Charles," Geneva said, "that you decided the right place for it was in your backpack?"

He shrugged as if the answer were obvious. "I just wanted to show it to my friends. A baby blue grandma gun! I didn't know there was such a thing. I wasn't going to use it or anything. And I had no idea it was loaded! If I knew that I never would have borrowed it. That would have been really dumb."

Tom zipped up the case.

"What are we going to do with it?" Geneva asked.

Helen stuck out her hand. "Well, return it to its rightful owner!"

"I don't think so," Tom said.

"I'll unload it, if it makes you feel better."

"You shouldn't handle a loaded gun when you've been drinking," Geneva said.

"I have not . . ."

"Save it. And right now, I'd appreciate it if you would go to your room before I say or do something I'll regret."

Helen appealed to Tom with a doleful look, but he stared her down, so she sighed heavily, hoisted herself to standing, and clanked down the hall.

"I'm really sorry, you guys," Charlie said. "I guess things got carried away."

Ella was curled in a ball with her arms around her knees. Her face was splotched from crying and her bangs were stuck to her forehead. Except for her gray clothing, she could have been five years old. Geneva pushed against the tears clouding her vision. If she hadn't allowed her mother to come here, none of this would have happened.

Tom picked up the gun case from the coffee table. "I'm going to run this down to the police station for safekeeping."

Geneva nodded and told Charlie to get busy on his homework. "Ella, I'm going to get a drink. Do you want anything?"

"Sure. Whatever. Just not iced tea."

• • •

Geneva preheated the oven for the frozen pizzas, then joined Tom in the backyard. She descended the stairs to the lawn, feeling off-balance and blurry, as though she had skipped a night's sleep. And a lost thought was nagging at the back of her mind, but she couldn't marshal the energy to ferret it out. If only she could take a weeklong vacation by herself, she might succeed in sorting everything out. But that wasn't on the menu. She'd have to settle for a phone call to Dublin after dinner. Maybe he could figure out how her life had spun out of control.

She took a chair next to Tom. "I wouldn't have thought it possible, but my mother's more of a loose cannon than I anticipated."

"Yeah, the gun was a shock, but I don't think we can blame her for everything."

"No, you're right. I think we have to accept that we are terrible parents."

Tom gave a short laugh.

"I'm not joking, Tom. We were a couple of lucky breaks away from having a kid with a rap sheet. And we haven't even broached the subject of smoking dope."

"I know. But they're still good kids. Good kids make mistakes, too."

She turned in her chair to face him. "I hope you're not thinking of going easy on Charlie. Because I'm not. Good kid or bad kid, serious mistakes call for serious consequences."

"If we come down on him like a ton of bricks, it might get worse instead of better."

"And if we close our eyes and sing a lullaby, maybe it will all go away."

"No need to get sarcastic, Geneva."

"It's either sarcasm or righteous indignation. Take your pick."

"What? So because you wanted to bankrupt your mother rather than help her out, and because you had some sort of women's intuition about what Charlie was up to, I'm to blame for all this?" He threw his arms wide and stared at her, incredulous.

"No, Tom, I'm not blaming you for this. But after being scolded for so long for worrying too much, you shouldn't be surprised I'm angry. I'm angry at my mother, at the kids, and at myself. And, damn it, Tom, I'm angry at you."

He looked away. His jaw muscle twitched. In a low voice, he said, "So what do you want to do?"

"I'm thinking the sooner my mother leaves, the better."

He leaned back in his chair and exhaled. "She's leaving? Did you tell her?"

"I haven't spoken with her. But I thought it was obvious that after what we just found out, she'd no longer be welcome here."

"Well . . ."

"Are you thinking of waiting until she actually kills someone?"

He put his hand on her shoulder. "Hey, it's been a rough day. A very rough day. But that's why it's not a good time to make decisions."

"Not a good time for you, maybe, but an excellent time for me. You may remember I wasn't completely behind her coming here in the first place."

Tom took his hand away and frowned. "Maybe it's fair to throw that in my face, but I also think that what happened with Charlie and Ella, or something similar, would have happened whether your mother was here or not."

"Mischief is one thing. Mischief with unlimited money and a loaded gun is another."

He put his elbows on his knees and held his head in his hands. As angry as she was with him, she could see he was struggling to know how to respond to what had happened, the same as she was. Still, she could not understand why he was so determined to have her and her mother remain in the same house and battle through their problems. Maybe he could see aspects of a relationship worth salvaging that she could not. Or, more likely, he couldn't imagine not being part of the kind of family he had, and stubbornly ignored the fact that the Novaks never had to assimilate anyone like Helen. Tom's intentions were as noble as they were misguided, but the time for Geneva to trust her intuition and her judgment—and make her own decisions—was long overdue. She hadn't held her ground when she knew welcoming her mother into their house spelled trouble. Helen was damaged beyond repair for reasons she did not understand, but now the reasons didn't matter. Helen had to go.

Tom said, "The last thing I want to do is fight with you."

"I feel the same."

"I'll go put the pizzas in. Are we feeding your mother?"

"Do we have a choice?"

* * *

Helen didn't respond when Geneva rapped on the door.

"Mom?" She opened the door a few inches. "Mom?" Her mother lay motionless on the bed facing the wall. The curtains were partially closed and a dusky light filled the room. The skin on Geneva's arms tingled. As she monitored the shape on the bed for movement, the room shuddered. She put a hand on the dresser to steady herself, then rushed to the bed. She took in the clear liquor bottle on the nightstand next to a small quilted bag.

"Mom!" She shook her mother's shoulder and turned her over. Her mouth was slack. Geneva bent and put her ear to her mother's nose, and heard a faint hiss.

She looked again at the nightstand. An inch of vodka remained. She picked up the bag and dumped the contents onto the bed. Amid the tubes and jars of makeup was a plastic sandwich bag containing a few white pills.

"Tom!"

She ran to the door and shouted down the hall.

"Tom!"

She patted the front pocket of her jeans but her phone wasn't there. Running back to the bed, she picked up the bag and examined the pills to identify them.

Tom appeared in the doorway. "What's going on?"

"Call nine-one-one! Tell them it's an overdose!"

She put two fingers on her mother's neck to take her pulse, willing the pounding of her own heart to quiet. The beat was faint and thready.

She grabbed her mother's shoulders and shook them. "Mom! Wake up!"

As she let go, she noticed a folded piece of paper sticking out of the discarded makeup bag. Without knowing why, she put it in her pocket, then tried again to revive her mother.

CHAPTER THIRTY-ONE

HELEN

From the time Paris turned sixteen until she left home for her internship in Columbia eighteen months later, Helen hardly had one decent night's sleep. She didn't want to go to bed before Eustace, not knowing what he'd get up to while she was upstairs, and once he was in bed, she'd wake up at all hours to make sure he was still there. She didn't have a clear notion of what she'd do if she caught him red-handed, but that didn't stop her fretting about it. Being up half the night took a toll on her looks, and did nothing to improve her temper besides. When she looked at herself in the mirror, she was frightened by how sharp her features had become, and how dull her hair and eyes. Eustace commenting on it didn't help matters, especially as Paris got prettier, in a womanly way, with each passing day. Helen tried to keep herself up, changing her hairstyle and experimenting with new beauty treatments, but she couldn't see it made a lick of difference. She was mutton, not lamb.

Some days her exhaustion became confusion and she thought she might be losing her mind. She'd wake with a start, the sun already pouring into the room, and panic upon realizing Eustace wasn't there. Throwing on her dressing gown, she would rush downstairs only to find her children, Paris included, sitting at the table, eating cereal and chatting away. Eustace would be leaning against the counter, holding a coffee cup, laughing at what one of them had said. Other times, she'd hear whispering coming from Paris's room. She'd run down the hall, Argus chasing her like it was a game. She'd brace herself for the shock, throw open the door and stand staring at an empty room. At times such as these, she doubted whether she had ever seen anything improper transpire between Eustace and Paris, and wondered if she should see a doctor. She went so far as to mention the idea to Eustace, who calmly agreed medication might help her insomnia. But she didn't go, because in her heart she knew as much as she craved sleep, she wasn't ready to pull a curtain over the nighttime.

Whenever Eustace went away on business, she slept the whole night through. In the morning she woke with her mind free of cobwebs and full of certainty she was, in fact, sane. This, and the glances and gestures she caught ricocheting between her husband and her daughter, told her he had not mended his ways, but only become more secretive.

In the spring of her senior year, Paris announced at the dinner table she was taking an internship in a law firm in Columbia. Eustace appeared to know all about it, because he didn't ask any questions, only smiled and patted her hand.

"That's flattering," Helen said, "but seventeen is much too young to live in a big city like Columbia on your own."

"I won't be on my own. I'll be staying with Aunt Clarisse."

Aunt Clarisse was Eustace's aunt, nearly eighty years old, and deaf as a post.

"Clarisse is lovely, of course, but hardly fit to chaperone a young girl!"

"No need to worry," Eustace said. "Her housekeeper—who's a sprightly thirty—comes every day. And almost every weekend, other members of my family visit."

"Sounds exciting," Dublin said, never one for tolerating relatives, especially the stodgy Rileys.

"Doesn't it?" Paris said, ignoring his sarcasm. "And, Daddy, promise you'll visit, too."

"I'm counting on it, princess."

"Maybe I'll go along with you," Helen said.

"You never liked the city."

"That was a long time ago. I might give it another try."

"Well, you might. But who's going to stay with the children, especially now that we don't have Louisa?"

. . .

Eustace visited Paris a few times he admitted to, and claimed he had business in places a good distance away more often than she thought likely. He never once let Helen come along, and the whole summer the girl came home to Aliceville just three times. When she was home, she wasn't particularly kind to her mother, nor particularly mean. The feeling Helen got was that Paris didn't care about her much one way or the other. She didn't rate.

That was more or less the way she treated Florence, too. Paris timed one of her visits to coincide with the father-daughter dance at the club. She hadn't been home two minutes before she came into the kitchen holding the dress she'd bought in Columbia for the event. Helen was dipping chicken in batter and Florence was shucking corn.

Paris held the dress up against her. "Isn't it fabulous?" It was yellow satin with a bubble hem. She flipped it around. "Don't you love the bow?"

Helen said, "It's pretty, but you might have asked Florence whether she wanted to go with your father this year, seeing as you've already been twice."

Paris looked at Florence as if she only just noticed her. "Well, I didn't mean to be presumptuous. You've talked to Daddy about it, then?"

"No, not yet . . . I was waiting for him to ask me."

"He probably thought you had practice or a game."

"It's over at two."

"I guess that might give you time to get rid of the sweat and fix up your hair." She appeared doubtful and put her finger to her lips in concentration. "I know. Let's let Daddy choose."

Helen had only wanted her to consider Florence's feelings, but now wished she hadn't opened this can of worms. "That would put your father on the spot."

Florence stared at the corn piled on the counter. "I'm not even sure I want to go."

Paris clutched her dress to her waist and twirled around. "That settles it then!" She ran out the door.

Helen watched Florence rip the husks off the corn with a bit more force than was required. She used to feel a little sorry for Florence because she'd never turn heads the way Paris did. But beauty could be a liability, no doubt about it, and everything else about the girl was just fine.

"Florence, honey, what do you say tomorrow night while those two are dancing with the snooties at the club, we take Dublin and Geneva and go see that new movie with Michael Keaton. You know the one."

"*Mr. Mom.*"

"That's the one. And have dinner out first. How would that be?"

"Sounds fun, Mom." She looked her mother and smiled. "Thanks."

* * *

In late August, Eustace helped Paris pack her belongings into his car and drove her to her dorm at the University of North Carolina in Chapel Hill. When he got home, he started in on the bourbon, and complained day and night about how the dorms were shabby and unsafe and too close to where they kept the boys. To hear him tell it, each and every one of those boys was a lout and a ne'er-do-well, unfit to share the same campus with his princess. Didn't take a genius to figure out what track his mind was taking. All along, Helen had figured Paris's going off to college would spell the end of it. Chapel Hill was a fair distance, and even a peculiar girl like Paris would eventually find a college boy who struck her fancy. Helen had been sure of it. And while she didn't think Eustace would give up easily—he was too stubborn by half—she reckoned he'd come to the revelation that his daughter had grown away from him.

But Helen had underestimated him. When she overheard him on the phone, trying to convince Paris she'd be happier in an apartment off campus, she knew he wasn't going to quit. Not now. Not ever.

CHAPTER THIRTY-TWO

GENEVA

Tom, Geneva, and Charlie followed the paramedics out the door and watched them load Helen into the rear of the ambulance. Tom headed for the truck and Geneva ran inside to get her purse from the kitchen. Charlie followed her in.

Ella pulled a pizza tray from the oven and set it on the counter. "They were burning."

"I completely forgot." She came around the counter and hugged her daughter tight. "We're going now. I'll call you as soon as we know anything." Ella's mouth was twisted with worry. Geneva kissed her forehead. "They came really quickly and that's good."

"Okay."

"And I'll call Ivan and Leigh on the way. They can be here in five minutes."

"Do you have your phone?"

Geneva removed it from the front pocket of her purse and showed it to her. "Got it. Now, if . . ."

"We're okay."

"Don't worry, Mom," Charlie said. "Just go."

She gave him a quick hug and left.

• • •

After they checked in at the reception desk, Geneva retreated to a quiet corner of the emergency waiting room and called Dublin.

"Hey, Ginny. Missing me already?"

"Yes."

"Uh-oh. Serious tone. Lay it on me. Or would you prefer one of our guessing games?"

"Mom's in the hospital. She overdosed on vodka and probably Demerol."

"Shit."

"The ambulance was fast. I think she'll make it."

"Damn her and her booze. Did she do it on purpose?"

"I don't know, Dub. It's possible. Today was a nightmare."

"What happened?"

"Do you have a few minutes? Because this will give you material for your shows for years to come."

• • •

An hour after they had arrived at the emergency room, Tom left to get coffee from a vending machine. When he returned, they stepped outside to find respite from crying children and anxious, ill adults. Wisps of fog slid out of the darkness and swirled under the floodlights. Geneva hugged herself against the air that seemed so much colder than when she and Tom had sat in the backyard, believing the worst of the day was over.

The pills were what worried her the most. She thought she had monitored her mother's pain medication, but apparently she was as good at that as she was at monitoring her children. But she had expected Helen would take extra pills to compensate for sobriety, not stockpile them. And without knowing how many were in the stash, she couldn't know how many her mother had taken, if any. A blood test would provide the answer, but would it then be clear whether she had overdosed on purpose?

The bag of pills might be a red herring. All on its own, the nearly empty vodka bottle—and all the others that preceded it— suggested drinking for the purpose of oblivion. The difference between what her mother had been doing for thirty years, and what she had done tonight, was only a matter of acceleration.

Tom put a hand on her shoulder. "I wanted to tell you something."

"Is this a good time?"

"I think so."

"Should I be bracing myself? Because I don't feel I have it in me right now."

"No, nothing like that. It has to do with why I've pushed so hard for you to be on better terms with your mother."

"I think I know why. Your family's so close and you want the same for me, however misguided that impulse may be."

"That's just it. I've never told you why my family is the way it is."

Geneva was about to sip her coffee, but lowered it again. "What do you mean?"

"It happened before I met you, and it was never the right time to bring it up. That and we're not supposed to talk about it."

"But now you're telling me?"

"Yeah, because I don't think it's fair for you to think your family is the only one with problems."

She ran her hand along the hedge lining the walkway. "I'm listening."

He took a deep breath. "While I was in college, my mom had an affair. A serious one. They almost split up over it."

Geneva studied his face for signs this was a joke, but found none. "Your mom? That's unbelievable."

"Now it is. But then it was a mess. Dad was so angry, and Mom . . . well, Mom was sorry, but also torn up about what to do. You remember Dad had a heart attack, right?"

"You mean that's when it happened?"

"Yeah. And Mom stayed with him, but I still wonder if she would have otherwise. And the kids, we all had our own lives. Unlike now, we didn't see them that often. But when they told us what was going on, everything changed. Of course we helped out because Dad was sick, but it went on long after he was better. We started dropping by, checking in, and inviting them to every game, every dinner party, every inane event."

"Did you and your siblings plan this?"

"No, not really. Juliana would call me and say, 'Let's have movie night at my place and invite Mom and Dad,' and then everyone would show up. We were holding them together by re-minding them of what they made together. Before long they were making excuses to have us over. And gradually they put the affair behind them. At least it seems they did."

"That's amazing. I can't believe you've never told me before."

"When they told us about it, we were sworn to secrecy. They'd be mortified if they knew you knew. I think by now everyone's forgotten the affair ever happened. Except maybe Mom. She must wonder what her life would be like if she'd made a different decision." He paused and looked away.

"What?"

He turned to her, his face soft with emotion. "I don't want anything like that to happen to us. I can't imagine losing you."

"Oh, Tom." She cupped his face in her hands and kissed him.

He pulled her close and held her as if she were a wild animal that might break free. "I love you. Please say you want to stay with me."

She was raw and jagged with the fear of losing her mother. The wall of frustration and resentment toward Tom she'd been building for so long crumbled. Her intuition about him, formed the day they met, had not been wrong. He was a good man. A true man. And she both wanted and needed him.

She wiped tears from her cheeks and looked into his eyes. "I never thought about leaving, and I never will."

He kissed her deeply.

They held each other until the wind rose and drove them inside.

. . .

They waited, talking little. Geneva worried she might lose her mother before she had a chance to understand her. When she realized this meant she truly did love her, she wept again. Tom wrapped her in his arms until her tears were spent.

. . .

Finally, after two hours, a doctor came to see them. She said they had pumped out Helen's stomach and her condition had stabilized.

The blood work showed she had taken Demerol, but earlier in the day. "Which was lucky," the doctor added, "considering her blood alcohol level." They would be keeping her overnight and, depending on her condition and state of mind, she could be released as early as midday tomorrow.

As they headed to the parking garage, Geneva texted the children to say they were on their way.

*   *   *   *

She slept fitfully. At quarter to five in the morning, she arose and walked quietly across the room to let Tom sleep, picking up discarded clothes along the way. Diesel stood when he heard her footsteps in the hall. He stretched his forelimbs in front of him and stuck his rear end in the air, yawning hugely, then met her in the kitchen. She squatted before him and massaged the skin behind his ears until his lids drooped with pleasure. When she stopped, he pushed his muzzle into her neck and licked.

"Yuck." She wiped her neck with the sleeve of her robe. He darted in for another lick, but she blocked his head with her hand and scratched him under the chin. "That's enough, thank you."

She turned on a single light in the kitchen, started the coffee, then proceeded to the laundry room, Diesel at her heels, to make inroads on the mountain of dirty clothes that had been accumulating all week. She sorted the clothes, going through pockets as she went, removing a stick of gum from Ella's hoodie and a parking stub from Tom's trousers.

In the jeans she had worn yesterday, she found the piece of paper she'd taken from her mother's bed. Staring at the worn pale blue paper, she felt for the wall behind her and slid down it until she was sitting on the floor. A hard lump of dread caught in her throat when she unfolded it and read Paris's name at the bottom. The date at the top was May 26, 1995. Twelve years after their father had died.

Mother,

This is the only and last letter you will get from me. I will make myself as clear as I can, then I'll have nothing more to say.

You say that because we were both victims of Daddy's "unusual desires," we should have sympathy for each other. I reject your premise. I have never been anyone's victim. I loved Daddy and Daddy loved me more than anyone or anything in the world. I don't believe in God or heaven but I do believe I was put on this earth to love my father. As much as you have tried to take that from me, you can't.

I've thought many times over the years of what might have happened if you had been able to give Daddy everything he deserved. Would he have turned to me if you had loved him better? Of course I believe he and I were destined for each other—and he believed it, too— but you seem to want to hand out blame, so you can take that share for yourself and live with it.

The idea that you were Daddy's victim almost makes me laugh. Are you too big a fool to see the irony in this? You were clever, I'll give you that.

You write that you want me to have a family and live a normal life. You mean, one like yours? No, thank you. I've had great love once, and that was more than enough.

*Now I have my work. If you stay out of my life, I will
have everything I ever wanted.*
  Paris

Her mind raced to make sense of what she had read, but the
ideas would not line up and instead spiraled away from one another. It was a language in which her understanding of the individual words was defeated by the syntax. *Destined. Blame. Heaven.
Irony. Desire.*

A wave of nausea flowed through her stomach, and she tasted
bile at the back of her throat. She suddenly felt sick but didn't
know why. She put a hand to her head and noticed her heart was
racing. She glanced at Diesel, who lay outside the room watching
her, his brow furrowed. Had she moaned or made a noise that
worried him?

She began to read the letter again, and got as far as "victims
of Daddy's 'unusual desires,'" and stopped. The ground became
fog that swam around and under her. She swayed and rocked.
Lowering the letter, she tipped her head against the wall to ground
herself and end the sickening pitching and swirling. She closed her
eyes and saw her father and Paris dancing in the living room. He
lifted his arm and she twirled under it, around and around, her
dress lifting as she spun.

Geneva's stomach heaved. She turned to the side and vomited
onto the laundry. She pushed herself upright and wiped her mouth
with a piece of clothing. In front of her, Paris was spinning, her
face close to Geneva's, her blue eyes sparkling, saying with each
turn, "Did you love Daddy? Not like I did. Did you love Daddy?
Not like I did." Diesel barked sharply. He pawed at her legs half
covered by her robe and barked again.

•   •   •

"Are you all right?" Tom scanned the scene, then knelt beside her and put a hand to her forehead. "You're really pale." Diesel peered at Geneva over Tom's shoulder. "It's okay, boy. I got it now. Go lie down."

She handed him the letter.

He gave her a questioning look, then sat down. She watched him read, the way one waits during a speech for the translator to begin. It was possible those words didn't mean what she thought they did. But then she saw him shake his head slowly, and wince, and knew that as much as she wished she had been mistaken, she wasn't.

Tom folded the letter in half, then raised his head to meet her gaze. "How could he . . . ? Nobody knew? And why didn't your mother . . . Oh, darling . . ." Tears shone in his eyes. He leaned forward and stroked the hair away from her face. "Let me help you up. I'll clean this up later."

As he slipped his hands under her arms, she saw a tear run down his cheek. She wiped a hand across her own cheek and looked at her fingers. They were dry.

Tom led her down the hall and asked if she wanted to go to bed. She shook her head.

"I think I'll go outside."

"It's not light yet."

"I know."

"You want me to come?"

"I'd rather be alone, I think."

"Sure. You get dressed and I'll pour you coffee."

"Thanks."

Her limbs were heavy and her fingers felt thick as she pulled on her yoga pants and T-shirt and zipped up her sweatshirt. She picked her robe off the floor and searched the pockets. She went to the kitchen.

"Do you have the letter?"

He pulled it out of his shirt pocket and handed it to her, along with a steaming mug. "Let me get the door."

Diesel followed her onto the porch and stood beside her, peering into the darkness in search of the reason they were outside at this strange hour. She sat on the top step and put down the mug. Diesel sat, too.

In her hand, the folded letter felt less like paper than the thin sueded hide of a small animal. The texture sickened her and she breathed deeply to stem the nausea. She concentrated on the outline of the redwoods against the sky, where a few stars lingered ahead of the impending dawn.

Diesel yawned.

"If one of those stars falls, be careful what you wish for."

She started to open the letter to read it again, to see whether this time the words it held would shock her less. Maybe if she read it again and again and again, eventually she would no longer feel as if she'd been turned inside out.

But the letter was a Pandora's box. The truth about her father had escaped and was running wild. The only question was what she was going to do about it. Already in the half hour since she'd opened it, the truth had trampled through her memories of her father, memories she had held dear for more than thirty years, and corrupted them like a virus. And Paris was no longer the eccentric enigma, but an abuse victim in absolute denial, a denial cultivated by her father, which made him even more despicable.

And her mother. She had a thousand questions for her mother, but only one mattered: How could you have let this happen?

An image came to her of Paris at sixteen, unwrapping a box and lifting out the nest Geneva had found in a dogwood tree. Paris held the nest lightly, respectfully, and smiled at her. Geneva glanced at her father, to see if he approved of her gift, too, but his eyes were on Paris.

The same age as Ella. Her throat clenched shut and pressure built at her temples. She doubled over to control the sobs racking her body. Diesel poked his nose into her neck. She threw her arms around him and hung there, trembling, until the first birds tentatively heralded the morning.

CHAPTER THIRTY-THREE

ELLA

There was no way she could go to school today. It wasn't because of the song, though yesterday that seemed like a reason to crawl in a hole and die. (And she still thought if she actually saw Marcus in this lifetime she would, in fact, die.) And it wasn't because of some post-traumatic stress from finding a gun in her brother's backpack, though that had seriously freaked her out. No, the reason she couldn't go to school—couldn't even get out bed, in fact—was because she had almost killed her grandmother.

If only she'd gotten a conscience a little earlier, like before Nana showed up, then her parents would have known the Prince was not a prince after all, but a sneaky little shit. Maybe they would've decided having a crazy alcoholic in the house wasn't such a hot idea, or would have let her come but kept him on a shorter leash. But Ella didn't say anything and the shit hit the fan, and Nana acted as if it was no big deal but then went to her room and downed a bottle of vodka and some pills, and the ambulance came and her mom said, "Don't worry," which was adult code for "major disaster," and Nana nearly died.

Good job, Ella.

The alarm on her phone went off a half hour ago. Usually if she didn't show up in the kitchen by this time, someone knocked on her door or at least yelled down the hall. Weird. She dragged her butt out of bed to see what was up.

Her dad was drinking coffee in the kitchen. He looked like crap. Worse than yesterday, which was saying something.

"Hey."

"Hi, Ella. I was letting you sleep in."

"I don't have to go to school?"

"No. I've got to take Charlie in, and maybe pick up Nana later, and I want you to stay with your mom."

"Why? I mean, sure, but what's wrong with Mom?"

He looked into his mug like there were tea leaves in there. "This stuff with Nana is tough on her."

She swallowed hard. "I thought Nana was gonna be okay."

"She is. But it's still tough."

Great. More collateral damage. "Is she sleeping? Can I go see her?"

"Sure." He got up and headed for the fridge. "Have some breakfast first?"

"Not hungry, thanks." She drew a slow circle on the wood floor with a toe. "Dad?"

"Yeah?"

"Is Mom going to be okay?"

He came around the counter and put his hands on her shoulders in pep talk position. "She's got you, doesn't she? And me." He smiled a little. "And Charlie."

For her mom's sake, she hoped one out of three was enough.

* * *

Her parents' door was half open, so Ella stuck her head in. Her mom was sitting in the rocking chair, but she wasn't rocking. She was staring out the window, which was strange all by itself. She wasn't the staring-out-of-windows type, unless there was a new bird at the feeder or a squirrel doing backflips.

"Mom?"

She didn't move an inch. "Yes?"

"Can I come in?"

"Sure."

There was only one chair, so she sat in front of it on the rug. Finally her mom turned to her. She looked worse than Dad. "Are you okay?"

Long pause. "Not really, to be honest."

"Do you want to talk about it?" Like she was a therapist.

She smiled a little. "No. I can't really. Someday I'll tell you about it, maybe. I'm sorry."

Ella felt half relieved and half left out. She'd had enough truth and drama recently, but she was also sick of secrets. But her main worry was that her mom looked sadder than she'd ever seen her. How could she help her if she didn't know what was going on?

"Have you called Uncle Dub? Maybe he can help."

Her eyes got all glassy. "It'd be great to call him with good news instead, wouldn't it?"

"Sure. But it's okay. He's your brother." And not the kind of lying rat fink hers was.

Her mom nodded, then turned to the window again. Ella sat there awhile, to keep her company.

Finally her mom got up and they went to the kitchen to get some food.

CHAPTER THIRTY-FOUR

HELEN

When she came to she didn't know where she was, but her head hurt so bad she didn't care. Like someone held a splitting wedge along her brow and was smacking it with a sledge-hammer. She closed her eyes again and hoped to God she would die.

Someone said her name and shook her. She squinted and saw a black man in a white coat. She tried to tell him to leave her alone, but her mouth was too dry to work. Reaching up to push his arms off her, she got tangled in something—tubes or wires—and gave up. Too weak to put up a fight and too numb to care.

Sleep was all she wanted but they wouldn't let her. Cruel, that's what it was. But she'd messed it up, got greedy with the vodka and then forgot about taking the rest of the pills. This was her punishment, lying in this bed, tubes stuck in her body, head split in two, being shook awake by a black man who knew her name but not a blessed thing about her. He was making it his job to keep her on this earth, as if he was her creator and the decision was his. She cursed him.

. . .

A woman bent over her and pulled the tube out of her nose, then stuck a straw in her mouth. The water tasted like tin. Her head was better, meaning someone was banging it against the floor instead of cutting it in half.

Hours later, Tom appeared at the foot of the bed. She asked him where Geneva was and he said she wasn't feeling well.

"Same here."

He didn't smile, but said he might be back later, depending on how the visit with the psychologist went.

This was news to her. "They want to see if I'm crazy?"

He glanced at the nurse who was checking Helen's drip. "Something like that."

"Tell them the truth and save them a trip, then."

"It's not funny, Helen."

"Who's joking?"

He stared at her, like he was thinking about saying one thing, then changed his mind. "Helen, did it ever occur to you that Geneva might need you?"

Now the nurse was staring at her, too. "She hasn't needed anything from me since she was out of diapers."

"I think you're wrong."

And he walked out without another word.

. . .

The nurse brought her a tray and told her the food would help her nausea. She ate and watched TV while she waited for the psychologist. Her headache had eased some, and wasn't much worse than an ordinary hangover. Must have been the oxygen and medication and whatnot they'd been pumping into her. That suited her fine. If she was going to live, she didn't want a darn headache.

She had already decided there was no point in fighting the system. What choice did she have? Stay here in the hospital? Volunteer for the mental ward? She didn't have a clear plan, but that was no different from any other day in the last thirty years. She could live with it until she decided not to.

Meanwhile she wanted out. Hospitals brought nothing but bad memories. Most people felt the same, she supposed, but she had her own particular reasons. Hospitals were more alike than they were different, and that was the problem. The week at the Good Samaritan after she crashed her car was bad, but the pain meds had dulled things. Now she was sober—or close enough to it—and everything about this room reminded her of ten days she would give her life to forget.

*   *   *

Paris had been at college six weeks and Eustace drank hard for all of it. In the middle of October he was playing golf—and drinking—and caught a heel in a divot. Went ass over teakettle into a bunker. Lay there for a good long time, the men at the club said, just staring at the sky. Wasn't until he finally decided to get up that he figured something wasn't right with his arm. Pointed in an odd direction.

His shoulder broke in two places, but he didn't take to being laid up, and insisted on carrying on as usual. He went to the mayor's office every day, and didn't let up on his socializing—or his drinking. Refusing to rest didn't help him heal, and he experienced considerable pain, especially at night. He thrashed something fierce and was up and down like a fiddler's elbow all night long. Desperate for sleep, Helen went downstairs and lay on the couch. She tried Paris's room once but it gave her the willies.

Between missing Paris, the encumbrance of the sling, and lack of sleep, Eustace was in a foul mood. The children gave him a wide berth and Helen didn't talk to him unless she had to. The last two weeks of October and the beginning of November went like that. Helen didn't know what was worse, Eustace's present condition, or what'd be going on when Paris came home for Thanksgiving.

One cold November morning, Helen picked up the paper from the front walk and sat down to read it before anyone else got up. That was the one advantage of sleeping on the couch—having a fresh paper all to herself before the others made a hash of it. She scanned the headlines for a story that struck her fancy. On page three she found one: RALEIGH MAN DIES OF TYLENOL OVERDOSE. Just last week she'd bought another bottle of Tylenol from Grether's. The doctor had given Eustace some medicine with codeine, but he objected to the way it hung in his head in the morning, so the first week after he broke his shoulder, he switched to plain old Tylenol.

Turns out the Raleigh man had a bad back. He'd been on the medicine for a while, but didn't take any more than what the label said he could, except for the night before he died, when he took maybe three times that. He didn't know he'd done it to himself. By the time the doctors figured out he didn't have the stomach flu, it'd beat down his liver and he was a goner.

She read the article again, then folded up the paper and hid it at the bottom of the pile of newspapers in the pantry. Then she put away the bedclothes in the living room, and returned to the kitchen to make the coffee.

• • •

She hadn't realized until she read the article how much she wanted to kill him. For a year or more she'd fantasized about him having a fatal accident—getting shot while hunting or during a robbery, or struck by lightning—but she hadn't considered taking matters into her own hands. Not seriously. Maybe all those murder mysteries she read gave her the notion that no one ever got away with it. There were too many nosy old ladies and clever detectives, and too many ways to get caught. She had three children aside from Paris to consider, two of them not even teenagers, and it wouldn't be fair to leave them virtually orphans. They'd go to Eustace's family, and she couldn't tolerate that.

But now she had a method. And the beauty of it was, with very little help from her, Eustace could do it to himself. That seemed right to her, because he'd brought it on himself, defying laws of man and nature both, and perpetrated this abomination upon her daughter. Paris might have been willing, but Helen lay that at his feet as well. A duckling will follow whatever it sees when it first opens its eyes, follow it straight off a cliff or right through the gates of hell. With hindsight, Helen wished she'd seen it and put a stop to it earlier. It was like a white bedsheet that grayed over time. One day you put it next to a clean one and can't believe you let the old dingy sheet next to your skin. She would live with the result of her blindness to her dying day; that was a cold fact.

But what was done was done. Putting a stop to Eustace was all that was left.

The first thing she did was drive thirteen miles to Layton and buy Extra Strength Tylenol. Every little bit would count. She bought a pair of slacks from her favorite store there, so if anyone asked, that was the reason she'd gone.

Luckily Eustace sent her to get pills and water at night, even though he was up every couple of hours anyway. He liked company for his misery. She'd taken to keeping the Tylenol on the dresser, and filled a glass with water before she went to bed. When she handed him the pills, he tossed them in his mouth without looking, then took a long drink. Couldn't have been easier to give him an extra one or two every time. After a week of that, she ground some up and put it in his coffee, and added extra cream.

Wasn't even two weeks later he started complaining about his stomach.

"Must've been something you ate at the club," she said, and headed upstairs for the Alka Seltzer. She ground up three Tylenol, mixed it with orange juice, and dropped two tablets in and watched them fizz.

He made a face when he drank it.

"New flavor. Don't you care for it?"

Helen didn't want him running to the doctor until she'd finished with him. Knowing bourbon didn't do his liver any favors, she played her last card.

Paris called him from Durham frequently, but he couldn't easily call her in the dorm, as there was only one phone on each floor and Paris was likely as not to be out. To stop them from talking, Helen left the phone off the hook whenever she could, and answered it herself the rest of the time. If it was Paris, she'd say Eustace was out, or lying down, then ask for a good time for him to call her back. Then she'd tell Eustace a different time.

She managed to stop them from talking for ten days—a record. During that time, she made sure the decanter stayed full and, on the nights he was home, joined him for a drink to help things along. When he groused about Paris "running around too much" and "forgetting her family," Helen topped off his drink. Once he was good and drunk, she added some Tylenol.

On the Saturday before Thanksgiving, he felt too poorly to attend a birthday party at the club for one of his golf partners.

"Let's have our own party, then."

She had Florence and Geneva put together some hors d'oeuvres and asked Dublin to pick out the music. Eustace felt right sorry for himself, and sat on the couch with his hand on his belly while the kids ate and danced. But he knocked back the bourbon the way she thought he would. He went to bed early, muttering drunkenly that he might have the flu. Helen followed him upstairs and gave him four Tylenol. He was too tight to notice. Then she went downstairs, turned down the music a bit, and had a cup of coffee.

At two o'clock in the morning, she woke Eustace up.

"You had a lot to drink." She held out four more pills and a glass of water. "Better take these."

"I already had some."

"No, you didn't. That was yesterday."

And he took them.

He stayed in bed half of Sunday—probably thinking it was a hangover, which it surely could have been—but woke up feeling dandy on Monday and set off to work. On Tuesday morning she heard him laughing on the phone to Paris and worried she hadn't given him enough. But that night he lay in bed groaning, then ran to the bathroom and vomited.

He'd planned to drive to Durham and bring Paris home for Thanksgiving, but he was sick as a dog and Helen couldn't see him leaving. Paris had to take a bus and didn't arrive until nearly midnight on Wednesday. When she saw her father in the morning, she wanted to take him to the doctor, but of course it was Thanksgiving.

"We'll take him tomorrow if he's not better," Helen said.

Needless to say he didn't have turkey and dressing with the rest of them.

His regular doctor's office was closed and Helen would've left it at that, but Paris insisted they go to the emergency room. They were short-staffed on account of the holiday and weren't looking at anyone too close if they didn't have a bone stuck in their throat or a bullet hole in their head. The nurse told them it was probably the flu and sent him home.

On Sunday morning Helen came upstairs from sleeping on the couch. Eustace was lying on his back, his face as yellow as a sunflower.

* * *

The blood tests showed plain and clear he'd taken far too much Tylenol. When the doctor at the emergency ward asked him about it, he admitted he'd taken a lot, but didn't know how much was too much. He'd have asked Eustace more questions, but Eustace took to moaning terribly. The newspaper article didn't mention that dying of liver failure was painful, but it began to look that way.

Paris was there, too, and wailed like a banshee when the doctor said there wasn't much they could do. Either he would live or he wouldn't, and probably he wouldn't. The doctor might have had questions for Helen, but she had her daughter to comfort.

She went to the hospital every day, taking turns with Paris when Geneva and Dublin needed minding at home. Florence came a few times, too, but didn't stay long. She couldn't bear the sight of her daddy's face—a terrible yellow-gray color, twisted up in pain. Helen refused to let the little ones visit at all. She couldn't see it would do them any good, and Paris provided all the bedside drama Helen could take. Watching Eustace wore on her, too. Day after day, playacting the loving wife terrified of losing her cherished husband, wringing her hands at his bedside, all the while wishing and praying he would hurry up and die.

If the doctors weren't particularly suspicious of the cause of Eustace's death, Paris was. Helen had expected it and stuck with her plan: simple denial. She'd been careful not to leave any ground-up pills or extra bottles around, so she knew Paris would be hard put to do anything more than speculate.

"How could he take so many pills without you knowing about it?"

"I don't watch him every minute. I figured he could read a label as well as the next person."

"But so many!"

"He drank a lot after you left, Paris. Maybe he lost count."

Guilt ran across her face, then, but she didn't back down. Not Paris. "You should've been taking care of him."

Helen knew her lines. "And you can't know how sorry I am that I didn't know what was happening. He's my husband, after all. We all thought he had the flu."

But then, after he'd been in the hospital five days, Helen's mind shifted. Maybe she relaxed her defenses a little, knowing she'd done what she set out to do. Maybe he was different now, no longer a perverted monster, but a middle-aged man in a hospital gown dying a slow, painful death. Under the fluorescent lights, surrounded by cold, hard tile, and machines with dials and tubes, where even the bed—meant to be a place of rest—had levers and wheels and rails, Eustace was vulnerable, not just because she had made him so, but because he was flesh and blood, same as everyone else.

She got to doubting herself a little. She thought back to what she had seen between him and Paris—the dancing, the tickling, the glances—and replayed the scenes again and again, as if her memory might be trying to sneak a truth by her. Of course, it wasn't the first time she'd had these recollections, but this was another thing entirely. This was reviewing the evidence in front of the jury of her conscience.

As Eustace moaned and twisted up the sheets, she saw Louisa standing at the door, then running away, and tried to remember exactly how her face had looked, and what she had said. Who said Paris's name? Had she? Or was it Louisa? She couldn't now recall anything Louisa said pointing directly at Eustace, aside from that he had fired her. Was it possible Helen had been so desperate to confirm her suspicions about her husband that she'd misunderstood Louisa? While she'd been poisoning him, she'd only thought about ways to get more pills in him. It was a game. Now that the game was over, and she was staring at the ugly consequences of her victory, her confidence wavered.

She wished she could ask Eustace what he had done, because surely he knew he was dying, and dying, like love, had a tendency to pull the truth out of folks. But the time for confession had passed, because he was delirious now, and didn't even know who she was.

. . .

The psychologist didn't appear to be more than twenty-five years old, and Helen doubted anyone that wet behind the ears could understand the first thing about a woman her age. But she had to give her credit. After a few questions about Helen's circumstances, she jumped right in.

"Did you try to kill yourself, Mrs. Riley?"

"There were pills left, so there's your answer."

"So you haven't been feeling depressed?"

"I've had better days."

"Are you referring to yesterday, or to a longer period?"

"I haven't much cared for going around on a walker and depending on people. I'm used to my independence." Helen didn't think she'd said anything interesting but the psychologist scribbled on her pad.

"And how much do you drink on an average day?"

"Lately, not as much as I'd like. But yesterday, maybe a bit too much."

"And the pills you took?"

"I bruised my hip the other day, and it was aching. I see now they don't go so well together."

The psychologist smiled a little and handed her a stack of brochures. The one on the top had a picture of a man with his arm around a woman. It read: Addiction Services. "I'll leave these with you. I hope your circumstances improve, Mrs. Riley, and, whatever happens, you think about your relationship to alcohol."

She'd think about it, all right. And then have a drink to it.

❧

CHAPTER THIRTY-FIVE

GENEVA

Geneva placed Paris's letter on the scanner and pushed a button to increase the contrast. She wrote an email to Dublin saying she had found the letter last night but only read it this morning, and asked him to call her once he'd read it. After checking to ensure the document was legible, she attached it. Her finger hovered over the Send button; the letter didn't belong to her and, while she had found it by accident, she was sharing it deliberately.

"Oh, well," she said, and hit Send.

Immediately she regretted it. She pictured him opening the email during a lull at work and having to rein in his reaction. So he wouldn't be blindsided, she called him. When he didn't answer, she sent him a text: Open my email in private only. Love, G.

Not knowing what else to do while she waited for him to call, she made the bed and changed the towels in the bathroom. Reluctantly, she entered Charlie's bedroom and surveyed the scene. The paramedics had knocked over the bedside table, and the bed was in disarray, but it wasn't the disaster she had imagined. Knowing her mother might be coming home later today, Geneva righted the table, wiped up the spilled water, and stripped the bed. She stopped in the kitchen on her way to the laundry and poured the last of the vodka down the drain.

Tom had not returned from dropping Charlie at school. Geneva told Ella, who was watching TV, she was taking Diesel for a walk.

"Want me to come?"

"No, that's okay. But if Dublin calls, ask him to try my cell."

. . .

The unmarked footpath lay beyond the blackberry brambles hugging the rear wall of the barn. Geneva nudged Diesel to the right, away from town, toward the creek and, eventually, the hills. The sun had no fog to burn that morning and bore down on the path where the arching branches allowed. Geneva called to Diesel to wait while she took off her jacket and tied it around her waist.

She wished she'd never seen the letter. The day should have begun here. This walk in the woods, her dog trotting ahead, sniffing the air, nosing the dew-laden bushes. This perfect June morning, the bees away from their hive and the possibility of the first larkspur or paintbrush around every corner. If she hadn't read the letter, she would be who she had been a month ago—a reasonably happy woman with an alcoholic mother and an estranged sister. Although imperfect, that person could enjoy such a morning.

How she envied Diesel. He could love someone without knowing them.

It occurred to her she didn't have to tell Dublin. She would stick her head back in the sand if she could, so why wouldn't she spare him? Sending the email had been a selfish move, as if sharing the terrible news would halve its impact. But they'd vowed nothing would come between them. If she hadn't told him, would the secret have moved them apart?

And she hadn't decided whether to tell Florence. At least Dublin could weigh in on that. Maybe Florence already knew, although over the phone she had talked matter-of-factly about the rivalry between Paris and their mother. If Florence could manage that sort of duplicity, Geneva didn't know her at all.

But she did know her mother had failed to protect her eldest daughter from her husband. Paris was undoubtedly a strange child, but she was nevertheless a child. Incest was not a gray area. Why didn't her mother shield her? Did she not find out until after Eustace died? Was it, then, shame that drove her to drink?

Diesel barked at a squirrel running up the path. She pushed the questions away and, turning for home, called Diesel to her.

A few minutes later, her phone vibrated in her pocket. Dublin.

"Hi. Did you get my email?"

"Yup. It just keeps getting better, doesn't it?"

His calm tone surprised her. "Did you read the letter?"

"Yeah, it's creepy, all right. But I'm not sure what it means."

"I thought it was pretty clear."

"What's clear to me is both Mom and Paris are completely batshit."

"I'm confused. Did you read it carefully?"

"I'm a good reader. Especially in English. I know some of it is suggestive, and I get why you're upset, but you've got to consider the source."

"Suggestive? What else could 'unnatural desires' mean?"

"I don't know. Dad's need for attention?"

"Then why use the word 'victim'? And Tom had the same reaction as I did."

"Look. I'm not saying it's completely impossible Dad was an abusive pervert. All I'm saying is that the letter isn't exactly a smoking gun."

"You're right. It doesn't prove anything. Still."

"Are you going to ask Mom about it?"

"I think so. How could I not?"

"I get it. The toothpaste is hard to get back into the tube, and inquiring minds want to know, but haven't you had enough drama for a while?"

"For a lifetime. But as much as I'd like to, I can't pretend I didn't read the letter."

"It's so implausible, Ginny. Think about it. Wouldn't someone else have known? Florence or Louisa, for instance? And we know Paris is weird. Can't you imagine her making up stuff about her and Dad just to get Mom's goat?"

"Well, I suppose . . ."

". . . and can't you imagine Mom tweaking reality a teensy weensy bit just to put a perverted spin on what was, in all likelihood, only a mildly twisted father-daughter relationship?"

Geneva sighed deeply. "She was jealous of Paris."

"Exactly. But the important thing, kiddo, is for you not to get all involved in it. I'm not going to. Join me over here in the I-don't-give-a-fuck-what-those-sorry-Southern-bastards-were-up-to part of the room. Paris is who she is and Mom is, God help us, who she is, and that's that."

"I'll give it some thought."

"It's what you do best, you little brainiac. Any word on Mom?"

"Nothing new. I think that means she's alive."

"Well, there you go. And once she's in L.A. again, and you don't have to see her every day, you'll say that as if it's a good thing."

. . .

Geneva did as she promised. She contemplated whether she could ignore Paris's letter. She pictured engaging in her normal, every-day activities—swimming, going to work, eating dinner with Tom and the kids—unsure who her father really was. Could she wall off the idea he might have been a monster, or at least a very sick individual, and live her life as before? She imagined turning the pages of the photo album, seeing his face, seeing Paris. A sour taste climbed into her throat.

Until she spoke with Dublin she had been certain of what the letter revealed. Was the doubt she now felt only wishful thinking, the same sort of denial that allowed her to turn a blind eye to her intuitions about Charlie and her mother's recent drinking? Her brother's attitude had a pragmatic what's-done-is-done appeal, but she wasn't sure she could adopt it and live with herself.

She turned the question on its head and asked why she shouldn't pursue the truth, whatever it turned out to be. She would have to ask her mother some hard questions, but it wasn't as if their relationship could deteriorate much further. She'd have no guarantee of straight answers, but so what?

As she turned off the trail and watched Diesel lope around the corner toward the driveway, another pebble shook loose in her mind. Florence had said their mother began drinking heavily after their father's death. If her father had been molesting Paris, wouldn't his death have come as a relief? Maybe Dublin was right, and the bad blood between her mother and Paris resulted solely from a poisonous mixture of jealousy and mental instability.

She came around the side of the barn. Tom stood in the drive, stroking Diesel, and looked up at her with concern.

"Hey. How're you holding up?"

"I'm okay."

"The hospital called. Your mom passed the psych exam."

"I'm not surprised. It's not a high bar. All they want to do is make sure she's not an immediate danger to herself."

"And they're releasing her around five."

They went inside. Several covered platters and plastic food containers lined the counter, including a jar of tomato sauce.

"Oh," Tom said, "Juliana stopped by. She said everyone sends their love and hopes your mom feels better."

"How did they know?"

He smiled. "They just do."

·   ·   ·

Tom and Geneva brought Helen home that night. She thanked them for not "tossing her out on the street" and went straight to bed. Early the next morning Geneva went to work, having called in all her favors over the last three days. Because it was Saturday, the clinic was swamped with visits that pet owners had put off during the workweek. Stan had left her a note, saying he hoped her mother was feeling better. Geneva hadn't told him the reason for Helen's hospitalization, and she appreciated that he hadn't asked.

She sutured the face of a cat that had gotten into a fight, spayed a young terrier, and monitored the animals her colleagues had treated yesterday and kept overnight. In her few free moments, she sorted through the backlog of emails and lab results, and made several phone calls to clients. Finally, she wrote notes to the staff thanking them for stepping up in her absence. She walked out to her car, breathing deeply for the first time in days. She loved her job most days, but today's hectic schedule was a godsend.

She drove slowly on her way home, collecting her thoughts. Once there, she stopped at the barn to say hello to Tom and Ella, and checked in with Charlie, perched at the kitchen counter with an open history book and a bag of popcorn.

"Hey, Momster. Guess what."

"After this week, do I want to know?"

He grinned sheepishly. "Yeah. It's all good. You know the Battle of the Bands? We won!"

Geneva paused, stymied by the moral arithmetic. "That's fine, Charlie. But if there was anything resembling a prize, your sister should get a cut."

"Nope. Just fame and glory."

"Have you seen Nana?"

He cocked his thumb toward the back door. "I've been keeping an eye on her for you."

Her mother sat on a chaise on the lawn, flipping through a magazine.

"How are you feeling?"

"Better. The sun feels nice."

"Yes, not a trace of fog today." She pulled up a chair. "Mom, I want to talk."

"Am I going to want to hear it?"

"Probably not." Her mother frowned but didn't protest. "There was an old letter to you from Paris on the bed last night. I read it."

"Well, now we know where Charlie gets his snoopiness." She lifted her magazine and turned the page.

"I'm sorry. But I can't pretend I didn't." Geneva leaned forward, elbows on her knees. "What happened between Daddy and Paris, Mom?"

She didn't look up. "What do you think?"

"Please just tell me."

"How is it your business?"

"He was my father. I want to know the truth about him."

Her mother laid her hand on the page as if it were a Bible, and looked her daughter in the eye. "There isn't one truth about anybody. You ought to know that by now."

Strangely, this felt like progress. "Did you see something?"

"I thought I did."

Geneva's stomach clenched. Sweat broke out on her palms. She willed herself to think, to ask the right questions. "That must've been terrible. I'm sure you wanted to stop it."

"I did try." She looked into the distance. "I got her that dog."

Argus. Why hadn't it occurred to her earlier how odd it was to give the first family dog to a sixteen-year-old? Helen returned to her magazine.

"Did you talk to Paris about it?"

"Oh, my." She let out a bitter laugh. "I sure tried to. Laughed in my face and said I was jealous."

Geneva imagined them sitting at the kitchen table, her mother's face serious and drawn, Paris haughty and smiling. "Obviously you didn't go to the authorities because no one would believe you—you weren't a hundred percent sure yourself—and Paris wasn't going to point a finger at Daddy."

Her mother appeared to be absorbed in an article on begonias, but Geneva thought she detected a slight nod.

"So all you could do was shield Florence." She swallowed hard to stem her tears. "And me?"

Helen closed the magazine, leaned in, and patted her daughter's knee. "I'm starving. That hospital food was garbage. Why don't we see what all Juliana brought us?"

Geneva got up and positioned her mother's walker in front of her, then followed her across the lawn to the back steps.

"You're limping a lot less."

"One step at a time."

Geneva boiled water for the pasta while Tom heated the sauce and meatballs. Juliana had included a container of freshly grated parmesan, a large green salad, garlic bread and her famous mud pie.

When they sat down to eat, everyone kept the conversation light, nerves jangled from the events of the last few days.

"Juliana was really sweet to do this for us," Geneva said.

"Her sauce is the best," Charlie said.

Ella picked up her third piece of garlic bread. "My favorite, right here."

Helen cut a meatball with the side of her fork and chewed

thoughtfully. "I believe these are the tastiest meatballs I've ever had, next to Louisa's."

Geneva's forkful of salad hovered in the air as she met her mother's gaze. Helen stopped chewing. Meatballs. The Christmas party. Geneva had put on her new red velvet dress and run downstairs to the kitchen to ask Louisa to put up her hair. Louisa had a knack for taming her thick dark waves. Her mother was taking a tray of meatballs out of the oven. She moved quickly and her face was flushed. "Where's Louisa?"

"She's not here."

"How come? She said yesterday she'd do my hair!"

Her mother yanked off the oven mitts and tossed them on the counter. "Your hair's the least of my concerns." She strode across to the refrigerator and Geneva jumped out of the way. "Don't get underfoot."

"But where is she?"

"How should I know? Your father's fired her and fifty people are coming through that door in an hour. Do something with your hair, then come down and give me a hand."

She hadn't seen Louisa since.

Across the dining table, Helen turned back to her plate. Geneva remembered Dublin postulating that if their father had molested Paris, Louisa would probably have known, and thought it a remarkable coincidence her mother had mentioned her on this particular day.

CHAPTER THIRTY-SIX

HELEN

Eustace took his time dying, as if he meant to punish her. Didn't matter he didn't know she was there. A week after he'd been admitted to the hospital, he mumbled what she took to be his last words. She wasn't there every minute, and couldn't be 100 percent certain he didn't say anything else, but from what she could tell, that was it. His lips parted, gray and cracked, and he puffed it out, like a weak kiss: "Paris."

She snatched up her handbag and left, nearly colliding with the nurse in the hallway. She desperately wanted to get revenge for that, but there was nothing she could do to a man nearly dead. A gesture would have been a start, but everything that came to mind—ramming her car into his, telling his parents what a monster they'd created, boycotting his funeral—only left her exposed.

She hoped she would feel better once the bastard was good and dead.

Paris was with him when his body followed the lead of his liver and quit for good. Helen expected her to carry on something fierce, but when she came home from the hospital and let her mother know he was gone, she was unnaturally calm.

"I'll pack now. I'm leaving in the morning."

"But what about the funeral?"

"That's a performance you can manage without me. I've said good-bye to Daddy."

She left in a hurry, with only a quick hug for Florence. Helen asked her to say good-bye to Geneva and Dublin before she left.

"I can't find them, and I'll miss my bus."

After the folks from the funeral parlor left, Helen went looking. She found them huddled at the bottom of their closet clinging to each other like baby monkeys, and wondered what in God's name she had done.

*   *   *

Because Eustace had been the mayor, Helen was required to grieve in the public eye more than she'd have preferred. She couldn't step out the front door without running into someone leaving a bouquet or a note. The mayor's office let a few days go by, then consulted her concerning each and every detail of the elaborate memorial service a man of Eustace's stature deserved. She pleaded overwhelming grief and referred them to Eustace's family, whom she knew would be only too happy to oblige. Luckily for Helen, people saw what they expected to see. She was remorseful for killing her children's daddy—and the man she had once loved— without absolute proof of his guilt, and feared she might be found out. But to the people of Aliceville, she was shocked and heartbroken.

Every day for a week, dozens of letters of condolence tumbled through the mail slot. She dutifully opened and read each one, then made a check next to the name in her address book or, if it was a business colleague, Eustace's. Using ivory cards bordered with black she had printed for the occasion, she penned her replies in a timely manner, making special note of gifts of flowers or food. Her handwriting was a bit shaky, but they'd expect that from a young widow.

One note was conspicuous in its absence: Louisa's. Desperate as Helen was to ask Louisa what she had witnessed, she knew better than to stick her neck out. Asking Louisa meant she was suspicious of Eustace and that gave her motive to kill him. If she had to bet, she'd wager Louisa wouldn't turn her in for meting out justice, but she wasn't taking any chances. She knew better than anyone a moral compass was a wobbly instrument.

. . .

After the trip to the hospital, Helen settled back in at Geneva's house, but she didn't feel settled. If the psychologist at the hospital had known how confused she was, she might not have let her go. Helen couldn't sort out her feelings, only that she was frightened. She had told the psychologist she hadn't tried to kill herself because it was the easiest thing to say. In truth, she wasn't certain. Or maybe she didn't care. But that didn't seem right somehow, because if she didn't care whether she lived or died, why was she so scared?

Lying in that hospital bed next to the memories of Eustace's demise didn't help matters. All the questions she'd never laid to rest were eating away at her, like rats in the dark. Whoever said time heals all wounds was full of baloney, and never had a daughter like Geneva, who wouldn't let the past rest. No, that girl had to dig up the yard until she found every single bone buried deep and long since picked clean. She was on a foolish mission to save them all. But, as Helen had discovered, while you were digging and inspecting and putting the pieces together, the past could eat you up and spit you out. Especially if you had plenty to hide.

She wondered about the pills she'd collected, which she'd told herself were emergency rations when booze got scarce. And the gun, which she'd told herself was for self-protection. Since she left the hospital, another thought had occurred to her: Both were self-protection, as in protection against herself, against the threat of living a minute more of her life. She'd been spending thirty years with her hand on the door handle. If things got really bad, she could leave.

Now that she saw what she'd been doing, she was sadder than ever. Because people with one hand on the door handle aren't living. They're biding their time, weighing each moment, daring it to be the one that tips the scales and sends them out of this life for good.

The gun and the pills and the vodka made a disgrace of hope. Helen had enough sense to see that. Problem was, she couldn't see any way around it. The past wasn't a guest you could ask to leave when you tired of its company. No, the past put up its feet and meant to stay.

CHAPTER THIRTY-SEVEN

GENEVA

While Ella and Charlie put away what remained of Juliana's Italian feast, Geneva googled Louisa. She didn't have to pause to remember her last name. When she was little, she made a birthday card for Louisa each year, and insisted on writing her full name on the outside, even though her mother said "Louisa" or "Miss Louisa" was sufficient. Geneva thought both names made the card more professional.

The unusual spelling of Louisa's last name—McCutchion—made her easy to find. Geneva was not surprised Louisa still lived near Aliceville, at an address she quickly determined was an assisted living facility. She didn't know Louisa's exact age, but she was older than Helen by at least ten years, maybe twenty. Even if Louisa had known about Paris and her father, her memory might be failing or she might not be willing to tell Geneva, a virtual stranger. Still, her instincts told her an inquiry was worth a shot. She sent an email to the contact listed on the facility's Web site, explaining who she was, and asked if Louisa could email or phone her.

* * *

The next day, Geneva awoke to a dawn muted by heavy clouds. Tom's pillow covered his head. She crept out of bed, pulled on a fleece jacket, and let Diesel into the backyard, where he sniffed the moist air for clues left by nighttime intruders into his domain.

Geneva retrieved her laptop from her bag by the front door and crossed to the living room couch. She scanned the list of new emails, all work-related except the last from grannymccutchion@gmail. com, sent that morning. She held her breath and clicked it open.

> Dearest Geneva,
>
> How happy I was to get your message after all these years! Naturally, I'm itching to talk to you. I use Skype to keep up with my grandchildren. (God blessed me with nine little angels.) I'd love to see your face—I can picture you as a little girl before me now—so please find me there. I'm granny.mccutchion.
>
> Hope to see you soon, dear one.
>
> Louisa

Geneva let Diesel inside and carried her laptop to the barn for privacy. She stood at the workbench and sent a request to Louisa's Skype account. While she waited for her to accept, she selected a handful of family photos and forwarded them to Louisa, knowing she would ask. Ten minutes later, the video call notice chimed. She clicked Accept, and Louisa appeared. Her short hair had turned white and her face was lined, but when she smiled Geneva would have known her anywhere.

"Look at you!" Louisa said.

They talked for a while. Geneva walked her through the photos of her family. As Louisa inquired about her husband and children, she felt a stab of regret for not including this woman in her life. Louisa had held her when she was ill, read her to sleep, and played Go Fish with her for hours at a time.

"What about Dublin, and your sisters?"

"If you don't mind waiting a minute, I'll send another batch of photos."

"Mind? I loved all of you like family."

She showed her Dublin's family, and Florence and Renaldo engaged in various sporting activities. Louisa chuckled. "Same as always." The last photo was of Geneva, Dublin, and Paris, taken by Whit at the Paleolithic Garden in L.A. the previous Tuesday. Louisa frowned as she examined the photo.

"We don't see Paris often," Geneva said.

"Don't you?"

"No." She waited for Louisa to turn back to the camera. When she did, her face was soft. "I was hoping you might know why. My mother and Paris haven't spoken in thirty years. My mother told me she suspected something, well, something terrible was going on between Paris and my father."

Louisa leaned back in her chair and gazed away. "I expected there was a reason you decided to look for me, after all this time."

"I don't mean to upset you. I know it's not right, bringing this up out of the blue. I'm sorry."

Louisa looked at the screen, presumably at the photo of Paris. "How is your mama?"

"Not so well, I'm afraid. She drinks too much. Last month she got into a serious car accident."

"That's a shame, a real shame. I always liked your mama. She's not fifteen years younger, but she was a daughter to me."

Geneva was surprised. "Then why didn't you stay in touch?"

"I couldn't say. I more or less expected to hear from her after your daddy died. He fired me, you know."

The barn was cool, but she felt a trickle of sweat run down her spine. "Why? Can you tell me?"

Louisa sighed. "All this time I thought your mama knew what he'd done. I reckoned she kept away from me because she didn't want reminding of it."

The bottom dropped out of Geneva's stomach, and her hand felt slick against the surface of the bench. She wanted to run for the door, but willed herself to stay. Louisa's face was full of concern.

"Oh, you poor thing. I know you loved your daddy. But you came here asking questions, so I figured you wanted answers."

"I did. I do." She rolled her shoulders up and back, and exhaled. "Louisa, if you saw anything, can you tell me?"

"I haven't told a soul."

"I don't want to know for me. I want to know for my mother."

"If you're sure."

Geneva nodded.

She shifted in her chair. "Well, it was the day before the Christmas party and your mama was in town, fetching the last few things. Your daddy asked Florence to take you and Dublin to the park, to keep you two out of the way. I'd gone around the back of the house with the trash and seen the back door wasn't shut properly. Figured it was Dublin, as that boy never could shut a door, even if you paid him.

"So I come through the back, and remembered I hadn't ironed Paris's dress like I was supposed to, so I went to get it. Of course, I usually knocked if a door was closed, but my head was spinning with all the things I still had to do before I left. It was my husband's birthday that day, and family was coming over, so you might say I was preoccupied. Anyway, the door wasn't locked—couldn't have been because it used to be the maid's room and they never had locks on them—and I went straight in."

Geneva was staring out the window beside the barn door. Louisa said, "You all right?"

"Yes. Please go on."

"I'm not telling anything I don't need to. I just want to make sure you know that I know what I saw. And there was no doubt about it. Not in the act, but Paris had her clothes off. She pulled the sheet over herself in a hurry, but didn't even blush." Louisa shook her head in dismay.

"And my father?"

"Had his hands on her, is all I'm saying. I'm not painting pictures for you. Then he looked me straight in the eye, and I was more afraid than I've ever been in my life, before or since."

Geneva stared at Louisa and saw the fear alive in her face. "What did he say?"

"He said if I breathed a word, he would ruin me. Not just me, my whole family. I believed him, too."

"What could he do?"

She lifted her hands as if the answer was obvious. "He ran that town, and his family ran the county. What couldn't he do?" She shook her head. "Didn't matter anyway. Because of Paris. She stared me down—the girl I helped raise—and said no one would believe me over her. When she said it, I knew it was God's honest truth.

"Lord knows I wanted to help her, but I couldn't see how. I suppose your mama was in the same position. Terrible as it was, I figured in a few months she'd be off to college, and it'd all be over."

Geneva's mouth went dry. Her gaze moved from Louisa to the far wall lined with oak cabinets. The grooved fronts shimmered, like a mirage. Time lurched backward for an instant, then jumped forward again, leaving her queasy.

Louisa continued. "Then, of course, your daddy died, and it was."

.   .   .

Tom and Geneva had set aside time for later that day to discuss what to do about Charlie's and Ella's transgressions. After everyone had showered and eaten, they went to their bedroom and closed the door. She told Tom what Louisa had said.

"So our take on the letter was right after all," Tom said.

"Unfortunately."

"It must have been hard to hear her talk about it."

"It was, and hard for her to tell me. But I was prepared for it. Mostly."

"Are you going to tell Helen?"

"I think so. At least she'll know she wasn't imagining it. But something's still bothering me."

"Really?" He grinned at her. "I thought all your detective work was done."

"I don't know. I have a feeling I still don't understand everything."

"I always have that feeling. I just go with it."

Geneva laughed a little. "Okay, let's talk about the kids."

After a long discussion, they decided Charlie would sell his purchases on eBay, or wherever he could get a good price, and give Helen the proceeds. Then he would have to earn the same amount over the summer and donate it to charity. They would take away his phone, Xbox, iPod and other toys, and require him to earn them back gradually. Ella would work to cover the truck repairs and missed SAT session. If she wanted to use a car during the summer, she'd have to do extra chores, including chauffeuring her brother. Finally, they would assess whether Charlie had in fact learned anything during the school year and arrange tutoring if necessary.

"They're going to be thrilled," Geneva said.

"Now, what about the possibility that Charlie's smoking pot?"

"Or Ella."

"Right. I did check his backpack and didn't find anything."

"Short of turning their rooms upside down or a home drug test, I guess all we can do is ask. And remind them of the consequences."

They left the bedroom and found Helen, Ella, and Charlie playing hearts in the living room.

Tom said, "Don't you two have finals starting tomorrow?"

"Study break," Ella said, scooping up an all-diamond hand.

"I swear she cheats," Charlie said.

"You can't cheat at hearts. Take it from me." Helen nodded toward the kitchen. "Juliana came by with more food."

"Why didn't anyone tell us she was here?"

Charlie said, "We would've, but when we said you were in the bedroom with the door closed, she said she'd catch you later." He raised his eyebrows theatrically.

Helen played a low heart, then held her cards to her chest. "I think Juliana brought supper again because she feels bad about that crazy dog of hers. Maybe she realizes now the only choice was to put it down."

Geneva wondered if this might be true. She inspected the containers on the counter: chicken curry, saffron rice, cucumber salad, and banana cream pie. If Juliana's guilt trip continued, they were all going to get fat. She opened the fridge and made space for the containers.

A creeping sensation ascended her spine. Unbidden, she heard the words her mother had said when she asked her what she had done to alienate Paris. *Not enough, and too much, all at the same time.* She saw the letter before her, and read the passage in which Paris noted the irony in her mother claiming to be a victim. Geneva's mind spun around and around like a flywheel. If not the victim, then the culprit. The perpetrator. The one who did the only thing she could to stop her husband, and the only thing Paris would never forgive.

She put him down.

The glass dish of cucumber salad slipped from her hand and smashed on the floor.

Tom was at her side. "Are you all right?"

"Yes." She closed the refrigerator, gripping the handle hard to steady herself. "What a mess."

Ella knelt behind her and picked up the shards.

"Don't cut yourself. I'll get a broom."

Tom gave her a worried look. "No, I'll take care of this. Why don't you lie down?"

"I do feel a little wobbly."

"Did you eat lunch?"

"No, I guess not."

"How about some cucumber salad?" Charlie said.

. . .

Geneva sat in the chair by the window, and finished the sandwich Ella had brought her. She put the plate on the floor. Rocking slowly, she watched a robin probe its way across the lawn.

She imagined being poor and sixteen, and falling in love with a tall, confident man from an important family. She imagined marrying him, and being afraid. She imagined easily her joy at the birth of her first child.

She imagined three more children, then the first again, becoming her husband's favorite. She imagined the first pinch of jealousy, then the growing concern, then the disheartening thought that because her concern was unfounded, she must be mad.

She imagined wanting to tell someone, but having no one to tell and nothing to tell them. She imagined appealing to her daughter, perhaps more than once, and feeling the burn of shame and scorn. She imagined the inevitable confrontation with her husband, the cold power of the stone wall he erected, the sting of his hand on her face.

She imagined wishing it would end, then realizing it would not, and fearing in either case it would begin again with another daughter she had given him. And another.

She imagined hoping he would die, then praying.

She imagined an opportunity. And she imagined taking it.

. . .

She found Tom alone in the barn, running his hand over a baluster carved with vines. He did this, she knew, not only to detect rough spots, but to feel how the design melded with the grain of the wood. The gesture was at once sensual and intellectual. She waited at the door until he set the piece down and beckoned her inside.

"I didn't mean to interrupt."

"That's okay. You look better."

"Yes. Remember I said a piece was still missing? I found it."

"Tell me."

She brushed the dog hair off Ella's chair, and sank into it. Tom pulled over a crate.

"First, I'm really sorry about what a disruptive mess our lives have been recently. I know it's not my fault—at least not entirely—but I'm still sorry."

"Hey. It's educational."

She smiled. "And *challenging*. Wasn't that the word all the child-care books used to call the terrifying stuff?"

"Yeah, we've both been challenged."

"And you've been incredible." She took his hands. "Really."

He gave her an embarrassed grin.

"Which is why I hesitate to ask you this."

"Uh-oh."

"It's worse than that, actually. I'm going to ask you a question, and if you say yes, I'm going to tell you something else. The deal is that after I tell you, you can't change your first answer."

"You're not usually this complicated. Why the hoops?"

"I need them. Trust me. Deal?"

"Sure, I guess. I mean, yes."

Geneva exhaled. "I'd like my mother to continue living with us. Indefinitely. Would that be okay with you?"

Tom startled. "Whoa. That was unexpected. Why? Does this have to do with what Louisa told you?"

"Yes, and what else I figured out. So, do you have an answer, or do you need to think about it?"

"Sure. I mean, we'd have to make a more permanent bedroom for her, but sure." He studied her face. "Aren't you worried about her drinking and corrupting our kids and everything else?"

"I'm hoping she'll finally agree to join a program."

He nodded. "That'd be great. Okay, so why did I have to agree not to change my mind?"

"Because there's no statute of limitations on murder."

CHAPTER THIRTY-EIGHT

HELEN

Something was going on. Ever since Geneva told her she'd read Paris's letter, Helen had been waiting for the other shoe to drop. Sunday morning—yesterday—she'd woken up and there was Diesel gawking out the window. Helen gawked, too, and together they watched Geneva leave the barn with her computer. Came inside and acted mighty peculiar, too. Later, she dropped that dish and stayed holed up in her room the entire afternoon. Since then, Geneva and Tom seemed to have their heads together constantly. Helen couldn't be sure what they knew, but one thing was certain: They had a plan for her. And she didn't cotton to other people's plans.

She hadn't wanted to come up here—it wasn't her plan—but what choice did she have? She pictured herself in her apartment with all her old furniture and bad memories, and dread crept up her legs like a nest of spiders. She'd managed to live with what she'd done (and hadn't done) up until now because nobody knew about it, except Paris. She could pretend, if only for a wink or two, none of it had happened. When that failed, she could drink. She never worried about passing out and not waking up. She never thought that far ahead.

But lying in the hospital she'd been plagued with recollections of things she didn't want to recollect, making her want to run away from herself faster than ever. Worse, the tubes and needles and the look on everyone's face told her she'd come near to dying. God help her, as much as she struggled to call what she did living, dying scared her more. Death was a cold and endless place. At least life served vodka.

If she was on her own again, with nothing to stop her from carrying on as she always had, she was either going to drink too much or drink too little. Neither choice would save her, so she gave up on the notion. She'd never been much of one for decisions anyhow.

. . .

They didn't keep her in suspense long. Monday night after supper, the kids were in their rooms studying, and she was reading one of her mysteries in the living room. Honestly, it was more like skimming. She'd figured out halfway through who'd done it and how.

When Tom and Geneva sat on the couch and said they wanted to chat, she closed her book and steeled herself.

Geneva started. "Yesterday I spoke to Louisa."

"Louisa who?"

"McCutchion."

"In South Carolina?"

"Yes. I Skyped her. It's a video service over the Internet."

"I know what Skype is." She wondered why Geneva would hunt down Louisa, but didn't get far because her daughter was talking again.

"She's well. She misses you."

"Does she? Now that's nice. But why—"

"Mom, I asked her about Paris and Daddy. I thought she might know. And she did. She saw . . ." Geneva twiddled her fingers, then looked at Tom as if the right words were inscribed on his forehead.

He said, "She witnessed a terrible act. She was certain of it."

Helen breathed in sharply. Everything came into perfect focus, as if she were squinting hard. Thoughts raced around in her head, but she couldn't snag one of them. She should have felt relieved, but truth was, as long as she hadn't been absolutely sure, she hadn't had to accept that Eustace molested Paris. Maybe it was easier to believe she had killed an innocent man than it was to believe he'd done what he'd done.

Geneva spoke low. "You were right about him. He was a monster."

Helen stared at her daughter, the child who'd idolized her daddy the most, Paris notwithstanding. All these years she'd let Geneva have her daddy the way she remembered him. The fantasy more or less ended when she'd read the letter. Now it was over for good.

Helen nodded.

"And," Geneva said, "I know you killed him."

Helen's heart fluttered in her chest. She opened her mouth to deny it, but her daughter reached out and took her hand.

"It's okay. We know, and it's okay."

She didn't hear that right. Too many emotions flying through her head had balled up her hearing. They would throw her out. They might even call the police, who'd dig Eustace up. She'd worried about this for thirty-five years and now it was transpiring. Detectives probably had new methods—like on *CSI*—and would pin the blame on her. No murderer was ever careful enough. She'd been right not to talk to Louisa. You never knew which way people would fall until you went and pushed them.

"Helen," Tom said. "Did you hear us? It's all right. We know you didn't think there was any other way."

"I don't know what I would have done in your position," Geneva said. "Maybe the same thing."

Helen took this in. A lump formed in her throat. Her nose started to run, so she searched up her sleeve for a tissue. She couldn't see too well, but blinking wasn't doing a bit of good.

"Oh, Mom. Don't cry." Geneva scurried off and reappeared with a box of tissues.

Helen dabbed at her eyes and collected herself. The stuffiness in her head cleared. Her emotional reaction was only the shock of having her secrets trotted out into the open after so many years.

She appraised her daughter—her broad, confident shoulders and intelligent eyes—and knew Geneva was wrong. No way on God's green earth would she have let her husband carry on with her daughter. She'd have packed up those kids and left him behind without a moment's thought for the consequences. She wouldn't have put her faith in a German shepherd or counted on her husband's decency to reappear by magic. She would have fought for her children, and wouldn't have worried about landing on the streets or in the same filthy shack she'd cut her teeth in. No, her daughter would not have been a coward.

Geneva regarded her patiently. If her daughter had more to say, she wasn't sure about saying it. She looked at Tom, who nodded. Spit it out. "Tom and I want you to stay here for as long as you need to."

"You do? I had the feeling you were counting the days until you were rid of me."

He said, "Well, it hasn't always been easy, it's true. And the invitation does come with a condition."

"A condition?"

"Yes," Geneva said. "We want you to attend a program to help you stop drinking."

Helen blew her nose and sat up. "So, if I don't go to AA, you'll tell the police."

Geneva shook her head. "No, nothing like that. We just think you could use the support. You remember my colleague Stan? He's one of the founding members of the local group. I'll even go with you if you want."

She pictured walking into a room with a circle of folding chairs filled with strangers who wanted to trade drinking for honesty. "I'll think about it."

Her daughter paused, as if she had expected a different answer. "One more thing to think about. I've obviously told Tom, but I haven't said anything to Dublin or anyone else. Not about what you did. What you had to do."

"You keeping secrets from Dublin? How long is that going to last?"

"It's not my place to tell. I found the letter and went from there. But whether you tell anyone is up to you."

Helen imagined the conversation and frowned.

"For what it's worth," Tom said, "don't you think Dublin and

Florence—and pretty much any other reasonable person—would understand?"

"I never thought about whether they would or they wouldn't. I wasn't taking any chances."

Geneva's eyes filled with tears. Helen couldn't remember the last time she saw her daughter cry.

Geneva said, "But you have. You've taken big chances, all this time—drinking yourself sick, burning things, having accidents, pushing people away, pushing your children away, pushing away people who love you." She buried her face in her hands.

Tom put his arm around her, then addressed Helen. "This is your second chance. We're here to make sure you don't blow it."

Helen walked to the kitchen and filled a glass with water. Geneva's face was splotchy and her forehead was creased like she was thinking hard.

"Mom, you didn't use your walker. You're barely limping."

"Oh, that." She drank from the glass. "I figured you wouldn't throw me out until my leg was better. Just keeping my options open."

CHAPTER THIRTY-NINE

GENEVA

Two days later, Dublin took a personal day and flew up to San Francisco. Geneva met him at the airport. He bear-hugged her at the arrivals curb. "I had to pay big bucks for a last-minute flight. Worse, I had to beg Talia's mom to help with Jack. Do you have any idea what it's like to haggle with a geriatric Muscovite?"

"No."

"This better be good."

"I'm not saying anything."

He threw his bag onto the rear seat. "I want popcorn. And beer."

Helen had asked Geneva to be there when she told Dublin. "In case I forget something." She followed Geneva's suggestion, and started at the beginning, with her first suspicions about Eustace and Paris. As Geneva listened, she realized she wouldn't know if her mother omitted anything, as she had never heard the whole story.

For once, Dublin didn't interrupt with jokes, although he did glance at Geneva occasionally, as if expecting her to suddenly laugh and point to a hidden camera.

"And once he'd taken that many pills," Helen said, "it was only a matter of time."

Dublin stared at her, immobile.

"I'm sorry," she said.

He ran his hands through his hair and sighed loudly.

"Aren't you going to say anything?" She turned to Geneva. "Why isn't he saying anything?"

He shrugged. "I'm digesting. I feel like one of those pythons on *Animal Planet*. I've swallowed a bush pig, or a gazelle, or maybe an entire rhino, and I'm waiting for it to break down a little. Right now, it's an awfully big lump."

Helen nodded. "It's a very big lump."

"Part of me thinks Dad's been dead for so long, how he died doesn't really matter. Especially now I know what a sicko he was. I was prepared for that part. Ginny told you she sent me the letter, right?"

"Without my permission, if you can imagine."

"Seems like small potatoes, Mom. Next to incest. And murder."

She lifted her hands as if to say she wasn't in a position to judge.

Geneva asked Dublin, "You said 'part of you thinks it doesn't matter.' What about the other part?"

"The other part is hoping none of this is genetic."

Helen leaned back in her chair. "So you're not planning on turning me in?"

"Are you kidding? And ruin my good name?"

"You're a good son."

Geneva winced. Even after opening her house to her mother, she hadn't received such praise.

"And the only one you've got," Dublin said. "Remember that, in case I piss you off sometime. And just to be on the safe side, I'm not eating or drinking anything you give me ever again."

* * *

At dinner, Dublin asked Charlie what his plans were for the summer.

"I'm Dad's slave. We're refinishing an old dresser and bed for Nana's room, and making some bookshelves."

Geneva leaned forward to catch her mother's eye, but she was intent on slicing her pork chop. Helen hadn't accepted their offer to stay, but everyone was working on the assumption she would. She appeared content and Geneva was certain she hadn't had a drop of alcohol since being discharged from the hospital. She decided to give her mother until the end of the week, then ask again. The woman had been through an ordeal.

Tom said, "Charlie's making amends."

"At least you get your room back at the end of it," Dublin said.

"And I still have to work a paying job 'cause I owe money, too."

"Your pockets will be empty, Grasshopper, but your heart will be full."

"Who's Grasshopper?" Ella asked.

"It's a cocktail," Helen said. "Sweet and green."

"It's from an old TV show called *Kung Fu*," Geneva said. "The wise teacher called his student 'Grasshopper' because he couldn't hear the grasshoppers at his feet."

"I can see how that would make an exciting TV show," Charlie deadpanned.

Dublin stood and bowed. "Spoken like a true Grasshopper."

CHAPTER FORTY

ELLA

Her last final ended and junior year was officially over. No one was around when she and Charlie arrived home from school, so she went straight to her room, dumped her backpack, and grabbed the bear. On her way out she noticed the door to Charlie's room was closed and figured Nana was taking a nap. Charlie was halfway inside the refrigerator when she came into the kitchen.

"I've got something to show you, bro."

"What? You found your brain?" He peeked around the fridge door, a slice of pizza hanging from his mouth.

"You might put it that way." She pulled out the bag of weed, the papers, and the lighter.

"Whoa. Are we partying, sistah?"

She shook her head. "Charlie, it's time to get real. When we had that shitstorm over the gun and everything, I didn't tell Mom and Dad about the drugs. Mine or yours. I kinda forgot. Or maybe I thought it was TMI on a day that already had TMI."

He'd stopped chewing. "What are you saying? Spit it out."

"It's time to stop."

He took another bite and grinned. "They asked me if I smoked, you know."

"What did you say?"

"That I tried it, but wasn't into it."

"They asked me, too."

"What did you say?"

"That I tried it, but wasn't into it."

They laughed.

Ella said, "Megan overheard you dealing in the park."

He rolled his eyes. "So, what? You want some? What's the game?"

"No, I don't want any of that stuff." She pointed at her stash. "I don't even want this anymore. And I want you to get rid of yours, too."

"Oh, I see. This is an intervention."

"Maybe. And maybe you need one. Dealing is really fucked-up, Charlie. You know it is."

He stared at the countertop.

"I've been thinking about Mom and Uncle Dub. One day, that's going to be us."

"That's scary."

"Not as scary as not having each other."

"I'm not dying or anything, Ella."

"No, but you're on your way to being a loser. We have to start doing the right thing. We might need each other, Charlie." She'd been plucking at the bear's fur. Now she stopped. "Are you listening to me?"

He chewed the inside of his cheek. Finally he glanced at her. His face was serious for once.

Ella said, "Get your stuff. Whatever you've got, okay? Let's do this together."

⋅ ⋅ ⋅

They walked down to the path by the river. After a while, they veered away from the water, into the woods.

"Why can't we just throw it in the creek?" Charlie said.

"There's fish in there. And frogs. Frogs are very sensitive."

At the edge of a clearing, she began digging a hole with the shovel she'd brought.

He said, "And nothing's going to dig this up? Because personally I think the squirrels could use a little chilling out."

"That's why the hole has to be deep." She handed him the shovel. "Your turn."

When the hole was three feet deep, Ella fished the drugs out of her pocket and dangled them above it. "To a clear mind and heart." She dropped them in.

Charlie cupped a small paper bag in his palm. "To staying out of juvie." He tipped the bag and a shower of pills and marijuana buds fell into the hole.

"Jesus," Ella said. She studied his face. "This is for real, right? You're not just doing this to get me off your case."

He nodded. "The whole thing was getting too intense anyway." He waved his hand over the hole. Against the dark earth, the pills looked like confetti. "No one tells you how stressful it is to be this cool."

CHAPTER FORTY-ONE

GENEVA

On Friday, the last day of school, Tom's parents hosted their annual beginning-of-the-summer barbecue. Tom texted Geneva at work to say Helen had a headache and wouldn't be coming, and that he and the kids would see her there. Before leaving the clinic, Geneva called home in case her mother had changed her mind. The call went to voice mail, so she figured Helen had fallen asleep.

Juliana greeted her at the door with a hug. "Are you hungry? I made the artichoke frittata you're crazy about. I'll get you a slice."

Jon squatted on the ottoman next to Grandma Novak's recliner, nodding as the old woman spoke, her hands carving the air like swallows at dusk. Geneva said hello to them, and followed Juliana into the kitchen. They chatted for a few moments—

Juliana asked about Helen's recovery and Geneva remarked she was happy to see Jon—then moved to the family room doorway. Ella, Charlie, Pierce, and Spencer were embroiled in a spirited game of foosball. Geneva was surprised to see her children on the same side. If they couldn't avoid each other, competition was the next alternative. Charlie flicked a handle and cheered as the ball disappeared into the goal. Ella high-fived him, and he beamed at her and winked. On the same team.

"Hey." Tom placed his lips close to her ear and slipped a hand around her waist. "I've got ribs on the grill, if you want one." He poked her rib with a finger.

She kissed his cheek and laughed. "Why is everyone trying to feed me?"

"I don't know. Maybe they care about you."

"In that case, I'd love some ribs." She pointed at Charlie and Ella. "They're suddenly getting along."

"I said they were fine, didn't I?"

Geneva raised her eyebrows, to remind him of the events of the past week and their resolution to not whistle in the darkness as parents.

"Well, *fine* may be too strong a word."

"How about *salvageable*?"

"Okay. We've got two very salvageable kids. I'm happy with that."

"Me, too."

•　•　•

She left the party early to check on her mother. Diesel's tail beat time on the floor as she came through the front door. She crossed to the kitchen and set the leftovers on the counter. The dog followed, toes clicking. She bent to stroke him and absorb his familiar smell of cinnamon and hay.

"Who's my good boy?" She let him into the backyard, where wisps of fog had begun to coalesce among the redwoods, muting the last light of the day. Diesel raced across the lawn in pursuit of a squirrel that narrowly beat him to a tree. She smiled, closed the door, and called down the hallway.

"Mom, it's me."

Remembering something, she returned to the kitchen, pulled an envelope out of her bag, and walked down the hall. No light spilled from underneath the door. She knocked lightly.

"Mom?"

She listened a moment, then twisted the knob slowly, pushed the door, and peeked in. A pale gray rectangle of light fell on the hastily made bed. Her eyes darted to the chair by the window. Empty. Geneva's hands went cold as she scanned the room. No reading glasses or folded magazine on the bedside table. No clothes discarded on the chair. She flicked on the light and yanked open the closet. The space along the rack she had created for her mother's clothes gaped at her.

Her stomach slid, queasy. She spun toward the bed and this time noticed a folded piece of paper leaning against the pillow. Her name, in her mother's tall script. Geneva sat on the bed and read the note.

> *Geneva,*
>   *I said I'd think about staying on with you here and I have, though it didn't take long to make up my mind.*

*You're probably mad at me for running out, but the last
thing I wanted was a drawn-out discussion. Stubborn as
we are, neither of us was going to win that one.*

*I know you think a better person is hiding somewhere
inside me. Now that you've ferreted out the truth about
your father and me, you think you can sober me up, drag
that person out, and have the mother you want. I can't
blame you for what you want, but I'm not going to
change. I haven't got the will or the courage. You and
Dublin might forgive me, but I can't see clear to forgiving
myself. There'll be no new tricks for this old dog.*

*I'm headed back to L.A. Maybe I'll stay there and
maybe I won't. Whatever I do, it won't be your problem.
You've had enough of those on my account.*

*Tell the kids good-bye from me. Thanks to you and
Tom for putting me up, and for trying. That's more than
most would have done, but it was never going to be
enough.*

Helen

*P.S. If I left something behind, don't worry. Whatever it
is, I doubt I need it.*

She'd been holding her breath, but exhaled sharply at the last
line, incredulous. Gone. Just like that. She'd been foolish to hope.
They all had.

For five weeks she'd been trying to break through to her mother,
to understand her. She'd discovered what she believed was the key
to ending her mother's self-destructive behavior. She'd offered her a
way forward, a chance to release the grip of the past, and pledged

herself and her family in support. Geneva hadn't forgiven her mother for denying her love and attention for so long, but she had found a measure of compassion, and wagered it would suffice. In a corner of her heart she even imagined her compassion as kindling that could not only ignite her tender and guarded feelings for her mother, but also jump across the void and ignite her mother's feelings for her.

Clearly, this was a fantasy her mother did not share.

The bridge of her nose stung. Her chest was hollow.

In her postscript, her mother had said not to worry about what she'd left behind. If you keep leaving things behind, Geneva thought, you learn not to need them.

She swallowed against the tears building behind her eyes.

No more tears for her mother. There'd already been far too many. Everything that could be said, had been. Everything she could do, she had. Enough.

She folded the note, placed it on the bedside table, and rose to stand at the window. Diesel sat on his haunches in the center of the lawn, facing the back door. He caught sight of her, and cocked his head. His jaw dropped open and his tongue slid out. Geneva smiled back at him, took a deep breath, and let it go.

The front door opened. For an instant, she thought it might be her mother, having changed her mind. But Charlie's voice floated down the hallway, and Ella's laugh in response. Geneva shook her head at her own foolishness, and left the room to greet her family.

• • •

Later that evening she entered Ella's room. She was lying on the floor on her stomach, drawing.

"Have fun at the party?"

"Uh-huh. Such a relief to be done with school."

"I didn't ask you earlier. How'd your psychology final go?"

"Piece of cake."

"Even though it's A.P.?"

"Yeah, but it's mostly common sense."

Geneva suppressed a laugh. Only in a multiple-choice test could human behavior appear commonsensical.

She sat cross-legged on the floor next to her daughter, who was drawing a cartoon dog on a leash. "What's that for?"

"An ad for my dog-walking service. I was hoping you could put some up at work."

"Good idea."

"At the bottom I'm going to put: 'Trained by a Veterinarian and Animal Behavior Expert.'"

She laughed.

"It's true, though. You showed me how to walk Diesel so he doesn't pull."

"I guess I did. Listen, Ella. You're not upset about Nana leaving so suddenly, are you?"

She looked up. "Kinda."

"Why?"

Her daughter frowned. "I feel like I messed up. If I had told on Charlie earlier, then the whole thing would've ended before he found the gun. And then Nana wouldn't have been so upset that she OD'ed. And I think she left because she was embarrassed about it."

Geneva laid her hand on Ella's cheek. "You made some mistakes, but what Nana did had nothing to do with you, in any way."

"Maybe you're just saying that."

"Does that sound like me?"

"No."

A slight breeze set the mobiles above her head in motion. Geneva had seen them nearly every day but had never observed them in action. The only light in the room came from a floor lamp near the desk, but faint moonlight, filtered through fog, spilled through the window. The white cards nearest the window had a ghostly cast, while the ones close to the desk were bright white on their illuminated side. In between were gradations of moonlight, darkness, and halogen light. The cards bobbed like corks in a gentle sea, and twisted coyly. The effect was mesmerizing.

Geneva pointed to the cards. "So, tell me how this works."

"The wordstorm?"

"I didn't know it had a name."

"Yeah. Well, it works best if you lie on your back." She set the marker down and demonstrated.

Geneva lay down beside her.

"Now you just open your mind to it. Let a word come to you. Then another one and another."

"And that's a poem?"

"Of course not! It's the seed for one. Maybe."

"Okay. Can I try it out loud, just for practice?"

"Sure. This doesn't have a lot of rules."

Geneva closed her eyes for a moment. When she opened them a card by the window faced her, then twisted away. "Whelp." And out of the corner of her eye: "Resilient. Palisade."

"Nice, Mom. I got 'sardonic machinations.'"

"This is fascinating, Ella. But I did notice one thing."

"What?"

"These are all SAT words."

"Oh, no!" Ella covered her face with her hands in mock horror, then rolled on her side and into her mother's arms.

Geneva held her close. Together they watched the wordstorm tilt and turn, the breeze, the moon, and the fog conspiring to create an infinity of unfinished poems.

HOUSE
BROKEN

SONJA YOERG

*This Conversation Guide is intended to enrich the
individual reading experience, as well as encourage us
to explore these topics together—because books,
and life, are meant for sharing.*

QUESTIONS FOR DISCUSSION

1. Helen's choices within her marriage were shaped by the nature of small-town life in the South during the seventies. Imagine, however, she lived in present-day California with a powerful and abusive husband and a daughter in denial of her victimhood. Would Helen have different options? Would she take them? If not, would she deserve forgiveness? Did she deserve the forgiveness granted her by Geneva and Dublin?

2. Geneva brought her mother into her home, despite her adamant belief that old dogs can't learn new tricks. Were there other instances where Geneva second-guessed her instincts? Have you ever made the right decision by ignoring your instincts?

3. The story is filled with dogs, and each plays a role in the plot, sometimes figuratively. Diesel is Geneva's faithful companion; who else stood by her? Which human character reminded you of Aldo, Juliana's Doberman, and how did Geneva come to make this comparison? What lesson did we learn from Argus,

Paris's German shepherd? Finally, the retriever at the rescue clinic is flawed, but not irredeemable. Who else could be described in those terms?

4. Paris is an intricate, disturbed, and disturbing character. How did you feel about her as a victim of incest? As Helen's daughter? As a sister to Geneva?

5. Ella and Charlie have a complicated relationship and keep many secrets from their parents. How do they evolve over the course of the story? What do you think happens to them over the next few years?

6. Geneva's brother is the one saving grace from her childhood. Discuss how Geneva might have become a different person without Dublin.

7. Paris notwithstanding, the Riley children become relatively well-balanced adults. Does this outcome justify Helen's actions? Dublin, in particular, appears bulletproof. Do you see this as a function of his personality or something else in the family dynamic?

8. At the beginning of the novel, Tom and Geneva bump heads over parenting. How are their approaches affected by their own family histories? How does this change over the course of the story?

9. Helen's children's views of their upbringing are as far-flung as the children themselves. How do siblings come to such different perspectives on the same events? Do you and your siblings hold similar views of your family life?

10. Geneva learns to forgive her mother, at least in part, and learns to let her go. What else did Geneva learn over the course of the story?

Turn the page for a sneak peek at Sonja Yoerg's second novel,

THE MIDDLE OF SOMEWHERE

Available from New American Library in September 2015.

Liz hopped from foot to foot and hugged herself against the cold. She glanced at the porch of the Yosemite Valley Wilderness Office, where Dante stood with his back to her, chatting with some other hikers. His shoulders shrugged and dropped, and his hands danced this way and that. He was telling a story—a funny one, judging by the faces of his audience—but not a backpacking story because he didn't have any. His idea of a wilderness adventure was staring out the window during spin class at the gym. Not that it mattered. He could have been describing the self-contradictory worldview of the guy who changes his oil, or the merits of homemade tamales, or even acting out the latest viral cat video. Liz had known him for over two years and still couldn't decipher how he captured strangers' attention without apparent effort. Dante was black velvet and other people were lint.

Their backpacks sat nearby on a wooden bench like stiff-backed strangers waiting for a bus. The impulse to grab hers and take off without him shot through her. She quelled it with the reminder that his pack contained essential gear for completing the three-week hike. The John Muir Trail. Her hike. At least that had been the plan.

She propped her left hiking boot on the bench, retied it, folded down the top of her sock and paced a few steps along the sidewalk to see if she'd gotten them even. It wasn't yet nine a.m., and Yosemite Village already had a tentative, waking buzz. Two teenage girls in pajama pants and oversize sweatshirts walked past, dragging their Uggs on the concrete. Bleary-eyed dads pushed strollers, and Patagonia types with day packs marched purposefully among the buildings: restaurants, a grocery store, a medical clinic, a visitor's center, gift shops, a fire station, even a four-star hotel. What a shame the trail had to begin in the middle of this circus. Liz couldn't wait to get the hell out of there.

She fished Dante's iPhone out of the zippered compartment on top of his pack and called Valerie. They'd been best friends for eleven years, since freshman year in college, when life had come with happiness the way a phone plan came with minutes.

Valerie answered. "Dante?"

"No. It's me."

"Where's your phone?"

"Asleep in the car. No service most of the way. Even here I've only got one bar."

"Dante's going to go nuts if he can't use his phone."

"You think? How's Muesli?" Valerie was cat-sitting for her.

"Does he ever look at you like he thinks you're an idiot?"

"All the time."

"Then he's fine."

"How's the slipper commute?" Valerie worked as a Web designer, mostly from home, and had twenty sets of pajamas hanging in her closet as if they were business suits.

"Just firing up the machine. You get your permits?"

"Uh-huh."

"Try to sound more psyched."

How could she be psyched when this wasn't the trip she'd planned? She was supposed to hike the John Muir Trail—the JMT—alone. With a few thousand square miles of open territory surrounding her, she hoped to find a way to a truer life. She sure didn't know the way now. Each turn she'd taken, each decision she'd made—including moving in with Dante six months ago— had seemed right at the time, yet none *were* right, based as they were on a series of unchallenged assumptions and quiet lies, one weak moral link attached to the next, with the truth at the tail end, whipping away from her again and again.

Maybe, she'd whispered to herself, she could have a relationship with Dante and share a home if she pretended there was no reason she couldn't. She loved him enough to almost believe it could work. But she'd hardly finished unpacking before her doubts had mushroomed. She became desperate for time away—from the constant stream of friends in Dante's wake, from the sense of sliding down inside a funnel that led to marriage, from becoming an indeterminate portion of something called "us"—and could not tell Dante why. Not then or since. That was the crux of it. Instead, she told Dante that years ago she'd abandoned a plan to hike the JMT and now wanted to strike it off her list before she turned thirty in November. She had no list, but he accepted her explanation, and her true motivation wriggled free.

The Park Service issued only a few permits for each trailhead. She'd faxed in her application as soon as she decided to go. When she received e-mail confirmation, a crosscurrent of relief and dread flooded her. In two months' time, she would have her solitude, her bitter medicine.

Then two weeks before her start date, Dante announced he was joining her.

"You've never been backpacking, and now you want to go two hundred and twenty miles?"

"I would miss you." He opened his hands as if that were the simple truth.

There had to be more to it than that. Why else would he suggest embarking on a journey they both knew would make him miserable? She tried to talk him out of it. He didn't like nature, the cold or energy bars. It made no sense. But he was adamant, and brushed her concerns aside. She'd had no choice but to capitulate.

Now she told Valerie, "I am psyched. In fact, I want to hit the trail right now, but Dante's holding court in the Wilderness Office."

"I can't believe you'll be out of touch for three weeks. What am I going to do without you? Who am I going to talk to?"

"Yourself, I guess. Put an earbud in and walk around holding your phone like a Geiger counter. You could be an incognito schizophrenic."

"I'll be reduced to that." She dropped her voice a notch. "Listen. I have to ask you again. You sure you feel up to this?"

Liz reflexively placed her hand on her lower abdomen. "I'm fine. I swear. It's just a hike."

"When I have to park a block from Trader Joe's, that's a hike. Two hundred miles is something else. And your miscarriage was less than three weeks ago."

As if Dante could have overheard, she turned and walked a few more steps down the sidewalk. "I feel great."

"And you're going to tell Dante soon and not wait for the absolute perfect moment."

Despite the cold, Liz's palms were slick with sweat. Her boyfriend knew nothing of her pregnancy, but her friend didn't have the whole story either. Valerie had made her daily call to Liz and learned she was home sick, but she'd been vague about the reason. Knowing Dante was out of town, Valerie had stopped by and found Liz lying on the couch, a heating pad on her belly.

"Cramps?"

"No," Liz had said, staring at the rug. "Worse."

Valerie had assumed she'd had a miscarriage, not an abortion, and Liz hadn't corrected her. Next to her deceit to Dante, it seemed minor. Valerie had made her promise she would tell him, but when Liz ran the conversation through her mind, she panicked. If she revealed this bit of information, the whole monstrous truth might tumble out, and she would lose him for certain.

"I will tell him. And I'll make sure I've got room to run when I do."

"He'll understand. It's not like it was your fault."

Liz's chest tightened. "Val, listen—"

"Crap! I just noticed the time. I've got a call in two minutes, so this is good-bye."

" 'Bye."

"Don't get lost."

"Impossible."

"Don't fall off a cliff."

"I'll try not to."

"Watch out for bears."

"I love bears! And they love me."

"Of course they do. So do I."

"And me you. 'Bye."

" 'Bye."

Liz put the phone away. She checked the zippers and tightened the straps on both backpacks. On a trip this long, they couldn't afford to lose anything. Besides, a pack with loose straps tended to creak, and she didn't like creaking.

Dante was still chatting. He glanced over his shoulder and flashed her a boyish smile. She pointed at her watch. He twitched in mock alarm, shook hands with his new friends and hurried to her.

"Leez!" He placed his hands on her cheeks and tucked her short brown hair behind her ears with his fingers. "You're waiting. I'm sorry."

She was no more immune to his charm than the rest of the world. The way he pronounced her name amused her, and she suspected he laid it on thick deliberately. He had studied English in the best schools in Mexico City and spent seven years in the States, so he had little reason for sounding like the Taco Bell Chihuahua.

"It's okay." She rose onto her toes and kissed his cheek. "We should get going though. Did you get the forecast?"

"I did." He threw his arms wide. "It's going to be beautiful!"

"That's a quote from the ranger?"

"*Más o menos*. Look for yourself." He swept his hand to indicate the sky above the pines, an unbroken Delft blue.

Things can change, she thought, especially this late in the season. Her original permit had been for the Thursday before Labor Day. It could snow or hail or thunderstorm on any given day in the Sierras, but early September was usually dry. She'd had to surrender that start date when Dante insisted on tagging along, because he didn't have a permit. They were forced to take their chances with the weather, two weeks closer to winter.

And here it was, September fifteenth. A picture-perfect day. Dante's beaming face looked like a guarantee of twenty more like it.

Photo © Sandy Payne Photography

Sonja Yoerg grew up in Stowe, Vermont, where she financed her college education by waitressing at the Trapp Family Lodge. She earned her PhD in biological psychology from the University of California at Berkeley, and studied learning in blue jays, kangaroo rats, and spotted hyenas, among other species. Her nonfiction book about animal intelligence, *Clever as a Fox* (Bloomsbury USA), was published in 2001.

While her two daughters were young, Sonja taught fine arts and science in their schools in California. Now that they are in college, she writes full-time. She currently lives in the Shenandoah Valley of Virginia with her husband. *House Broken* is her first novel.